A Tracy Brubaker Mystery

MURDER ME TWICE

Book 3

John Carter Stell

Midnight Marquee Press
Baltimore, MD, USA

Tracy Brubaker Mysteries

#1 The Big Nap
#2 Crossed Stitch
#3 Murder Me Twice

Cover Design by Susan Svehla

ISBN 978-1-936168-83-5
Library of Congress Catalog Card Number 2018952712
First Printing September 2018

Dedication

To Mena...for everything

Who are you going to believe, me or your own eyes?
—Chico Marx

A Tracy Brubaker Mystery

Chapter 1

Wagner House had a reputation as one of Baltimore City's finest (and thus most expensive) restaurants. But Professor Andrew Braxton, J.D. truly thought it had the best food in the downtown area. So whenever he had cause to be visiting the Harbor or its nearby environs, he made it a point to secure a lunch reservation. Today, however, would be slightly different in that he had invited a guest to join him. She had been one of his favorite students when he was teaching Legal Reasoning, Research, and Writing. Teacher and student had kept in touch over the years and he was not at all surprised by the success she was having. He had ceased being a law school instructor for several years now, instead doing some consulting work that kept him active in the legal community but allowed him a very flexible schedule. He was 68 years old but looked like a man in his early 50s, and he was committed to thoroughly enjoying his golden years.

When Braxton saw Tracy Brubaker being escorted to his table he immediately rose to greet her. She was by nature, he had learned shortly after knowing her, a hugger and so he opened his arms for their customary embrace. "Tracy, you look marvelous," he began. "Life must be treating you well."

She smiled. "I have my fair share of ups and downs but you won't hear me complaining. You look terrific yourself—you must be keeping busy."

"Yes, I am. Veronica is a traveler par excellence so we are quite the globetrotters."

"I hope to do some traveling at some point. What places have you been to?"

"The obvious ones: United Kingdom, France, Ireland, Italy, Scotland, Switzerland, and others I've forgotten. There's a very beautiful world out there, Tracy. I hope you do indeed find time to see some of it. If I recall you're Italian on your mother's side."

"Yes. My mother's family is from Sicily."

"Italy is full of beautiful sites, and is so rich in history. We've been there several times and always find something new to see." Dr. Braxton's travel pitch was interrupted by the arrival of their waiter, a short, thin fellow dressed in a tuxedo-ish uniform who was looking very serious. Dr. Braxton did not allow the man a chance to speak. "I'd like your house salad and the Chicken Chesapeake, with the garlic mashed potatoes and the vegetable medley."

"Very good sir," the stoic-faced server said. "And for you ma'am?"

Tracy had been quickly scanning the menu while her former professor was decisively placing his order. This was her first time here and she really would have liked more time to study the establishment's offerings. Now the clock was ticking. "Um, I'd like a cup of your Cream of Crab soup, please."

"Excellent choice, ma'am."

Tracy smiled. "And I'll take the Stuffed Shrimp with mashed potatoes and the string beans."

"Another excellent choice. Can I get you anything to drink other than water?"

"Oh, water will be fine."

"Very good then. My name is Benjamin. Please let me know if you need anything else. Your soup and salad will be out shortly." And then Benjamin gave a slight bow and headed to submit the orders.

Tracy had, up until now, kept her curiosity at bay. But she was no longer able to contain it. "So Professor, what may I ask is the reason for you treating me like a queen?"

Braxton laughed. "Oh, so you think my request for the pleasure of your company holds an ulterior motive?"

She smiled and nodded.

"You're quite right of course. I read that the Paganini trial ended on Monday. So I wondered if you had any other major cases on tap."

She was sipping from her water glass. "Nothing major," she said after putting her drink down. "It was a pretty intense experience, though. And it's only been a couple of days since it all ended. I'm still kind of decompressing." It was Thursday, March 26, 2015, and Tracy was still playing catch-up at the office. The Monday just passed she had exposed a killer in court; she still felt drained by the experience. However, the least she could do was hear what the doctor had to say; he was picking up the tab for this feast, after all. "What's on your mind, Professor?"

Braxton smiled as Benjamin returned with the doctor's salad and Tracy's soup. "It concerns a client of mine from 27 years ago. Have you read or heard about the man who was arrested for stabbing and killing an acquaintance of his?"

Tracy shook her head. "I haven't been paying much attention to other murder cases." Then she added, "Professor, this is the best Cream of Crab I've ever tasted. It's so good I'm having a hard time staying focused on what you're saying."

          A Tracy Brubaker Mystery

He chuckled. "You haven't changed a bit, Tracy."

She grinned. "I hope I'm a little wiser, Professor. Now: about your client..."

Braxton nodded. "About 27 years ago, when he was 17, he was arrested, tried, and ultimately freed on the charge that he murdered his own father. The police have nevertheless continued to believe in his guilt; that he got away with murder."

Tracy wiped the corners of her mouth with her napkin. "A murdered father," she thought. Her own father had been murdered. He had been a detective with the Baltimore Police Department and was gunned down over 10 years ago while protecting a witness. She was thus instantly sympathetic to people whose fathers had been taken from them by anything other than natural causes. "So this was back when you were practicing criminal law," she commented.

"Yes. I was actually friends with his father's business attorney; that's how I wound up defending the son."

"I see."

"Now, as you have no doubt surmised, he has been arrested again. This time the victim is someone he hardly knew. They had met just a few weeks prior to the murder. Then, one night while they were at dinner, they had a heated argument, witnessed by both the restaurant's patrons and staff. A few days later, the other man was found dead in his apartment."

"In your client's apartment?"

"No: the man's own apartment. My client's fingerprints were found on the knife, however, and he doesn't have an alibi for the night of the murder. Of course he denies it completely. And I have to admit that I believe him."

The diners finished their first courses as Braxton continued to give Tracy some details on the past and present crimes of which his client was accused. When their main courses finally arrived Tracy thought, "If they taste anywhere near as good as they smell, this is going to be heaven." Benjamin placed their entrees in front of them and asked if they needed anything else. The diners each smiled and answered in the negative. Then Benjamin left them. Tracy sampled her selection: perfection, absolute perfection. Braxton noted the expression on her face.

"It meets with your approval, no doubt," he said smiling.

"Professor, why haven't you brought me here sooner?"

He laughed. "Well, now you know all about it. Get your beau to bring you here some time."

Her beau; she was currently beau-less. But she had a date with her former love tomorrow night, so maybe her situation would in fact be changing shortly. She took another sip of water. "Over the phone you said there was something unusual in nature about what you wanted to talk to me about. So far it sounds like a pretty standard circumstantial case."

Braxton nodded as Tracy spoke. "Well, I haven't yet told you what the police think his motive is."

"Oh," was all Tracy could think to respond. "What is the alleged motive?"

"Well, first I must mention that over the past 20 years or so my client has been pursuing his own leads in his father's murder. Occasionally he'd think he'd be onto to something, only to have it lead nowhere. And at one point, he even was telling people he thought his father would come back, reincarnated, to unmask his killer."

Tracy put her fork down and studied her host. "Reincarnated? Are you serious?"

"Very. This victim, this near stranger, befriended my client just a few weeks before he was killed, as I told you. And my client remarked that he had some things in common with his father: a slight limp with the left leg, similar tastes in music, and various other small details."

Tracy opened her mouth a bit. "Are you saying your client thought this guy was his reincarnated father?"

Braxton shook his head. "I'm saying that that is what the *police* are saying my client thought. And that he killed this man out of some sort of self defense, thinking that it was a kill or be killed situation."

Tracy frowned. "That's screwy."

Braxton chuckled. "Perhaps; but there is one other detail I haven't told you about."

"And that is?"

"The victim in this case, Tracy, was born on the very same day that my client's father was murdered 27 years ago."

Tracy blinked a few times. "How do you know this?"

"It's been confirmed already by the police, hence my client's arrest."

"That's…that's…I don't know *what* that is."

Braxton sat back in his chair. "My client assures me he didn't really believe in this reincarnation business. It was just bar talk, brought on after one too many. But at the same time, he was keeping an open mind."

Tracy nodded. And yes, she was intrigued, at least to the point where she wanted to meet Dr. Braxton's client. "You win, Professor. I'm officially curious. What's the current status of the case?"

"He's in jail; denied bail. He called me after he'd been arrested, not realizing I didn't actually practice anymore. I recommended someone I'd heard good things about to him whom he used through the bail review, preliminary hearing and arraignment. He wants my client to plea it out."

"Let me guess: the client doesn't want a plea bargain."

"No. And then I found myself following your case, and what you were able to do. My client has told me wants a new attorney, so it's not like I'm doing something behind anyone's back by meeting with you."

 A Tracy Brubaker Mystery

"You told your client about me?"

"No. I didn't want to say anything until I talked to you."

Tracy smiled appreciatively. "Okay Professor. I can at least talk to him I guess; but no promises."

"I understand completely. When can I arrange a visit?"

"Will Monday work? I think my morning is pretty clear."

"That would be excellent, Tracy. I will arrange things then. Now, let's finish this exquisite meal before things get too cold for me to enjoy them."

And so the two colleagues did just that. Afterwards, Dr. Braxton told Tracy he'd be in touch with a meeting time. They hugged their goodbyes, and then Tracy made her way back to her law office.

"That's Rod Serling territory right there," Neal Bennett said after his employer relayed the details of her lunch meeting.

"Freaky, is what I call it," Rebecca Dietz, Tracy's secretary and administrative assistant, added.

"Right on both counts," Tracy agreed, "so you can see why I had to agree to at least meet with the guy."

"Who is he?" Neal asked.

"Based on what the professor told me I think his name is Colin Richmond. The newspapers have some stuff on the arrest. The victim, Timothy Pane, was stabbed in his apartment. Richmond and Pane were seen arguing at Denzinger's Steaks and Chops, a steakhouse in the city. It's the old circumstantial chestnut."

Neal shook his head. He didn't like the idea of regularly defending possible murderers. He had been with Tracy for five years now, since she started her own law firm. Her practice, up until almost a year ago, didn't get involved in murder cases, or, for that matter, anything involving violence. The reasons had to do with Tracy's own belief that getting murderers off for a living would be a slap in the face to her father, a man who specialized in putting criminals *behind* bars. But Tracy had had, within the last year, two successes in defending clients falsely accused of murder. Not only that, in each case she had handed the police the real killer. When Tracy's own mother basically told her that it was her *duty* to help the wrongly accused, even if the crime they were accused of started with 'm', that pretty much sealed the deal for the firm's future. Just yesterday Tracy had told her staff of two that they may be taking on future clients charged with taking the life of another, *if* Tracy felt the potential client was indeed innocent of the charges. That was very risky, of course; someone who murdered someone else wouldn't hesitate to lie about it, even to their attorney. But Tracy had made up her mind, and Neal loved her like a kid sister. So he agreed to stay on in spite of his reservations.

"So I should keep Monday morning open?" Rebecca asked.

"Yes. Hopefully we'll have a time by early tomorrow."

"Righto."

"Well, I guess that's it for now folks. I'll let you know how it goes." She smiled at both Rebecca and Neal, and then returned to her private office located in the back of the suite.

"It's so good to see her happy again," Rebecca said to Neal. "She had a rough few weeks." That was putting it mildly: a seemingly impossible case, death threats, her mother's stroke, all within a short span of time. But all of that seemed to be old news that was now filed away in the "memories not to be revisited" cabinet.

"She does seem to be her old self, doesn't she?" Neal asked rhetorically. "I just hope jumping into another murder case so soon doesn't do her more harm than good."

"I think she'll be fine. Remember, those other two cases involved people she knew personally, people she was close to. That wouldn't be the case here."

"True. But you know Tracy, she makes friends fast."

Rebecca didn't respond. Neal was right: Tracy had a "glass is half full" approach to life and she tended to view each person she met as a potential friend, even her clients. That had worked very well for her for the most part. But it had also increased the stress levels, in Rebecca's opinion, to more than what were really warranted at times.

Sensing there was nothing left to talk about, Neal returned to his workspace so he could pursue the relatively safe world of business contracts, trust agreements and the like. Maybe Tracy wouldn't end up taking the Richmond case after all; maybe she'd take one look at the guy and know the cops had arrested the right person.

"Good luck tonight," Rebecca said to Tracy. "I'm homeward bound."

"Thanks, Beck. Goodnight." Tracy had let Rebecca know she had a dinner date with Brian Shane; well maybe not a date—closer to an outing. Regardless, Rebecca gave her boss a big grin and then headed out the door. It was after 5:00 p.m. on Friday; Brian would be picking her up at her condo around 7:30 p.m. She should be making her way home soon herself.

"Goodnight Tracy," Neal said, popping his head in the doorway.

"Have a supreme weekend Neal," she responded.

"You too," he said grinning. And then he was gone too. Shortly thereafter Tracy checked the coffee pot (already emptied and washed), turned off the lights, set the alarm, and locked the office doors. She had made her date with Brian on Monday, when he called to congratulate her on the Paganini case. And she had been thinking about tonight ever since.

Brian Shane: the man she fell in love with while dating him in college; Brain Shane: the man who gradually used alcohol more and more to fight

　　A Tracy Brubaker Mystery

his inner demons. Brian Shane: the man she regrettably said goodbye to when he refused to seek help. Brian Shane: the man who was accused of murder almost a year ago, the man she ultimately proved was innocent. He had been her first love and her first murder case. Seeing him again had been bittersweet. But he had told her was going to join Alcoholics Anonymous and get his life in order. He told her he still loved her, even after all the time that had passed. She was sure she loved him too, although she knew they couldn't just pick up where they left off. But based on the phone call just a few days earlier he had sounded like the Brian she remembered: friendly, enthusiastic, considerate, and charming. It had been almost a year since he said goodbye to alcohol. Tracy at least wanted an update. She'd be 32 next month and she was wondering about her personal future. Her business was doing just fine. But she wanted a family; she always had. Still, she couldn't just rush in—or rather rush back in—to something without being sure that Brian was ready also. But how would she know this? "Stop getting ahead of yourself," she scolded. "Just enjoy tonight and see where it takes you."

Tracy was now at the condo she called home, staring at the contents of her closet: what should she wear? Something sexy: like the black dinner dress that stopped just above the knee? "Hmm, that may be too much." How about just a blouse and jeans, the uber casual look? "Well, I want him to know that this could be more than just two people hanging out. Besides he mentioned reservations, so I need to look somewhat presentable." Okay, something in between—sexy casual. "Huh? What's that?" She frowned. The heck with it; she grabbed the sequined black dress and dolled herself up. A little makeup (she didn't typically wear much) and a dash of perfume (she rarely made use of the stuff) completed her uniform. "I'm giving you a real shot here, Brian," she thought. "You better not blow it."

Time passed slowly; it was before 7:00 when she emerged from her bedroom ready for the night. Now she was sitting on her couch. Memories of their first meeting—at her friend Crystal Shane's July 4 party—were playing in her head. She didn't attend that summer party looking for a hookup. Crystal hadn't told her too much about her only sibling, her brother Brian, who was just a year older than she. But there he was, helping set up the tables, cooking the food, and serving as gopher. There he was, looking like an Adonis in shorts and t-shirt, sandy hair, and sparkly smile. Crystal introduced them. And then Crystal suggested Tracy help Brian set up some of the stations since she'd arrived early. And then Tracy suggested to herself that she find ways to help Brian the rest of the evening. So when he asked for her phone number as she departed the Independence Day party, she didn't hesitate to supply the requested information.

Her doorbell rang. She rose slowly, took a deep breath, and went to open the door. She felt a little silly. It's not like this was some first date with a man she hardly knew. "I'm being ridiculous," she told herself. She grasped the handle and pulled.

Brian Shane stood in the doorway clad in a button-down shirt and gray dress slacks. They looked at each other a moment. "Tracy you look…you look incredible," he said, his mouth slightly agape.

She smiled at him. "This old thing? Why don't you come in before you get arrested for loitering in the halls?"

Brian smiled and did as suggested. The two embraced firmly. "I can't tell you how great it is to see you again," he said into her ear. "You're as beautiful as ever."

She pulled back to face him. "It's great to see you too, Brian. You certainly look like you lost the weight you told me about. What was it: 10 pounds?"

"Well, closer to eight."

She laughed. "Oh, well, what are a couple of pounds between friends?" They looked at each other a few minutes more. "Should we get going?"

"Huh?" he asked. "Oh, the dinner—right. I promised you dinner."

"My tummy's going to start grumbling soon, Brian. It's past her feeding time."

He smiled. "We wouldn't want that. Let's go then." Brian moved back toward the hallway and Tracy followed after turning out the lights, grabbing her winter coat and small purse, and pulling the door shut. She was on the fourth floor of her building so they opted to use the elevator. Waiting for their chariot to arrive they found themselves looking at each other again, each with stupid grins on their faces. The bell rang, the doors opened, and the two entered the car holding hands.

Brian's automobile—a 1975 Mercury Cougar XR7 that he had taken care of for over 15 years—was parked along the street just outside Tracy's building. He moved quickly to the passenger door and opened it for his date. After she made herself comfortable and he closed the door, she reached over to unlock the driver's door for him. They had gone through this pseudo ritual too many times to count when they were dating. It was Brian's gentlemanly courtesy that was one of the reasons she felt so attracted to him, especially in an age where, she believed, courtesy was on its way out.

"I can't believe you still have this thing; that it still runs," she said after he pulled away.

"I've had to replace a lot of stuff of course. But it's the one indulgence I haven't stopped indulging in." She was looking at him, smiling. He wanted to look at her. But that wouldn't be a good idea given he was in charge of the wheel. "Hey, listen to this." Brian pushed the power button on the auto's sound console and Boston's "More Than A Feeling" started flowing from the speakers. Tracy may have been born in 1983 but she loved 1970s rock, probably thanks to her father who enjoyed that era too.

"You're really laying on the nostalgia, aren't you?" she asked teasingly.

"If I had a time machine, Tracy; if only I had a time machine." He didn't expand any further on what he meant.

The couple arrived at Culpepper's Steak and Seafood Shanty early for their 8:30 p.m. reservation. Brian eschewed the valet parking option and decided to park slightly further away. Tracy put her coat on, and Brian put his arm around her, pulling her close to him, for added warmth. They checked their coats, and then Brian spoke briefly with the hostess. He turned to his date. "It won't be long."

Tracy smiled. Another one of the area's highly acclaimed restaurants that she had never visited before. Could she handle two consecutive days of rich seafood?

"This way please," the hostess said approaching the couple. Soon they were seated across from each other; their table was along one of the several wall-like partitions that seemed designed for romantic dinners for two. Tracy was reviewing the menu the hostess had given her.

"Uh, Brian..."

"Yeah Tracy?"

"There are no prices on this menu."

"So?"

"Well, I…I mean…"

"Tracy, don't worry about it. You know I can afford it."

"Yeah, but…"

"Order what you want. That's kinda how this is supposed to work." He was smiling at her. Tracy had always been money-sensitive due to the economic environment in which she grew up. Her father's pay wasn't the highest on the compensation scale and her mother was a homemaker. Brian, on the other hand, was a millionaire several times over thanks to his inheritance. His father had founded a snack food company that made the Shane family wealthy; Crystal at present was continuing the tradition. But it was something the two rarely discussed. He had never considered for a minute that Tracy's interest in him was financial, something that couldn't be said of the other young women Brian had courted prior to meeting her.

"Well, I'll just get an entrée."

"Tracy, stop that," he jokingly admonished her. "If you see something you want, go ahead and get it. We could share an appetizer if that makes you feel any better. But for tonight, the sky's the limit. Can you remember that for me? Please?"

She smiled and looked at him. "Okay. But knowing me I'll order the most expensive things on the menu."

"And that would perfectly okay."

"Okay Brian; if it's really alright."

Tracy still wasn't comfortable throwing caution to the wind. She decided she'd find out what Brian was going to order and order the same thing, at least the entrée. They both then had crab cakes for their main course. That was preceded by a shared appetizer of crab dip and bread. Each also ordered the garden salad; neither would most likely have room for dessert. During most of the dinner, they engaged in small talk. Brian told her about his job in the computer field, and how having Crystal as his boss was actually pretty cool. Tracy told him details about the Paganini case that had not been made public. He was clearly impressed. After their plates had been cleared away and their after-dinner coffee served, Tracy started fiddling with the salt shaker that was near her.

"So tell me about AA. How are you doing with that?"

"I'm already down to one meeting a week, even if I don't think I need it. It keeps me humble, aware that I'm not perfect and need others. Does that make sense?"

"Sure," Tracy said sincerely. "I know I've been guilty of over-confidence. In fact, I'm lucky to have people like Rebecca and Neal, who always seem to know when something needs to be said and what to say."

Brian nodded. "I really think it's great that you have that kind of relationship with the people you work with, or rather who work for you. I don't believe that's very common."

Tracy smiled. "Well, sometimes they treat me like their baby sister or something. They're both older than me."

"They look out for you, huh?"

"Yeah; that's a good way of putting it." She cleared her throat. "Haven't you been tempted to drink though; haven't there been times when you really wanted a belt?"

Brian looked at her seriously. "Sure there've been. There will be in the future. But I know the consequences; I know no good will ultimately come of it. I just think of that when I'm tempted. And then, like I said, I still go to meetings. It's not always easy, but it *is* getting easier."

Tracy smiled at him. "I think that's wonderful Brian. After all this time, to be able to put your demons in check in less than a year's time; well, I just can't help but be proud of you."

Brian looked at her seriously, and then reached for her hand. "Can we go back to your place? I'd like to talk some more; but I'd rather not do it here."

Tracy put her head down. Then she looked back at him. "Okay Brian. That'd be fine."

     A Tracy Brubaker Mystery

Shortly thereafter Brian Shane had taken care of the bill, mildly irritating his date since he refused to reveal the grand total. Then he again opened the car door to allow Tracy's entrance. There was mostly silence on the way back to Tracy's abode. Brian was rehearsing his speech mentally, and Tracy was trying to guess what that speech was going to be and what, in turn, would be her response. Finally, she just said, "Thanks for a great dinner Brian. It really was top notch."

He smiled. "Only the best for my Tracy."

Tracy's eyes widened a bit. What exactly was going through Brian's mind? He arrived at Tracy's building and again found nearby street parking. He reached for her hand as she exited his car, and kept on holding it as they made their way back to her unit.

"I'll need my hand back to get the key," she teased.

"Oh, sure. Sorry." She removed her key ring from her purse and then opened her door. Brian followed, pushing the door shut behind him. She hung her coat up in the closet, and motioned for Brian to hand over his covering. He obliged.

Tracy went into her kitchen. "Do you want anything to drink; water maybe?"

Brian was looking at her while he answered, "No." Now they were looking at each other. They both remained still for several moments. And then Brian moved toward her, gently placed each of his hands on her respective cheeks and kissed her. She kissed him back. She put her hands around his neck and the two were locked in passion. Then Tracy suddenly pulled herself away, and went to the opposite end of the room. Both were now breathing heavily. There were no words or even looks exchanged for what seemed liked hours. Finally Brian spoke.

"I'm sorry Tracy. I told myself I shouldn't try anything physical. But… you just look so beautiful. And I just couldn't…I…I just…I'm sorry."

Tracy turned to face him. She cleared her throat. "Well, it's not like I pushed you away; at least not initially." She paused. "I guess I'm just not sure what…I mean part of me really wants us to try again. But another part of me is…"

"Tracy: you're not the one who owes explanations. You're the good guy here."

"Well, I don't know about that."

"Please don't do that. Please don't take on responsibility for something you didn't do. It doesn't make me feel any better, quite the contrary."

"I'm sorry —"

"And don't apologize. You're not the one who owes anyone an apology." Brian started moving toward where Tracy was standing, still keeping some distance. "Look: I've gone over in my head again and again what I was going to say to you tonight. And in typical Brian Shane fashion I screwed things up."

"Brian: you haven't screwed anything up yet."

Brian snuffed. "Yet...that's telling."

Tracy shook her head. "I shouldn't have said it like that."

"Tracy, I love you. I probably fell in love with you the night I met you, if I'm honest with myself. And ultimately I took you for granted and just made a mess of it all. I hate who I was and what I did and what I said. I wish I could take it all back. But I know that's impossible. And I wish too that I had been able to make good on the promises I made to you and your father. I'm so ashamed of that too. I know you said that I couldn't look at our relationship as my ultimate goal; that I had to get sober for myself. But I won't lie to you Tracy. The two of us getting back together—that possibility—has been the light, right or wrong, at the end of this tunnel that I buried myself in.

"I once told your father in front of you that you were my world, and I meant that. And ever since I made that terrible decision to leave your home, turn down your loving offer to help me, I've felt like a wandering astronaut, desperate to get back to his home." Brian was in tears now, not something that Tracy had seen too often, even when they were dating. "So while I have absolutely no right to ask anything from you, I'm going to ask anyway. Tracy, I need to know if there's a chance you could love me again, the way you once did. I need to know if given time there's the chance you might want to marry me and spend your life with me. Because if there is no chance of that ever happening, I need to know now, before I start thinking about, hoping for something that will never be." He paused again. "And don't worry about saying there isn't a chance. I won't be heading to a bar if that's how you feel. I meant it when I said I was done with the drinking. I might need to go to 10 meetings a day for a few years, but don't factor in what I may do when answering me. I know you're an honest person, so I am asking for you to be honest now. I'll do anything you ask me if you want to put conditions on your answer; I mean, anything. I just ask for one more chance. Please Tracy, just one more chance. I don't know who said it was 'better to have loved and lost than never to have loved at all,' because they're full of crap. Losing you has been a living death for me. I know I deserved it. But I...I just hope..." Brian stopped talking; his sort-of-rehearsed, mostly improvised speech was done. He had thrown himself on the mercy of the court. He couldn't think of anything else to say in his defense, probably because he really had no defense.

Tracy looked at him, the man who mere moments ago was smiling and joking with her, much as they used to. Here was the one and only man she had given herself to, a decision that went against her faith but nevertheless formed a permanent bond with him as far as she was concerned. He had ultimately asked only one thing from her tonight: honesty. In spite of his crimes, the guilt of which he wasn't denying, she believed he was telling

    A Tracy Brubaker Mystery

her the truth tonight, the truth about everything. Maybe she was being foolish to even consider giving him another chance. But she was tired of wondering about the two of them, tired of playing what-if games, and tired of being alone. If this was a mistake, she'd beat herself up over it later. But she was still feeling vulnerable thanks to the events of the last few weeks: the death threat, her mother's stroke, and the fear of failing in her defense of Max Paganini. How much better it might have been for her emotionally if she had had someone to confide in, to know that she was loved, cared for, and protected in ways only lovers could do. Yes; yes, she would be honest with him.

"Tennyson," she said.

"What?"

"Alfred, Lord Tennyson said that about loving and losing."

"Oh."

There was more silence. "So you'll do anything for me; anything I ask?"

Brian straightened up, and moved closer still to her so they were now face to face. "Anything..."

"Can you be trusted to make me one more promise? Can I trust you, Brian?"

He nodded and said, "Yes," his voice cracking, his whole body overcome with the realization of what he believed was going to be her answer.

She put her hands on his cheeks and looked into his eyes. "You have to promise me that you will never, ever hurt me again like you did. Never."

Tears came down his cheeks but he was smiling, shaking his head. "Never," he repeated softly.

She continued her study of his eyes. "There won't be a third chance, Brian. Quite honestly I'm not sure I could survive going through that again a second time but..."

He continued shaking his head. "I won't need a third chance."

She smiled. "That doesn't sound very humble."

"On the contrary that's exactly what it is: I don't want to lose you again. You're the only woman I've ever truly loved and I'm going to make sure every minute we're together that you know by everything I do and everything I say that I love you. How can I be any more humble before you? Just don't ask me to kneel; I might rip my pants—they're kinda tight."

Now they were both smiling and it wasn't long until their lips were reintroduced, a totally mutual decision. Brian moved his lips to her cheek and then toward her neck. "I love you, Tracy," he said between signs of affection.

"I love you too Brian," she returned. And shortly thereafter the now-recommitted lovers moved to a different room in the condo, a place where more than their bodies would be laid bare; a place where, in spite of the darkness, they could still look into each other's eyes—the mirrors of their soul mate—contemplating a future once thought lost that was now, again, within reach.

A Tracy Brubaker Mystery

Chapter 2

When Brian Shane opened his eyes he realized he was alone. He checked the nightstand clock: 8:38 a.m. Wow, did *he* sleep in. He was usually up by 6:00. Of course it had been a late night; a wonderful night, as it turned out, far better than he dared imagine when he called just five days ago. He heard some noise from outside the bedroom. "Probably making us breakfast," he thought. He pulled on his slacks and headed in the direction of the gently crashing cookware.

Tracy was dressed in her bathrobe and barefoot. He observed her moving a spatula around a frying pan. He moved closer but dared not sneak up on her. "Good morning," he said softly.

She turned to face him, a warm smile across her face. "It certainly is. How do you want your omelet? I have shredded cheddar, diced ham, diced tomato, and diced green pepper as your choices."

"Just make it the same as yours," he said, now with his arms around her waist.

"Two everything omelets it is." He started kissing her neck. "You're going to make me burn the eggs, Romeo."

"I don't care about the eggs," he said now nuzzling her.

"I'm hungry; you wouldn't like me when I'm hungry."

He started chuckling. "Where are the plates, glasses, and silverware? I can at least set the table if my hands aren't welcome here."

She poked him in the ribs with her left elbow. "Don't be a sourpuss. The plates and cups are in the cabinet to my right, and the silverware in the first drawer right below it."

"Gotcha." Brian had the table set in a flash. "Do you want milk or OJ, hon?"

"OJ—a nice tall glass." Tracy brought her pan over and divided its contents more or less evenly between the two plates. Brian filled each neighboring glass with the juice. Then she took some butter and strawberry jam from the refrigerator and placed them on the table. When the toast was ready, she grabbed the two pieces and dropped one each on the plates. "Breakfast is served," she announced.

"Can I have a good morning kiss first? That should last me through breakfast."

"Oh really?" she asked smiling. "Well, okay, if you really think you need one."

The early meal was a mostly quiet affair. They exchanged frequent glances and smiles, but there was a certain comfort in the silence. "How are the eggs?" Tracy finally asked.

"Perfect."

"And the toast?"

"Perfect."

"And the juice?"

"Perfect."

She was softly laughing now. "You're too easy to please."

"Hardly; nobody but you pleases me."

She grinned. "You can stop with the pickup lines, Don Juan. I think you have my attention."

Brian blushed. "Sorry, I'm no Tennyson when it comes to romantic expression."

Tracy looked at him. "I thought what you said last night was rather beautiful."

"Really? I thought I just rambled."

"Ramble, shmamble. I thought you said what you wanted to say very effectively. I mean, I believed you."

"I meant every word of it, Tracy."

She smiled and returned to finishing her meal; she hated cold eggs. "So what do we do now?" she asked quietly. "I mean, after all the thought you put into last night, what did you see happening if things went your way?"

He swallowed his last drop of orange juice. "If I tell you I'm afraid I'll scare you off."

She continued looking at him. "I want to know, scary or not."

"Alright, I'll tell you. I thought last night would end with us saying goodnight and you telling me to call you some time; that you weren't quite ready to resume our relationship but that you would give me a chance. That's the most I was hoping for."

"And what was your real best case scenario? There was nothing scary about what you just told me."

He looked down at his plate. "Well, I guess, my best case one was pretty much how it went, except that I asked you to marry me and you said yes, and we were getting our license this morning. But of course I know you've always wanted a church wedding, so that was never gonna happen."

She was now wearing a sympathetic smile. "I don't think I'd call that scary; ambitious maybe."

He looked back up at her. "I guess it's not like riding a bike, is it? We really can't just pick up from the last good memory and pretend the rest didn't happen."

She leaned back in her chair. "I wish we could; I wish it were that easy. On the other hand, what's the point dwelling on the past?" She leaned toward him. "What do you want for our future Brian? Do you really still want what we talked about all those years ago?" She started rubbing his shins with her feet.

He leaned in, enjoying the massage. "Yes—marriage, kids, a house somewhere nice; the whole Norman Lear thing."

Tracy started laughing. "I think you mean Norman Rockwell."

Brian didn't smile. "I'm serious Tracy, imperfect as my expression may be."

She nodded. "Okay. Would it bother you if I had to work late every night for weeks on end on a case, or had to work some weekends on occasion?"

"I could bring you dinner. We could share a quick meal."

"I can get stressed out over cases sometimes; would you be able to deal with Bitchy Tracy?"

"I helped you study for how many exams while you sweated bullets? It couldn't be worse than that."

"Would you go to church with me every week and on holy days? Would you agree to raise our kids Catholic?"

"I actually have been going to church again as part of my program. I'd love to go with you; for us to go as a family."

"And would you keep secrets from me, even if you had the noblest of intentions?"

"What do you mean?"

"Like if you learned you had some inoperable brain tumor or something, and you thought by waiting to tell me you'd spare me some pain?"

"Oh. If you want to me tell you every time I get a splinter or paper cut I'll do it."

"And if you got the urge to drink, because you learned I was dying of cancer or something, would you be able to ignore it and stay sober?"

Her question stunned him; why was she getting so dark? His own mother had died of cancer when he was 14, a fact Tracy was very much aware of. He hated to consider such a thought. "I don't want to even contemplate something like that."

"I'm asking you to contemplate it. Could you stay sober if your world was dying?"

He gulped. Somebody must have been doing some rehearsing of her own while preparing breakfast. He hadn't been prepared for any tough inquiries. "I would need a lot of meetings and support to help get me through something like that. But I wouldn't drink." Then he smiled. "I wouldn't do that to God."

"What?" Tracy asked starting to laugh.

"I could see you up there in heaven, demanding an audience, ready to give God an earful for taking you from me and thus causing me to drink again. You'd have to vent to *someone*."

She was laughing heartily now. The dark cloud had apparently dispersed; they were both wearing smiles again. Soon that's all they were wearing. Years of pent-up passion and loneliness were going to be aggressively made up for, in part, for the remainder of the weekend. There was no logic to thinking that way; but for once Tracy didn't care about logic and thinking. These next hours would be for feeling, for canceling her reservations about being with Brian again. And as the weekend hours went by, she became even more passionate, more aggressive. She was in love again, madly in love again; the prodigal Brian had returned. And she had forgiven him. The future was tomorrow so she wasn't going to think too much about that. Here and now was all she cared about for the moment. Tracy Brubaker: Wild Child. She liked the sound of that.

It was early Sunday evening and Brian was preparing to leave. He didn't want to go of course; he would have asked to move in with her if he thought she would say yes. But in spite of what they had shared during the last 48 or so hours, he knew Tracy was at heart pretty old fashioned. She hadn't taken communion at Mass earlier in the day; he could guess the reason why. "Can we meet sometime tomorrow; for lunch, dinner, or a snack?" he asked as they were embracing by her front door.

"I have a client meeting at 11:00 a.m.; I'll probably eat lunch in a hurry. But dinner's a possibility; no promises though."

"I'll bring you dinner if you have to work late."

She smiled. "We'll see. I may be starting a new case tomorrow and I'll be pushing my little gray cells hard. I'm not going to want distractions. And you would be a distraction." She looked up at him and then kissed him. "I'll call when I'm certain about how tomorrow will go. Okay?"

"What choice do I have?" he smiled back.

"None really."

"You're going to enjoy wielding your power over me, aren't you?"

She chuckled. "Maybe a teensy weensy bit, yeah."

"I can take it." Then he kissed her firmly and gave her another squeeze. "I love you," he told her.

She met his eyes with hers. "I love you too. Now shoo." He opened her door, moved in for another not-that-quick-really smooch and then entered the hallway. She watched him as he stood waiting at the elevator. Then he disappeared into one of the cars, smiling and waving at her. And then the electronic doors closed.

Back inside she sat down on her couch, each hand rubbing the opposite upper arm. She was smiling. And she was missing him already. How was it possible she could just pretend the past didn't matter anymore? Because: suddenly it didn't. She was looking solely ahead. She wanted Brian Shane with her wherever her future was going to take her. Not perhaps, the wisest move. But her gut told her he was his old self again, the one she fell

                                   A Tracy Brubaker Mystery

in love with all those years ago and was in fact still in love with. She was happy and in love again and the hell with what her more practical side was trying to tell her. Tell her? She suddenly wondered what her mother would say when she found out. It was close to 7:00 and Tracy figured she should probably call her mom now, lest the woman start playing Let's Make a Worst Case Scenario in her mind. Tracy picked up her phone and dialed Violetta Brubaker's number.

"Hello?" the familiar voice asked.

"Hi Mom; just checking in. Everything okay?"

"I was starting to worry. You usually call Saturdays."

"Sorry about that. Something came up, again and again." And then Tracy started laughing at her very private, and rather dirty, joke. She had a hard time calming down.

"Tracy, what's the matter? When did you start drinking?"

Okay; that helped stopped the merriment. "I'm not drunk Mom, not the way you mean it."

"How else can one mean it?"

"Well you could be drunk on life, or happiness, or…love."

There was silence. "When did you start drinking? It was after my stroke, right?"

"No, Mom. For the last time I'm not drunk and I haven't even been drinking *at all*."

"Then what's going on; I can tell in your voice something is going on."

Tracy paused. "Mom, do you remember last year that I helped out Brian Shane?"

"Yes, I remember. I still don't understand that; he was so cruel to you."

Tracy gulped. "We're seeing each other again. We went on some dates this weekend."

More silence. "I thought he was a drunk."

"He's been getting help for that. He's been sober since his dad died last year. He's not that person anymore. He's the man you and Dad met at dinner that one time; the man you and Dad both liked."

"I never said I liked him."

"Oh yes you *did*."

"You're getting him confused with someone else I liked."

"I'm not the one who's confused here."

"You're being disrespectful."

"You're not going to spoil my mood Mom. If things work out, you could be getting what you've been nagging me about for years."

"I don't nag you about anything."

Argh, this woman. "Whatever Mom."

"Tracy, you shouldn't get your hopes up just because you spent a nice weekend with this man. You've been so alone for such a long time that any man who asked you out would probably do."

Unbelievable! "MOM! I think I'm done talking to you about this." Tracy took a deep breath. "Remember the Paganinis invited us over for Easter dinner next Sunday. I want to bring Brian with us."

"Well, that's not up to me."

"I know. And I know that Mr. P would have no problem with it."

"He doesn't know him; why should he have a problem with it?"

"You'd have to be nice to him."

"You don't get to tell me what to do, Tracy. I am *your* mother."

Tracy was officially irritated. "Maybe I'll just bring Brian with me then, if you're going to be that way about it."

"Tracy, how dare you talk to me like this?"

"Oh stop it! That routine isn't going to work with me here." Tracy had thought the experience of her mother's stroke had brought them closer together; helped them understand one another better. Now they were right back in their familiar pattern.

Violetta paused. "I want you to bring him here next Friday; Good Friday, for dinner."

"What?" she asked mildly panicked.

"I want to see the two of you together before you introduce him to Massimo and his family."

"Why? Are you going to poison his fish or something?"

"Oh, you difficult child. Just bring him over for dinner. You were coming over here anyway."

Tracy scratched her forehead. "Well, okay, if he doesn't already have plans saving the world or something."

"What does that mean?"

"Oh, didn't you know? Brian's now a superhero; he gallivants and traipses all around the globe saving those in trouble, except when he has time to stop by my place and give me some of that fine hot lovin'."

"I don't know what I'm going to do with you. You think you're so funny."

"I'll let you know about Good Friday, Mom. Now I think I hear a knock at my balcony door. Brian-man may have a new shield he wants to show me. I love you."

Tracy couldn't see her mother shaking her head, confused expression on her face. "I love you too, although I've given up on ever understanding you."

"Not possible to do Mom; I'm *way* too complicated. Ciao!" And then Tracy hung up. She stared at the receiver a moment as if it had just stuck its tongue out at her. "Oh, that woman sometimes!" she cried aloud. Then she forced a smile. She wasn't going to let this brief albeit exasperating phone call spoil her mood; no siree Bob.

She went back to sitting on her couch, still a bit grumpy. Then her phone rang. She grabbed the receiver. "Hello," she said flatly.

 A Tracy Brubaker Mystery

"Hey beautiful; miss me yet?"

She grinned. "Is this the plumber who keeps asking to check my pipes?"

Brian started laughing. "No."

"The dry cleaner who wants to… clean my dryer…dry my…OK, I don't really have anything for that."

"Tracy you crack me up." She could hear him laughing.

"At least I amuse somebody."

"What?"

"Are you free for dinner Good Friday?"

"I'm free for the rest of my life as far as you're concerned."

"My mother wants us over for dinner."

"Your *mother*?"

"I just spoke with her a few moments ago."

"Holy moley Tracy what did you tell her?"

"That we tried every position in the Kama Sutra this weekend and then made up some of our own."

"You…oh very funny." Tracy of course couldn't see how red Brian's face now was. "Seriously, what did you tell her?"

"Just that we were seeing each other again; I left out what exactly we were seeing."

Brian chuckled. "Tracy, for such a button-down type you can be… well…"

"So I can tell her we'll be there?"

"Sure, I guess."

"How about Easter Sunday? I have a previous engagement but I know I could bring a date."

"Will your mother be there?"

"I'll make her ride in the back and put her at the kids' table."

More laughing. "Count me in then."

"Good," Tracy said without much enthusiasm.

"Good," Brian returned, a bit confused.

"Well, okay then," Tracy said, still sounding a little irritated.

"Tracy, do you want me to come over and give you a massage or something? I can *feel* the tension all the way over here."

Now Tracy finally laughed. And then she lied to him. "No, you don't need to come over. I'm fine."

"You sure? Say the word and I'm there with bells on."

"And nothing else I bet."

"Tracy, you're killing me talking like that."

"Sorry, I don't want you dead quite yet. Plus, I do need to be up early tomorrow."

"Well, alright. But I'm missing you already."

"Keep the thought. I'll call you tomorrow."

"Okay. I love you."

"I love you too. And thanks for a…a perfect weekend. I love you." And then she hung up before she told him how much she wanted him there with her right now. The button-down side of her however, for better or worse, still wielded some control.

Based on the look on Rebecca's face as she entered Tracy's office early Monday morning, the five-foot-five, auburn-haired attorney suspected that her secretary had spent the whole weekend wondering about Tracy's date. "Good morning Tracy. So how did it go?"

"How did what go?" she teased.

"You're in a good mood — translation, it went rather well."

Tracy smiled, blushing a bit. "You could say that."

Rebecca smiled broadly. "So you two are officially seeing each other again?"

"Yup, we're officially seeing a lot of each other again."

Rebecca's eyes widened. "Tracy: *that* good a weekend?!"

Tracy just grinned and nodded. "I don't know what came over me, Beck. I just kind of tossed all doubts, inhibitions, and the rest of it aside. The pressure of the last few weeks had been so overwhelming, so awful, I just said the hell with all. You know what I mean?"

"You bet. I know *exactly* what you mean."

"Now don't tell Neal anything about this."

"No way."

"Thanks. I like to keep my private life private, you know. But if things go okay, I may not be able to keep things private for very long."

Rebecca's expression was now set for stunned. "Tracy, you don't think you're — "

"Oh, no. I should be fine. I know my cycle well enough. I just meant that Brian may be stopping by for late night dinners and things."

"Oh; gotcha."

"But let me be the one to deal with Neal."

"Hey, no problem. I'm so psyched things are looking good for you. I mean, you certainly deserve some happiness, especially after all you just went through." Rebecca flashed Tracy another wide smile and then moved toward the office coffee pot. The schedule over the next few days would be a light one given it was Holy Week. The office would be closed on Friday. There were going to be plenty of opportunities to daydream. But for now Tracy was going to look up everything she could find on the Timothy Pane murder, and what was being said about the man arrested for it, Colin Richmond. She also was curious what she could learn of Richmond's father's murder. Normally she'd have asked Neal to gather this info together. But since she had no idea if Richmond would in fact be a client, she decided she'd be the only one spending time on the case for now. Unfortunately there was little she could find on the older murder, and there wasn't

 A Tracy Brubaker Mystery

much more on the more recent one that Dr. Braxton hadn't already told her about. Well, she'd let Neal work his magic if she ended up agreeing to defend Colin Richmond.

Tracy was led through the halls of the Baltimore City Detention Center to her 11:00 a.m. meeting with Colin Richmond. He was dressed in the customary orange jump suit, and looked older than the 44 years she assumed he was based on what Dr. Braxton had told her last Thursday. He was an average looking man of average height, a conclusion Tracy reached when Richmond stood to shake her hand. It was a soft handshake.

"I can't tell you how much I appreciate this, Ms. Brubaker," Richmond said quietly.

"Please call me Tracy. If we're going to be working together it will make things easier." Tracy removed her yellow letter-sized notepad and a pen from her briefcase.

"Okay. Fine."

She could tell he was nervous; the worried eyes were those she recognized as resembling Brian Shane's and Massimo Paganini's at one time or another during their ordeals. But it was way too early to be reaching conclusions.

"What did Dr. Braxton tell you about me?" she asked him.

"That you were a great attorney, one of the best students he ever had. And that I could trust you."

"Well, I meant more along the lines of my experience in murder trials."

"Oh; not much really."

"I've only handled one murder case that's gone to trial before."

"But you won that one, right?"

"Yes. But one success does not guarantee another."

"Yeah; I get that. But the guy I have now says I should just take the State's offer: 10 years."

"Voluntary manslaughter?"

"I think so."

"The cops' theory is that you had another fight and this time you stabbed him?"

"I'm not sure."

"You don't know what the exact charges are against you?"

"Well, I think it's actually second-degree murder. The deal is for voluntary manslaughter."

"Okay; that follows. Look, I need you to fully understand that my experience in murder trials is practically nonexistent. I'm not some superstar."

"This guy I have now doesn't care if I really did it or not. He keeps telling me trials are about proof, not truth. He's got all kind of jingles like that."

"Jingles?"

"Sayings, one-liners."

"Oh, I see. And you want someone who believes you're innocent to defend you."

"Right."

"But how can you expect anyone who doesn't know you to be able to talk with you a few minutes and know you're innocent? There are people out there who've been married to their spouses for years and are shocked when they learn dark secrets about them, usually during their arrest."

"Yeah, I guess you're right."

"Did you know that an attorney, if you confessed your guilt to her, cannot get up in front of a jury and say, 'My client is innocent of these charges'?"

"No, I didn't know that."

"That's why maybe your attorney didn't want to know; he didn't want you to confess and tie his hands."

"Maybe."

"I just mean there could be reasons other than him not caring for not specifically asking about whether you're innocent or not."

"I see what you mean. But I think he just wants me to plead this out."

Tracy sighed. "Okay, Colin. So tell *me* what you wanted to tell *him*. Did you kill that man?"

He looked at her. "No, I didn't. I hardly knew him."

"What about your father: did you kill him?"

"No, I didn't kill him either." His face started getting red. "I mean I was cleared on that. But they brought all that up at my bail review hearing. How can they do that when I wasn't sent to jail for it?"

"I'm sorry Colin. That's the law. You'll note that verdicts in cases aren't guilty or innocent; they're guilty or not guilty. It's a subtle but to my mind obvious position that our legal system has: if we arrested you, you're probably guilty. But if you're sent home, it's not because you're innocent, it's because we just didn't prove you were guilty."

Richmond started nodding. "Yeah; yeah I can see that. You really nailed it there."

"Don't misunderstand me though Colin. I still believe that we have the best legal system in the world and the lion's share of people involved in it—from the judges all the way to the investigating officers—do their best to make sure the wrong people don't get arrested. But they're human, and mistakes get made."

"They've made a mistake here. I didn't kill that guy."

"Do you know how your fingerprints got on the knife?"

"No. I'd never even been to his apartment."

"Had he been to yours?"

   A Tracy Brubaker Mystery

"No. We just had casual meetings: a few beers at the bar, small talk about the Ravens; in fact the night he freaked out was the first thing like that we had. You know: something formal."

"Where were you eating again?"

"Denzinger's Steaks and Chops; we were at the one just off Cathedral Street."

"Sure, sure; I've heard of it. There are a few of those places throughout Maryland."

"Yeah, right. So Tim makes the reservation, we're having a nice talk about whatever—I mean I had some wine so I'm not sure what exactly we were talking about. Then all of a sudden he throws his napkin down, stands up, and starts yelling at me. I didn't know what was going on. Then he just leaves, and everybody's staring at me. I mean…Jesus."

"So you have no idea what set him off."

"None; and that's the absolute truth. I never saw him again. He was… dead a couple days later. I…I just don't understand it."

Tracy studied him. "Do you know if anyone saw you at his place, or rather claimed to see you there?"

"I'm not sure. The cops just talked about the knife and the argument and that got them what they needed. My lawyer said they may not have divulged all they had though. The State wouldn't want to—let's see how did he put it—show their whole hand?"

Tracy nodded. "Right. And how did you meet this Pane guy again?"

"I was in line buying some lottery tickets for the office, and this guy comes over to me swearing he knows me. I'd never seen him before. A couple days later I'm at a bar downtown—Ritchie's Digs—and I hear someone whistling my father's favorite song, just like my father used to whistle it."

"And it turns out to be Tim Pane."

"Exactly. So I go over to him and when we're walking back to the bar counter for another round I see he's limping like my father used to. My dad broke his leg as a baby and it never healed right; at least that's what I remember being the reason given. So we have a few drinks, talking about stuff, and I find out he likes the same kind of music and food and other things that my dad liked. Then a couple days after that we're at the same bar *again*, but this time he insists on picking up the tab. When he pulls out his wallet I see his license and can't help but notice the birth date."

"The day your dad died."

"Right. So, yeah, I was getting pretty creeped-out. I didn't even know what I believed yet."

"Hmm. Very interesting indeed." Tracy paused a moment. "Colin: are you sure Mr. Pane understood that the two of you were just pals. I mean, could he have thought you were—how shall I put this—interested in him?"

He looked at her, and then the color took a beeline from his face. "Wait—do you mean like he wanted to date me or something?"

"Well, maybe you were having those drinks of yours, and you made some remark that offended him. You know, like guys sometimes kid around with other guys and call them names that might be offensive to gay people."

"What?" he asked angrily. "You sayin' I'm a homophobe or something?"

"No Colin; relax. I'm saying you may have, without any intention of being mean-spirited or cruel, nevertheless said something he took as offensive, and that's why he left. We live in an age of hyper-sensitivity."

The color returned to the incarcerated one's cheeks. "Oh, I see what you mean. I crossed a line or something without meaning to."

"Exactly."

"Well, I don't know. He never said anything that sounded like a come on. I guess I never really thought about it."

"Your lawyer didn't bring this possibility up?"

"No. I swear you've spent more time talking to me today than the other guy has during the last couple months."

"Oh." She looked at her notepad. "Colin, it sounds to me like you were set up."

"That's what I've been saying this whole time. But nobody will even listen to me. It's just like the last time."

Tracy looked at him sympathetically. "Luckily you were cleared of that."

"Maybe in the courtroom; not in the cops' minds though. I think they may have something to do with this. Maybe they helped frame me."

"That's a very dangerous alley to walk through, Colin; believe me."

"Well, it's not right. I was just hearing how one of those cops that busted me is getting rewarded for taking down some crooked real estate guy; huh, some hero."

Tracy's head perked up. "Reginald Walters?" she asked, referring to the man that Tracy helped bring to justice via her defense of Max Paganini.

"Yeah, that guy."

"And what's the name of the officer that helped bust you?"

"Well he's a big-deal detective now: Detective Elias Tanner." Tracy's heart sank as Richmond continued. "If there were any justice in this world they'd throw that Tanner prick in the slammer along with the man who really killed my father."

     A Tracy Brubaker Mystery

Chapter 3

Tracy had been prepared to take Colin Richmond's case. She believed he'd been honest with her and she felt great sympathy for him. But the revelation of the involvement of her father's former partner, someone who had been like a second father to Tracy in the years after Peter Brubaker's murder, had given her pause. Richmond had no way of knowing about Tanner's exceptional record and reputation in the Baltimore Police Department; that his run-in with Tanner 27 years ago was most likely being remembered through something less than rose-colored glasses. But as part of her defense she was going to have to poke around into Richmond's previous arrest; there was no way around that. Her reasoning: if Richmond was innocent, then he was set up, and the victim Timothy Pane *had* to be involved in that set up. Of course Pane had no way of knowing his own murder was part of the ultimate plan. But Pane had approached Richmond initially; *Pane* had started the ball rolling. So the murderer had to have set the whole thing up using Pane as an accomplice, and Tracy had to wonder just how the mastermind found Pane, a man with a birthday matching the elder Richmond's date of death. There was no way this was all a coincidence. Both murders had to be linked. So Tracy had been silently working through theories as Richmond answered her questions.

Now Tracy was wondering what kind of person would have access to that kind of private information: not too many people. Unless the villain turned out to be a friend or acquaintance of Pane's, how did he learn the date of Pane's birth? Someone with access to computers located at BPD could have. Tracy didn't like the thought that a law enforcement person could be involved in this; in fact, she outright loathed it. But Richmond's suggestion that the police had framed him was now involuntarily being factored into her preliminary theory.

"What is it Tracy?" Richmond finally said.

"What?" Tracy asked, her ruminations having been interrupted.

"You just kind of stopped talking."

"Oh, I'm sorry Colin," she said a bit sheepishly. "I took a trip to Planet Tracy for a moment. Sorry about that."

"Oh, no problem." Richmond cleared his throat. "So what do you think? Will you take over my case for me? I mean, I like you. I could see working with you."

Tracy paused. "There may be a problem."

"What?"

"To be blunt: I'm friends with Detective Tanner; more than friends actually."

Richmond stared at her, mildly shocked. "What, you two are hooked up?"

Tracy couldn't help slightly laughing. "Oh, no; not that. He was my father's partner many years ago. He's a close friend of the family; he is family."

Richmond looked as the table in front of him. "Oh," was all he said.

"That could work to your advantage in that I have a source that is more likely to talk to me than anyone else you may hire to defend you. On the other hand, I think rather highly, to put it mildly, of Detective Tanner. I refuse to believe, even almost 30 years ago, that he would knowingly arrest someone he thought was innocent. He's a good man."

Richmond looked to the side. "Well, he…he pushed pretty hard. It was clear he thought I did it right from the beginning."

"Look, Colin: I wasn't there obviously so I'm not going to presume to tell you what he did or didn't do or say. I'm just trying to be honest with you about a bias I'm going to have here. Is that going to be a problem for you?"

Now Richmond was looking at her again. "You know what? It won't. I won't let it. I want you as my lawyer. I like you."

Tracy smiled. "Okay Colin. Inform your current counsel about your wish to change. You'll have to sign some papers to allow him to release to me whatever information he has, as well as speak to me about any private communications you two have had."

"Sure; whatever you say."

She smiled again. "I'll have a standard letter of engagement prepared which you can then sign to make this all official. I'll be in touch." Tracy rose to her feet and returned her notebook to her briefcase.

"Thanks, Tracy. Thank you so much. I promise you I didn't do this." He offered her his hand once again, and they shook.

"I believe you Colin. I promise I'll do whatever I can." She smiled one last time at him for the day and knocked on the exit door. The guard was soon there to release her and she made her way back to her car. She found herself smiling again, this time thinking of Professor Braxton: so that's the real reason he thought of her for this case. He would have interviewed and cross examined Tanner all those years ago, and she was sure he knew about Tanner and her relationship. "Sneaky, Professor," she thought. But she wasn't mad at him. Nevertheless she planned to tease her mentor about it at some point, maybe to the point of getting another expensive meal.

Still in her car she decided to phone Rebecca. "Beck, I'm done with my 11:00. I'm going to stop at BPD before coming back though."

"Okay."

"I'll probably be back around 2:00."

"You have a 2:30 p.m. in-house meeting."

"Right—shouldn't be a problem."

                    A Tracy Brubaker Mystery

"You need anything?"

"I'm good Beck. See you about 2:00."

"Righto." Then Rebecca clicked off.

"Might as well get this out in the open now," Tracy thought as she left the detention center and headed for an impromptu meeting with Detective Elias Tanner.

"Hi El," Tracy said as she entered Tanner's office. "How's the wonderful world of you?" She gave him a quick hug, which he gladly accepted, and then she sat down in the chair that faced his desk.

Tanner smiled. "Don't mind making yourself comfortable."

"Ha," she smiled back. "Not much comfort here, El. But I'll make it work."

He chuckled. "Why don't you just start bringing your own chair then? There's nothing in the budget right now for furniture upgrades."

"Oh, you're cute," she grinned.

Tanner sat down. "You seem to be in great spirits. Things are good?"

"Yes, they are." She paused. "I have something personal to share. And then I have what I hope isn't too unpleasant business."

Tanner gave her a curious look. "Okay—what's your good news?"

She grinned again. "I'm seeing Brian Shane again. I didn't plan for it to get so, um, let's say serious so fast. I mean, in spite of the years gone by I…well, it's like we just…well, like we picked up from where we left off… kind of."

Tanner was grinning. Tracy wasn't one to hem and haw; she usually said what she wanted to say with little hesitation in saying it. "I see," was all he said. "So he's been staying sober then?"

"Yes. I'm so proud of him, El. He really seems to be the person I remember before it all went bad. I…I just thought I should tell you for some reason."

He nodded. "And have you told your mother about this?"

Tracy sighed. "Yes. She invited Brian over for dinner Good Friday. I guess she wants to see for herself his—well, let's call it a rebirth."

"Well good luck, Tracy. You two certainly picked an appropriate time to meet up again. I mean: Easter is about redemption and forgiveness, right?"

Tracy smiled widely. "Exactly, El. That's exactly it. I don't want to be mad at him anymore. I want to give him another chance. I think it's going to work out. I still…I still love him, El."

Tanner looked at her seriously. "I hope it works out for you two. I really do."

"Thanks El," was all she could say.

"Now: what is the good news?"

"Oh, you're funny."

He laughed. "Sorry; couldn't resist."

"Uh-huh. Well, I guess you heard Colin Richmond got arrested for another murder."

Tanner stared at her and immediately passed "go." "You're his new attorney, are you?"

"You're as quick as ever, El. I met with him this morning. I didn't know you were involved with his first case until then."

Tanner looked toward his office window. "So, now that you know, you're here to what exactly?"

"Just to get your impressions of him. I know it was like 27 years ago or something. You were what, 29?"

"Yes, I was 29. Six years as an officer, about to make the leap to detective."

"And this case helped with that leap?"

"Not exactly; my next case did though, and I started a partnership with a certain person you may be familiar with."

Tracy grinned. "Okay. So what do you remember about Richmond?" Tracy didn't want to suggest any adjectives of her own.

Tanner looked back at her. "To be honest Tracy: I thought he was a punk. He was mouthy and defiant, not sad and helpful like you'd expect someone who just lost their father that way to be. He was confrontational the entire duration of the investigation and the trial. I didn't like him. And there was plenty of evidence against him to continue to make me not like him."

Tracy nodded. "So he didn't seem that upset by his father's death?"

"He was too busy trying to play a tough guy. He fought with his father all of the time. As soon as we started interviewing neighbors they all asked if we talked to the son; they all said he probably killed Jackson Richmond."

Tracy nodded again. "I haven't really gotten into the details of the old case yet. Would you mind telling me what you remember?"

"Why should I mind? You can go through the transcripts at some point. It was August 1987; someone made a 911 call reporting a body. Me and another officer responded and found Jackson Richmond dead from blunt force trauma, a couple blows to the head with a high school baseball trophy or something like it that belonged to his son, Colin. Neighbors we talked to said they heard arguing that night. Colin wasn't there though when we arrived."

"What about Mrs. Richmond?"

"She'd been out of the picture for a while; just up and left one day."

"Oh."

"We were still at the crime scene when Colin showed up. Said he was at the movies — *The Lost Boys* is what he went to see if I remember correctly."

"Did he go to the movies with anyone?"

"No — said he just decided to up and go. He had already seen it five times or something like that, escapist entertainment and all."

"So how did he react when you told him his dad was dead?"

 A Tracy Brubaker Mystery

Tanner paused. "He seemed surprised; then we started asking questions about the evening, then got more specific about *his* evening. That's when he started giving us grief, using profanity, that sort of thing."

"You hadn't accused him of anything yet?"

"No; we were just asking questions. No accusations were made. He was told again and again we were just trying to get a time line together to narrow down the events of the evening. But that's not how he saw it."

"Teen rebel type, huh?"

"Complete with black leather jacket and greased-back hair, believe it or not; and perhaps a guilty conscience."

"Oh. What was the evidence? I assume his prints were on the murder weapon."

"Yes; we had that, the history, his refusal to cooperate, and a witness to the crime."

"A witness?" Tracy asked, mildly shocked.

"Yup; a 45-year-old librarian who was across the street sitting on her balcony sipping iced tea and reading a book on…what was it? I think it was philosophers or something like that."

"A librarian? Did she wear glasses?"

"Yes. But she had them on. She heard the yelling, looked over, and saw Colin beating his father."

"Wait a minute: she positively identified Colin? Actually saw his face?"

Tanner shifted a bit in his chair. "From the angle she was sitting at she saw his leather jacket and jeans."

"So what she really saw was someone dressed like Colin hitting his father."

"At the end of the day that's what Colin's defense attorney had the jury believing. A pretty big coincidence if you ask me though."

"Well, black jackets and jeans isn't that unusual an outfit. Still, the jury acquitted him on just that?"

"Acquitted? It was a hung jury. The State decided not to re-try it after they found out half the jury voted not guilty. They thought the same thing would just keep happening, so they dismissed the charges."

"So basically everybody thought a murderer walked."

"Bingo," Tanner said without amusement.

"Well, there were no true eyewitnesses, and of course Colin's prints would have been on the weapon anyway since it was his trophy. Maybe the SA moved too quickly."

Tanner nodded. "You may be right about that; hindsight is 20/20 though."

"Sure. Did he sue the city or anything?"

"No, he just kind of slithered away. I've tried not to give it too much thought since then. But I must admit I'm surprised by how vivid the details still are. I guess I always remember the ones that got away best."

"Sorry El. I…wait. The other lawyer didn't come to see you about this?"

"Nope."

Tracy shook her head. "Okay. I thought he might have. Well, I'm sorry I had to bring it up. You're not involved at all in Richmond's current case?"

"No. Danbury has it. She's a good detective, Tracy. I think you'll like her. But she won't like you that much."

Tracy looked taken aback. "El, everybody loves Tracy. I should have my own sit-com."

Now Tanner was laughing again. "Not Shandi. Trust me Tracy, she's been divorced almost a year now and we still are hearing about her ex."

"What does her ex have to…Oh, I see. Was he criminal or civil?"

"Divorce was and is his specialty."

"She married a divorce attorney?"

"Yes, Tracy. Divorce attorneys get married too you know."

Tracy scowled. "I don't handle divorces; they're too depressing."

"I don't think Shandi will care. Plus, you're representing Richmond. She doesn't like him either."

"Well, you could put in a good word for me, couldn't you El?"

Tanner smiled. "I'm going to stay out of this as much as I can. Anything else?"

Tracy closed her notebook. "I guess not then. Time I skedaddled." Tracy rose and headed toward Tanner's office door. "Happy Easter, El."

"You too, Tracy. Tell your mother I said hello."

"Thanks."

"And good luck with your new fellow. I hope it works out for you."

"Thanks squared." She put her hand on the doorknob and then looked at Tanner. "Are you angry at me for taking the case?"

Tanner shook his head. "Of course not, Tracy. I think you've picked a bad horse this time out. But I'm not angry at you for doing your job."

Tracy smiled. "Okay; good. 'Bye." And then she was out the door. "So, a hung jury the first time around," she thought as she navigated her way to her auto. "And Richmond's lawyer never bothered to talk to El about the first case either. Am I missing something here?" Tracy tossed her coat and case in the backseat and then started her trek back to her office building. She found herself wondering about Shandi Danbury and how to approach she who hates attorneys. "Maybe a chocolate Easter bunny would work," she thought smiling to herself, having Easter on the brain. "Everybody may not love Tracy but most people love cute chocolate bunnies." And then Tracy made a mental note to add such a thing to her shopping list.

Tracy's 2:30 meeting lasted until past 5:00. An older couple, their accountant, and Tracy went through several permutations of various trust agreements for the pair's four children. At the end of the day it had been a

 A Tracy Brubaker Mystery

good meeting, with thanks given to everyone by the parents. Tracy was escorting her clients to the exit when she noticed the sharply dressed gentleman standing in her lobby. After everyone left he approached Tracy before Rebecca could make introductions.

"I'm Nick Fallston," he said offering his hand.

"Hi, Mr. Fallston. I'm Tracy. What can I—"

"Up until a few hours ago I was Colin Richmond's attorney."

Tracy went slightly pale. "Oh. Well, I want to assure you—"

"May we have a few moments?" he interrupted again.

"Um, okay. Follow me to my desk." Once inside her personal office she offered him a seat.

"I'll stand. So I understand you're pretty new to criminal law."

"In practice, yes."

"It's a different ballgame from business and civil matters."

Tracy's color was returning, and now in danger of hitting the red zone. "Yes, Mr. Fallston. I made Mr. Richmond perfectly aware of my lack of court experience in criminal cases. He still decided to retain me."

"He doesn't understand the reality of his situation. Do you?"

Danger, Will Robinson. "I beg your pardon."

"That the jury is going to find out about his past crime, even though he was never convicted."

"A judge won't admit that into evidence."

"That's not what I said, is it? I said they'll find out about it, no matter what the rules say."

Tracy scowled at the now unwelcome visitor. "What is it I can do for you, Mr. Fallston?"

"I want to make sure your new client and you understand that a plea is the best thing for him here."

"Uh-huh."

"The jury will look at him like someone who got away with murder once, and so they'll convict him on this crime to make up for it."

"You're sure of that, are you?"

"Yes, I am. I've seen it happen several times, on evidence less compelling than what the State has this time."

"Even if he's innocent?"

"That has nothing to do with it. Trials are about proof, not truth."

"Catchy."

"Huh?"

"That's a pretty cynical look at things, don't you think?"

"Do you know how many years *I've* been practicing criminal law Ms. Brubaker?"

"How about a hint? Do I get a prize if I guess correctly?"

"Twelve years."

"Oooooooooo..." Tracy exhaled widening her eyes in the process.

Fallston blinked, momentarily at a loss for words. "What is your problem?"

"You are," she answered quickly. "Who do you think you are coming into my office and then acting all high and mighty? Did somebody hurt your *feewins* or something? This is a cynical-free zone Mr. Fallston. Do not bring your 12 years of cynicism here."

Fallston's mouth slightly dropped. "Okay, look. I'm sorry. You're right, I guess I came off like a…Well, I really didn't mean to show you any disrespect."

Tracy's blood temp was returning to normal but she still wished Fallston would leave. "Again I ask: what can I do for you?"

"Believe it or not I just want to make sure you know what you're in for with this case. The police have another shot at a guy they think got away with murder before. You are going to find that, if you have any contacts or friends with the BPD or the SA's office, they're suddenly going to stop returning your calls. You think I'm cynical. Wait until the first time it happens."

"Okay, Mr. Fallston. You've made your point. I understand where you're coming from. But Mr. Richmond, as you know, says he's innocent. And I'm not going to force him to take a plea, nor will my defense suffer because of it."

"I wouldn't have pursued any less vigorous a defense. I wasn't given much of chance to do so."

"I had nothing to do with that."

"I know that. But you've only had one criminal trial. I'm well aware it worked out quite successfully for you. But they all aren't going to go that way."

"No, I guess they all won't at that."

"Okay. Well, I wish you luck. Oh, and here," he said handing Tracy a piece of paper. "Just sign below Mr. Richmond's signature there and I'll send you what I have by way of interviews and the like. I've already alerted the SA that you're now Richmond's attorney."

"Let me run this through my copy machine and then you can have it right back," Tracy said after adding her name as instructed. Seconds later she returned. "Here you are Mr. Fallston: all nice and official now."

He looked at the paper. "Fine." He sighed. "Look, I'm sorry again for being disrespectful. I'm only concerned that Mr. Richmond doesn't fully appreciate his situation. I hope I'm wrong and that you're right and that he'll be okay at the end of the day."

Tracy sighed too. Maybe Fallston wasn't as uncaring as Richmond made him out to be after all. "Let's just forget about all of that then," Tracy said smiling. "Let me show you out."

He smiled in return. "Thank you. And of course you can call me with anything that's not clear in what I forward to you; which reminds me:

here." He offered her his card. She accepted it and gave him one of hers. Then he said "Goodbye" and was on his way to the elevators.

"Everything okay Tracy?" Rebecca asked.

"Oh sure; just a little misunderstanding. I guess Mr. Fallston cared more about his former client than said client thought. He just needed some work on his Tracy skills."

Rebecca laughed. "Is he skilled now?"

"I think so," Tracy grinned. "Where's Neal?"

"He left. He said if you needed anything to feel free to call him."

Tracy looked at her watch. "Oh! It is well past 5:00, Beck. You can brave the streets if you wish."

"Only if you don't need anything. Are you working late? Do you want me to order you something before I go?"

"Nah. I have dinner covered I think."

"Oh, I see," Rebecca said giving her boss a suggestive grin. "Well, then maybe I should get out of here pronto."

"Oh stop it," Tracy laughed. "Don't make me regret sharing my innermost secrets with you."

Rebecca chuckled. "Okay. Goodnight Tracy." And then Rebecca left the office, locking the door behind her. Tracy looked at her watch again: nearly 6:00. She smiled. She quickly returned to her office, picked up her mobile phone and punched in Brian Shane's number.

"This is Brian," he answered.

"I'd like to place an order for delivery."

There was brief silence on the other end. "And what shall it be tonight ma'am?" he asked, a smile obviously on his face from the sound of it.

"Got any specials?"

"I'll try to make anything you order special ma'am. What are you in the mood for?"

"Oh, maybe some exotic chicken and pasta dish—yes, chicken and pasta in a cream sauce. And a side salad."

"Okay. Where am I delivering tonight?"

"My place; 7:00 is a good time. Will that work for you?"

"I'll make it work."

"What discounts do you offer if you're late?"

"I guess we'll have to work something out. I wonder if maybe I *should* be late."

Tracy laughed. "If you want to take your chances…"

"I'm leaving now. Do I get a bonus if I'm early?"

"I'll see you around 7:00, Brian."

"Right. Oh, by the way: I love you."

"Hey you flirt—I'm just ordering dinner here." She paused to let Brian get his chuckles out of the way. "But I love you too. See you shortly."

Brian was, alas, late. He didn't ring her doorbell until 20 minutes after their agreed-upon meet time. She opened her door. "I'm going to have to speak with your manager boy. Now get in here."

"Sorry, ma'am. The cook was slow."

"The cook huh?"

Brian put the food on the kitchen counter. When he turned around Tracy was in front of him. She moved toward him, put her hands on his neck, and pulled him toward her. Their passionate hello lasted for several minutes. Finally she pulled away, grabbed his arms turning him 180 degrees, and removed his coat.

"Wow; I get this for being *late*?"

Tracy moved toward her front closet. "Just imagine what you would have gotten if you were on time, or early."

Brian's eyes widened. "Not fair," he said. "Circumstances were beyond my control."

Tracy laughed. "What do you want to drink, tardy boy?"

"I…I guess just water."

"Sure — how many lumps?"

"What?"

"Ice cubes; work with me here, Brian."

"Oh, right. How could I forget that? Two should be fine."

Tracy gave him another smile and then filled two glasses. From the cabinet she removed two plates, divided the contents of the takeout container, and then grabbed two forks and knives from the silverware drawer. Brian just watched her. She placed the filled dishes, utensils, and glasses on her four-person dining table and sat down. Brian was *still* looking at her.

"Come on Brian: right foot, left foot, right foot, left foot…" She was still smiling.

"I…oh, sure. I don't know what's with me tonight." He smiled an embarrassed smile and then joined her. They said evening grace and then sampled the late-arriving vittles.

"Not too bad, Brian," Tracy said. "Cream sauce is just right, chicken is good; pasta could be better."

Brian smiled. "You should let me cook for you next time. I could even make some more acceptable noodles *now* if you have any tucked away."

Tracy chuckled. "It's fine Brian. I'm still thinking of last Friday's dinner. Anything is going to pale in comparison to that for the next few days."

Brian nodded. "It *was* good, wasn't it? Did I tell you that was my first time there?"

Tracy's eyes widened a bit. "No, I don't think you did."

"Crystal recommended it."

Tracy smiled. "Oh, I see. And what have you told Crys about us? I keep meaning to call her."

"I just told her we were officially seeing each other again. That satisfied her I think."

"Okay."

"I didn't want to go too much into it."

Tracy felt her cheeks flush. "Oh, well I…She doesn't need to know all about that."

Brian put his fork down; not that it mattered, as he had hardly eaten anything. "Oh, I didn't mean it like that. I would never go into details… Not even with Crystal."

Now: her whole head was as red as a beet. "Brian, look…um…I kind of just let loose this weekend. I don't know what came over me…Yikes…I mean…I can't believe I…"

"Tracy," Brian said starting to laugh. "It's alright. I think I know what you're trying to say and I feel the same way about it. I mean, I think we both went a little crazy. I hope you're not saying you're sorry for it though."

Tracy shook her head. "Oh, no no no…that's not it."

"Well good. I know that was probably just a once in a lifetime thing."

"Yeah, that's what I was trying to say. At least until we're married." Tracy stopped chewing her food. Again, she was saying things out loud she didn't mean to. So now Brian knew for certain what she was thinking. Why did it bother her that he *did* now know? Well, she had lost a little of her power; knowledge was power after all. She put her head down. "Oh dear," she mumbled.

Brian was smiling at her. He reached for her free hand. "Tracy, what's wrong?" he asked.

"I shouldn't have said that," she answered quickly. "I mean, we still need some more time together, don't we? I mean, before we start talking about…well, I just shouldn't have said it."

"But you *know* I still want to marry you."

"Yes, I do. But I still think we should give it some time. Right now we're in the 'excited to be back together' phase. And that's great and all. But what about when that phase is done? You see what I mean?"

He shook his head. "Not exactly. My feelings aren't going to change; why would they? I think what you're trying to tell me is that you need some more time to work through it, in your mind anyway. And that's fine; I didn't expect to re-sweep you off your feet really. But Tracy," he said, leaning closer to her, "I think you do really still love me. And I think deep down you know I've righted my life. And there's only one course I'm trav-elling." They were very close now, eye to eye, feeling the other's breath on their cheeks.

"Brian, don't you want to finish dinner?" He shook his head. "Then what do you want to do?"

"Is that a trick question; I mean, seriously."

"We both have to work tomorrow."

"I'm not asking to spend the night," he said, now almost whispering. "You're still the practical one."

"One of us has to—" But she didn't finish her sentence. Brian and she had found other uses for their lips. Soon their unfinished plates sat lonely at the table.

It was almost midnight when Brian put his coat on to leave. He looked at her seriously as he turned to say goodnight. He kissed her and then embraced her. "So how long then?"

"What?" she asked in return.

"How long do you think it will be when you've moved on to the next phase?"

She pulled back so that she was facing him. "I don't know Brian. I don't know how I could possibly answer that."

"I'm sorry; unfair question."

She smiled. "You don't have to apologize. You don't have to apologize for loving me and wanting to marry me. I wish I knew why I'm hesitating."

Brian nodded. "I think I know."

She looked at him quizzically. "Oh you do, do you?" she asked him, now smiling. "Well could you please enlighten *me*? I'd really like to know."

He started stroking her cheek with his thumb. "Because this is all too good to be true. I know I think it is. I still can't believe you've let me back into your life after all these years. And I think part of you—that practical part of you—still can't believe, after being apart for so long, that we could be together again feeling like we felt all those years ago, now in a position where we can act on it. But *I'm* going to believe it. And I just hope soon you'll believe it too."

She closed her eyes. Then she started contorting her face. Brian asked, "What's wrong?"

"I sent my non-practical side over to my practical one to have a few words with her and now they're arguing and I think there will be blood."

Brian started laughing heartily. "Oh, Tracy I love you. I love you I love you I love you." And then he was kissing her again. Then he said softly, "I hate leaving you. I hate it."

She gave him a gentle push. "You have to shoo."

"I want to see who wins," he protested.

"Sorry, you'll have to find out who won later. Thanks for dinner…and dessert."

"No, thank you for dessert," he corrected.

"I need you to go Brian," she said, her voice cracking.

"Tracy, what is it?" he asked concerned.

"Nothing. I just need you to go before…I don't."

"Tracy—"

"Brian, please go. I love you; now please…"

"Okay, Tracy okay. I'm really not trying to upset you."

"I know that. Goodnight. I love you."

"One more kiss and then I'm gone." She obliged, and then he did as he promised.

Tracy put the uneaten food away in containers, washed the dishes, and then readied herself for the night's rest. She sat on her bed, which seemed such a lonely place now. She found herself staring at her reflection. Then she looked away. "This is nuts," she thought. "This guy's loved me for what, 15 years? Do I really think he's playing some con game here? He knows what I'd do to him if I found out he was; well, he should anyway. Am I going to keep seeing him, making love with him and then suddenly change my mind about him? Hah, not likely. What am I supposed to do, contrive some test to see if he'll drink? I could tell him I hate him and that I never want to see him again, and then see what he'd do. And then, if he passes the test, go back and just say, 'Kidding!" Oh dear Lord: I'm losing it again." She lay down and slid her legs beneath the covers, her eyes on the blades of the disengaged ceiling fan. "Oh forget this! If he asks me, I'm going to say 'yes.' That's exactly what I'm going to do. If he were to call me tonight when he gets home and ask me, I'd say 'you bet.' He might call. He probably *will* call. Maybe I should wait up. But I'm so tired; so tired. I'll just lie here. I can hold out another 20 minutes or so. I can do that."

But she couldn't and she didn't. She didn't hear the phone when it rang, and she didn't hear the message Brian left until the next morning. "You know who this is, beautiful. I just called to cast my vote for the non-practical side for the win. And of course to say how much I love you." She would have told him who won had she been awake to answer.

Chapter 4

Tuesday morning Neal was getting his marching orders: find out all he could about Timothy Pane and find out all he could about the murder of Colin's father, Jackson Richmond. Tracy was going to arrange another visit with their new client; she wasn't going to wait for Nick Fallston's material.

"Not sure what luck I'll have on ye ole information superhighway with a 1987 crime," Neal told his employer. "The internet wasn't in full swing back then."

"I hear you," Tracy told him. "But the court transcripts are an option. And I can probably arrange something through El to review potential evidence that may still be stored somewhere."

"Hmm. Why should we be spending all this time on an almost 30-year-old crime though? Shouldn't we be looking into Colin Richmond's life right now?"

Tracy leaned back in her chair. "Well, what are the odds an otherwise innocent person would be wrapped up in two murders during their lifetime?"

"Umm, I give up."

"I bet it's close to zero. I have to think that the motive for the current crime is tied to the past crime. 'The Child is the father of the Man' you know."

"What?"

"Didn't you pay attention in your English classes, young man? William Wordsworth—"My Heart Leaps Up When I Behold." Any of this ringing a bell?"

"Uh, I never liked poetry. I know Roses are red, Violets are blue…"

"Oh good grief; I am amongst the heathens."

"Who said *that*?"

"Who said what: good grief? Charlie Brown I guess."

"No, the heathen thing."

"I did; just now."

"You—oh never mind."

"What were we talking about again?" Tracy asked furrowing her brow.

"You thought the two murders are connected."

"Oh right. I know Colin's been looking into his father's murder on and off through the years. Now: if Jackson Richmond's killer knew about this, what do you think he'd do?"

Neal started nodding. "I get you. You think the purpose of the second murder was to stop Richmond from investigating the first."

"Ding ding ding ding ding ding ding…"

    A Tracy Brubaker Mystery

Neal chuckled. "Okay, okay. But don't you think this reincarnation set up is a might elaborate? Wouldn't it be easier just to run junior down in a parking lot or something? This whole spiritual angle is wacky."

"And what if Colin has a box or flash drive or something else of gathered information? The police find it while looking for a motive for his murder. You see?"

"Right. The killer wouldn't necessarily know what Colin had found out or what kind of records, if any, he kept. So he might not want to risk attacking Colin directly."

"And the crowd goes wild."

Neal shook his head while laughing. "Boy you're in a *good* mood." He paused. "But I still think it's a risky way to frame somebody. I wonder how he got Pane to go along with it."

Tracy shrugged her shoulders. "Any number of ways; he could have just paid Pane, telling him it was all a practical joke, for example. My only question is how he could have found out about Pane's birth date. *That's* not something that typically pops up in casual conversation."

"Yeah, good point. Employment records would have that info."

"A killer couldn't just start looking through a company's payroll records…unless of course Pane works or worked at one time for his killer. Make sure you check out Pane's employment history."

"Sure."

"And then of course police or DMV employees have access to that information. I wonder if Pane had any run-ins with the cops. I wonder if our killer works at a state government agency." Tracy leaned forward. "You see why I am so interested in the 1987 murder?"

Neal started nodding again. "You win, Tracy; I'm with you. I'll start looking into what we just talked about."

"You're a good man, Neal Bennett."

Neal stood and took a few steps away from her desk. Then he joined his hands together and pressed them against his heart. "I will take my leave now. But, alas…'Parting is such sweet sorrow'." And then he skipped out her doorway. She started laughing, gently at first, then rather intensely. She *was* in a good mood. She just hoped *Romeo and Juliet* wasn't the play that was going to be representative of her and Brian's renewed relationship.

Tracy was once again seated across from Colin Richmond at the Baltimore City Detention Center. He seemed a little more relaxed this time out, apparently pleased that Tracy Brubaker was now officially his attorney. "Wow, two meetings in two days; I can't believe it," he said as his greeting to her. She smiled in return.

"I'm just trying to get up to speed as fast as I can."

"Whatever you want to know, just ask me."

"That's a great attitude to have. You need to be honest with me, even if that means sharing some things about yourself that may not cast you in the most positive light. I'm interested only in clearing you of these charges; I'm not here to judge you as a person. Do you understand what I'm saying?"

Richmond nodded. "Yeah—like if my alibi for the night of the murder is that I was stealing some car, you'd want me to tell you that."

Tracy looked at him curiously. "Well, yeah, that's one way of looking at it I guess. My point is that nothing you tell me leaves this room, unless of course I can use it for your defense." Richmond nodded again. "Okay; now, since your prints were on the knife we're going to assume you were framed. And if you were framed then either someone had it out for you specifically, or they witnessed the argument you had with Pane in the restaurant and took advantage of the situation, meaning they had something against Pane, not you. You were just in the wrong place at the wrong time. Now you of course wouldn't be able to shed any light on the second scenario, so I want to talk about the possibility of the first."

"Right; I see what you're saying."

"Good; so is there anyone you can think of in your life right now, or someone who exited your life in the not too distant past—an old girlfriend for example—that, shall we say, doesn't care for you all that much?"

Richmond narrowed his eyes and scratched the stubble on his chin. Then he started shaking his head. "No, I can't think of anyone I've pissed off *that* much, enough to want to do something like *this*."

"Well, what about from a business perspective? What is it you do for a living?"

"Oh; office layout and office renovations; I and my partner own a small company that specializes in readying office space or renovating office space for businesses, any size. We coordinate the furniture, the carpet, the computers, the cubicles…just about everything. We take care of all of that stuff so the new tenants don't have to worry about it."

Tracy nodded. "That sounds like a good business. What's the name of it?"

"Richmond and Carruthers Office Planners and Specialists."

"Carruthers is the name of your partner, then? How long have you worked together?"

"Jon and I are best friends; we have been since high school. We've had the business now almost 10 years."

"I take it Jon is overseeing everything now."

"Yeah; Jon's a great guy, the only one who's stood by me this whole time, even back when…well, he's just the best friend anyone could have."

"I'll want to talk to him of course, see what the police have been asking him."

"Oh sure, no problem."

                    A Tracy Brubaker Mystery

"How many employees do you have?"

"Well, we kind of just bring people in if the current job is too big; pay them as contractors even though Jon and I are doing the work too."

"Oh I see. But you probably have regulars that you use if they're available."

"Oh sure, we have a go-to list. Jon can get those names for you."

"I'll talk to Jon then. Any irate customers not happy with your work?"

"Oh no; we have a perfect reputation; we're always getting referrals."

"Great. Do you and Jon hang out outside of the office?"

"Well, he's a family man; he's got two kids, seven- and three-year-old boys. His wife was his high school sweetheart: Janie. Nice girl, Janie. They've been married, must be 15 years at least."

Tracy was smiling; thoughts of playful little ones always made her do that. "So Jon was mostly at home when he wasn't working."

"Yeah; not that I blame him. Like I said: good guy."

"So I guess he and Janie were together the night your father was killed?"

Richmond blinked. "Uh, yeah; from what I remember. Why would you bring that up?"

"As a segue to my next area of discussion: your father's murder."

"I don't think I understand."

"Well, I could be completely off my rocker thinking this, but if you say you have no enemies in the present then maybe we should be looking at your past. I mean, you are still following up leads after all these years."

"Damn straight. And I will continue to do that."

"Exactly my point, Colin. Now what if your father's killer knows what you're doing?"

Richmond's eyes widened. "You think *he* may have set this up?"

"Or she; let's be open-minded here."

"Oh, I didn't mean anything by the 'he' comment."

"Oh I know that," Tracy said grinning. "But, while we're on the subject, any lady friends I may want to talk to?"

Richmond looked at his lap. "Well, truth is, I just broke up with someone; Linda's her name."

"Oh, I'm sorry," Tracy said sincerely. "How long ago?"

"About the time that Pane fellow entered the picture; a little before that."

"I see. Can I ask what happened?"

"Well, nothing major. I mean, I guess I just didn't see any kind of future for us. She's a few years older than me, and she wasn't interested in getting remarried. I guess, even though I'm no spring chicken, I'd like what Jon has someday."

Tracy nodded. She understood Colin Richmond on this point; she understood him completely. "So Linda is divorced huh?"

"Yeah—twice. She's a pretty lady, so guys hit on her all the time, even when we were together and I went to get us drinks or something. I'm sure she's hooked up with someone else already."

"You've never been married then?"

"No."

"Ever been close?"

Richmond shook his head. "Not really."

"Okay Colin. What's Linda's last name?"

"Schumacher." He spelled it for her.

"I'll probably just want to have a few words, you understand."

"Sure; whatever."

"Uh, Colin, when was it you pursued your last lead in your father's death?"

Richmond's eyes narrowed once again. "I guess about two years or so ago."

"And what was the nature of this lead?"

"I found out there was a company installing carpet in the building that evening. It was just one of those things where I ran into someone from the neighborhood and we got talking. And I told him about what I did for a living, and then we're talking about best quality carpets for offices, and then he mentions he remembered some carpet van being there the night my father was killed. I didn't remember that; I'm not sure if it came up at trial at all."

Tracy perked up. "So what was the name of the company; did you find out?"

"Let me see, what was the name: Waverly Carpet Installers? Yeah that was it, or Waverly Carpet Installation maybe. But they're out of business now; have been for quite a while. I really couldn't do anything with it when all was said and done."

"I might be able to; I have someone who works with me who's very good at that sort of thing. Did you go to the cops with this?"

"You're kidding, right?"

"Oh; sorry. I guess that was a stupid question."

"No. Sorry. I didn't mean to sound like a dick."

Tracy chuckled. "Don't worry about it Colin. I just ask questions, not always thinking that the answer is obvious."

Richmond smiled. "Good. I want you to know I really appreciate what you're doing. I like you and I don't want to piss you off."

Tracy laughed gently. "As long as you're honest with me, that is not going to happen. I save my ire for people who deserve it: liars, killers, and people like that."

Richmond smiled and nodded. "Okay. Anything else I can tell you?"

"Well, let's talk about the night of the murder—Pane's I mean. You hadn't seen him since the fight?"

 A Tracy Brubaker Mystery

"Right. That was a Friday—February 20 this year."

"And when again did you first meet?"

"It was the Monday right after the Super Bowl."

"Okay—that makes it February 2."

"That sounds right. So anyway we have that fight. He was killed that Monday, so that would be the 23rd."

"And you were home alone at the time of the killing?"

"Yeah; I went to my place straight after work; got home that night— must have been before 7:00; microwaved some dinner and sat in front of the TV until bedtime. I guess I turned in before 11:00; didn't watch the news or anything. The next day I'm at a job site when these two cops come to talk to me. Then on Friday they arrest me. I've been in jail ever since."

Tracy shook her head. "I'm sorry Colin. I can look into getting you another bail review hearing; maybe I'll find something."

"I thought they just looked at whether you'll show up for trial and whether you're a danger to other people."

Tracy nodded. "True; I'll still look for another approach though. Do you think you could post bail if I were successful?"

"I don't know."

"Jon would probably help you, wouldn't he?"

"He probably would; yeah."

"Okay. Now, how about just a brief rundown of the night your father was killed. What were you doing just before you left for the night, and then where were you before you came back and learned what happened?"

"Uh, well, Dad and I had just finished dinner. It was early—5:30 or so. I called Jon and he said he and Janie were doing something and that he'd call me or would stop by after he dropped her off at her house. I figured I wouldn't be seeing him that night. So I helped clean up dinner, and headed to my room, put the headphones and chilled for a bit. The next thing I knew my old man is ripping the phones off my head yelling about me promising to help him with something or other. Well I'm pissed off now so I take off."

"What did you do?"

"Went to the movies; I love the movies."

"Me too, old ones though."

"Really? Old like what, *Dances With Wolves*?"

Tracy smiled. "Older—like *Gone With the Wind*."

"Oh—I've heard of that."

"I do really like Dances though. You know, I think there was a different Kevin Costner movie out the summer of 1987; *No Way Out*?"

Richmond was smiling, nodding vigorously. "Yeah, yeah I did see that one. That was great; he's a military guy asked to investigate a murder and the people don't realize he was screwing the victim."

"Uh, yeah," Tracy agreed. "Did you know that movie was a remake of a film from the 1940s called *The Big Clock*? It starred Ray Milland and Charles Laughton."

"No, I didn't know that. You really know your movies, huh?"

"Well, not really. My dad was a fan of noir and mystery and I kinda learned a lot through him. He actually told me about *No Way Out* but wouldn't let me watch it."

"Why not?"

"Because I wasn't 17 at the time; the film has bad words and bare boobies."

Richmond started laughing. "Oh, I see. Protective father."

"Yes. So what *did* you see that night?"

"*The Lost Boys*, one of my favorite movies of all time. I still love that movie; spin it every now and again. I just wanted to live like that—you know, sleep all day, party all night. No authority to rein you in."

"But weren't those partiers the bad guys?"

"Well, youth are always the bad guys as far as adults are concerned, right? Was true then, probably is still true now."

"And that was your thought when the cops questioned you after you got back from the movie?"

Richmond blinked a couple of times. "They didn't waste any time in accusing me. My dad was dead, beaten to death by someone, and they start in on me practically right away." He was starting to get angry; his face turning red.

"Okay Colin; no need to relive that night in full. So you didn't notice anybody hanging around your building when you left for the movie."

"No, but I wasn't really paying attention. I just wanted to get out of there."

"You fought with your dad a lot, huh?"

Richmond gulped and then nodded. "He hated me."

"What? Why would you say something like that?"

"Because he hated my mother for leaving us and I reminded him of her, so he was always yelling at me because he couldn't yell at her. He didn't used to yell like that, before she left I mean; we used to be pals."

"Oh, Colin. I'm sorry. That wasn't fair of him. That must have been awful for you." She reached for his arm. "What was your mother's name?"

"Amanda," he said through clinched teeth. "I hate her for what she did to us. I still don't know why she left. I come home from school one day and she's not home. My dad called the police; filed a missing persons report. Then I learned from Dad that some of her things were missing, like she packed a bag. The police lost interest soon after that."

"I see. The police thought she was having an affair and ran off with the guy?"

 A Tracy Brubaker Mystery

"You got it. I know my parents weren't the happiest people but I didn't think my mother would do something like that."

"How long had she been gone when your dad died?"

"I guess about, uh, a couple of years at that point."

"Where did you stay after your trial was over?"

"I stayed with Jon's family. His parents are great people like Jon; I guess that's where he learned it."

"Wow, so you actually lived with Jon for a while?"

"A couple of years; then I got my own place while I worked some part-time jobs. My dad had saved some money so I was eventually able to go to community college and get a business degree. Then I hooked up with Jon and we went into business together. I owe him so much."

"I bet he's come to visit you."

"Some Saturdays, yes. The week is so busy for him; and he is working weekends to keep up. Tracy I…" Richmond's voice started to crack.

She rubbed his arm again. "What is it Colin? What can I do for you?"

He shook his head. "Just please help me get my life back. I didn't do this thing. I can't believe this is happening again."

"I promise you I'll do what I can. Now I think that's enough for today. Do you have any questions for me before I go?"

Richmond shook his head. "No; I'm sorry. I just want to get out of here."

"I'll look into another bail review hearing. Hang in there Colin. I'll be in touch." Tracy rose to make her exit, and then she was shortly on her way to her car. She was surprised when she realized she was wiping away some tears that had crept into her eyes. Whatever doubts she may have had about Colin Richmond were gone; she was convinced of his innocence. But now another thought, a rather ugly thought, had entered her mind. What if Colin's mother didn't just run off with a lover? What if something happened to her? And what if Colin's father, after almost two years after his wife's disappearance, had learned something? Could Pane's killer be guilty of three murders? She was now itching to see everything there was on the Jackson Richmond killing. Would Tanner be willing to scratch?

"You're going to have to give me some time to pull everything together, Tracy," Tanner said to her. Tracy was sitting in her car in the detention center parking lot, on the phone with her late father's partner.

"Oh, I understand that. I just really want to look at what you have. Is next week realistic?"

"Sure, I think that will be fine. You think you have something?"

"I don't know. Do you recall if Colin's mother's disappearance factored into your investigation?"

"I don't recall; I guess not in a major way since nothing's ringing a bell."

"Okay; how about some carpet people being there the evening of the murder? Do you recall if they were questioned?"

Silence on the other end. "No, that's not ringing any chimes either."

"Well, okay. That's why I want to see everything. Who knows, maybe the killer's DNA is resting on something in a box somewhere."

Tanner cleared his throat. "I think you know what I have to say to that."

"Alright El. Just let me know when I can come by to go through what you have."

"Sure Tracy. Anything else?"

"Uh, I have a question about Detective Shandi Danbury."

"Really?"

"Do you know if she likes chocolate bunnies?"

"What?"

"Never mind then. If I don't talk to you before Sunday, have a Happy Easter El."

Tanner chuckled. "You too Tracy. Don't get any cavities."

"Hah. 'Bye El. Love to you and yours."

"'Bye Tracy. Best to your mom." The two ended the call simultaneously. Tracy looked at her watch: almost 2:30; time to feed the belly and then back to the office. Ideas were already taking shape and she wanted to test them out. She felt as excited as kid with a sweet tooth on Easter morning.

"You with me then Neal?" Tracy asked after bringing her associate up to speed.

"Yup. I've got Waverly Carpet Installers or Installation, Jon Carruthers, Linda Schumacher, and Amanda Richmond added to my list of inquiries."

"And Janie Carruthers too; she was with her future husband in high school."

"Right. Is that it?"

"For now. I'm sure I'll have more after El gets that old case stuff together."

"Well, I was going to go through the transcripts of the trial."

"Oh sure. But I wouldn't be surprised if I find some things that aren't in the transcripts."

"Okay. So you're really feeling good about Richmond being innocent."

"Yes; I'm convinced of it."

"Well, you're two for two, so far be it from me to doubt you."

"You are wise in your generation."

"Okay—what poem is that from?"

"Not a poem; *Bride of Frankenstein*."

"No kidding?"

"No kidding. I've probably seen all the old Universal monster movies at some point or another."

"I didn't think you liked horror movies."

                    A Tracy Brubaker Mystery

"I don't as a rule. But great movies are great movies, you get me?"

"Right. Well, I shall then once again take my leave. Absence makes the heart grow fonder, you know."

"I thought it was out of sight, out of mind."

"Oh, forget it then. See ya." And then Neal left in a mock snit as Tracy laughed. She next turned to her computer, searched for Richmond and Carruthers, and found what she was looking for: a phone number. She dialed it.

"Richmond and Carruthers Office Planners and Specialists," the voice said.

"Is this Jon Carruthers?" Tracy asked.

"Yes, ma'am, it is." Tracy introduced herself. "Oh, I'm glad Colin found somebody he liked," Carruthers said after listening. "I know he didn't like that other guy."

"Well, I want to help Colin. I'd like to meet with you and just talk about some general things. I think you'll make a great character witness if nothing else."

"Oh, sure; anything for Colin."

"I guess you're really busy now. Is there a time that we could make work? I'm available evenings too."

"Well, I couldn't swing tonight. How about tomorrow night, around 8:30? You could come to my house; the kids are in bed by then; at least they're supposed to be."

Tracy chuckled softly. "That would be great Jon. Can I have your address?" He gave it to her. "Is this the best number to reach you?"

"Yes, it is."

"Okay, I'll plan on being at your place around 8:30 tomorrow. If you need to push it back or change the date just let me know."

"It shouldn't be a problem."

"Thanks Jon. I know you're super busy so I really appreciate you finding the time."

"Like I said: anything for Colin. I'll see you tomorrow then. Have a good night."

"You too Jon. See you tomorrow." Tracy smiled as he closed her phone. Jon Carruthers sure sounded like the kind person Colin had said he was. The fringe benefit of her job was that she frequently met nice people she otherwise never would have. Of course, it was rarely under ideal circumstances. But she was nevertheless looking forward to her Wednesday evening appointment.

Tracy checked the corner of her computer screen: 5:09 p.m. She smiled. She wouldn't be able to see Brian tomorrow most likely so she wanted to make sure she saw him tonight. She placed her call.

"This is Brian."

"Hey, handsome; how's it going?" she greeted.

"Oh, hi Tracy. How are you?"

Tracy scrunched her face. There was something less than enthusiastic in the way he was speaking to her; where had his smile gone? "I'm fine, Brian. Are you okay? You sound a little down."

"Oh, I'm sorry. I guess I'm just tired."

"I guess we'll have to make it an early night then, huh?"

"Well, maybe we should catch up on our sleep tonight."

Tracy gulped. What was going on? "Well, I won't be able to see you tomorrow night probably. I have a late meeting connected to my new case."

"Oh. You did tell me you'd have to work nights sometimes, didn't you?"

Tracy didn't like this. "Brian, what's wrong?"

A brief pause and then, "I told you. I'm just run down."

"Well, I could come over to your place so you wouldn't have to make the drive. I'll shoo when you tell me."

Another pause; "Okay, I guess that would be fine."

"That's better," she said. "Where is your swinging bachelor pad exactly?" He told her. "When do you think you'll be there?"

"After 7:00; anytime after 7:00 should be fine."

"Okay; great, I'll see you at 7:01 p.m. then." She heard him laugh—hurray!

"Okay. See you then."

"Right." She paused. "I love you Brian."

"I love you too Tracy." He paused also and then added, "God, how I love you." And then he hung up.

Tracy sat confused for a moment. Something was bothering him, but what? Had he not told her something and was feeling guilty about it? Maybe he was just having a bad day, struggling with his sobriety. Maybe he wanted a drink and she called him at a bad time. No point in guessing though; she'd be seeing him in two hours and she would find out why he sounded so blue. She hoped it was nothing she couldn't handle.

Tracy suddenly realized Rebecca was looking at her. "Anything wrong Tracy?" she asked.

"I hope not Beck."

"You need anything?"

"No, I'm good."

"Well I was going to head home then."

"Oh sure Beck; go on home."

"Okay." Rebecca hovered. "Are you sure you don't want to talk about anything?"

Tracy shook her head. "It's okay Beck; thanks."

"Alright; goodnight then."

Neal popped his head in a little after 6:00. "I'm heading home Tracy; want to walk out with me?"

 A Tracy Brubaker Mystery

"No thanks Neal. I'll be here another half hour or so. Thanks for asking, though."

"Are you okay?"

"Peachy keen."

"You seem a little lemony."

That brought a smile to Tracy's face. "Off with you Sir Fruit of the Loom. Don't darken these halls until tomorrow morn." She waved a dismissive hand at him. He chuckled.

"Night boss." Then Neal Bennett took his leave. She was anxious for the time when she could take hers.

Brian Shane lived in an apartment complex in Baltimore County; one that had numerous amenities including indoor and outdoor pools, a tennis court, a gym, and possibly other gems that Tracy didn't notice as she guided her blue Audi to an appropriate parking space. The guard at the security gate had been helpful in directing her to Brian's location, and she promptly found the visitor parking area. She was practically running to his building after exiting her vehicle. She buzzed his unit—3C—from the building's lobby. She was immediately allowed entrance. When she arrived at his door, it was already slightly ajar so she just came in and called out, "Brian?"

"Back here in the kitchen Tracy," he immediately answered back. "I'll be right there." And he was.

Tracy scanned his fully furnished apartment. A brown suede sofa and loveseat set surrounded a glass coffee table, which matched the table that served his dining room. Four black-cushioned chairs looked like comfortable seats for dinner guests. His kitchen had dark oak-colored cabinets and a center island where the stove burners rested, with plenty of room on either side if needed. The plants she noticed were artificial, but you can't have everything.

"Wow, this is *really* nice. I mean, I never realized you had a future as an interior decorator." Now he was in front of her, and he pulled her toward him; he kissed her intensely. Tracy returned the sentiment; she was feeling some relief.

He pulled away from her. "Don't let this fool you," he said smiling. "We have some corporate apartment units we keep for nonlocal business associates. We put them up there when they're in town for budget meetings or other functions. I happened to like they way some of them looked, so I had my apartment furnished and set up pretty much the same way. I mean, I paid for everything and all; I just can't take credit for how it looks."

Tracy laughed. "Well, I think you have good taste then. It really looks nice."

"Thanks. Can I get you something to drink? I have water of course, and orange juice, and 1% milk. Or I could make you some tea, hot or cold."

"I'm fine Brian."

"Are you sure? It'd be no trouble."

"I'm good Brian." Tracy sat on the brown loveseat and kicked her shoes off. "The carpet feels nice too," she said as she massaged her feet with its fibers. "Now come and sit next to me and tell me what's wrong."

He stood there a moment. He brought his right thumb to his mouth and started moving his thumbnail up and down the space between his two front teeth as if something were stuck there. Then he started to shake slightly. And then he started crying; not a gentle sob, but really crying. The smile left Tracy's face as she stood back up. "My God, Brian; what's *wrong*!?"

He struggled to get the words out. "I…I can't forgive myself." He finally said. "I can't do it."

Tracy went over to him and embraced him. "For what Brian?" she asked. "For what?"

"For hurting you like I did. I…I just can't get past it."

"Brian, you're going to have to get past it," she said gently.

"I've tried," he said, slightly, but only slightly, regaining his composure. "But last night I had another one of those nightmares."

"Nightmares?"

"When I remember that night in your parents' house; the night I turned my back on you and left. The night I hurt you so…so badly."

"Brian: that was a long time ago." They were still standing, now rocking gently from side to side.

"But I still remember it; I wasn't so drunk that night that I don't remember. I remember everything."

"Brian, you can't keep thinking about it. The past is the past."

"But you said just a few days ago that I needed to promise not to hurt you again."

She removed her head from his shoulder so she could face him. "I know I did; I meant that as a way of telling you that I wouldn't tolerate any drinking. I didn't mean that you should keep beating yourself up over something you did when you weren't even really yourself."

He nodded. But then the tears returned full force. "I love you so much, Tracy; how can I ever make something like that up to you? How can I forget—how can you forget—something like that?"

Tracy took Brian by his hands and started moving in the direction of the loveseat. "Sit down with me Brian." He obeyed. "Now listen, I just spent the last few weeks yelling at people I cared about because a case wasn't going as well as I wanted it to. I yelled at my own sick mother as she lay there in a hospital bed. I've hurt people too, Brian."

He shook his head. "Not like I hurt you."

"Brian, people who love each other hurt each other all of the time, even though they may not mean to. But that's why there are things like forgiveness and understanding. I *know* how bad you feel about that night; I believe you when you say you're sorry for it. And I forgive you for it. Do you understand that Brian? I have no intention of ever bringing that up again. Doesn't that matter to you?" He nodded his answer as she wiped his tears away with her thumbs. "Then I guess we need to add an addendum to your promise to me; you need to promise to forgive yourself for the past. I couldn't stand it knowing this will continue to haunt you like it has been."

He nodded again. "I can try; sure."

"Try not; do," she said trying unsuccessfully to sound like Yoda. He chuckled. "That's better," she smiled. "Do you think you should go to a meeting? I'll drive you."

He shook his head. "No, I don't need one. I'm well aware that while I could get drunk trying to forget it that ultimately I'd pay a bigger price. I don't feel the urge to drink. I don't need a meeting."

"Well, okay."

"I'm sorry Tracy; I didn't mean for this all to come out like it did."

She was now stroking his cheeks. "It's okay Brian. I don't want you keeping things from me, especially something like this that's been eating away at you. We really do need to try to look to our future; clean slate, you know?"

He nodded. "Tracy?"

"Yes?"

"I really need to blow my nose."

She laughed and then released his face so he could do just that. "Are you better now?" she asked when he was done.

"I love you," was how he answered, as he now took her face in his hands.

"I love you too."

"Do you really Tracy? Do really love me?"

"Yes." She was smiling at him, the warm smile he remembered from their many times together which consisted simply of each looking at the other. "Yes, I do really love you."

"And you believe that I'm once again the person I once was; that I've put my life back on track?"

"Yes, I do," she said without hesitation.

"Then marry me, Tracy. I'm asking you to marry me."

She looked at him seriously for a moment; then she allowed her smile to return and stroked his hair. "Yes Brian, I'll marry you."

Brain blinked. Did she just say what he thought she said? "Uh, you *will?*"

"What—are you deaf now?" she teased. "Did you think I'd let you sample the goods if I didn't think you were going to purchase?"

"What? Oh never mind." And then the two kissed again, bodies entwined; hands stroking hair, the only two people in the world. "Hey," Brian said, breaking the silence.

"What?" she whispered.

"You know what I want to do right now?"

She grinned. "I bet I can guess."

"I bet you can't."

"Okay; what then?"

Brian pulled back slightly so he was looking at her. "I want to go shopping."

"*What?*"

"For your ring."

Tracy's eyes widened slightly. "Hey, yeah; where *is* my ring?" she asked in mock irritation.

"Well, you're low maintenance so I didn't want to get you something myself; you probably would have refused to wear it and make me take it back. It was hard enough getting you to order dinner last Friday."

"You have a point." She was smiling ear to ear.

"I know this place not too far from here: Hastings Jewelers. Crystal's bought some stuff from there. They have everything on site to put together the perfect engagement ring. I think they close at 8:00 but I can call them and I know they'd stay open for us."

Tracy was looking at their joined hands. "Okay."

"We can pick out something that will make your eyes widen but not cause them to fall out." She let out a gentle laugh. "And then when people ask about it you can tell them, 'Brian Shane, the man who loves me with all of his being, gave this to me'."

Now she was looking at him again, and soon their lips made contact. They were silent as they readied themselves for the visit to Hastings. They left Brian's apartment hand in hand. Their future together was just getting started.

Chapter 5

Tracy looked through her office door Wednesday morning. Rebecca was at her desk, as she usually was by 8:00. Tracy opened the door and quickly placed both hands behind her back.

"Hey: morning there Tracerino; how are you?" Rebecca greeted, looking up from her stack of papers.

"Oh, I'm okay," Tracy answered as she slowly approached the reception desk.

"Good."

"And how are you Beck?"

"I'm perfect."

"Yup."

Rebecca looked at Tracy curiously. "Are you okay?" she asked.

"Well, Beck to tell you the truth: I've put on some weight."

Rebecca looked skeptical. "I seriously doubt it."

"I seriously have."

"Tracy, come on: how much are we talking about—half a quarter of a pound or something?"

"Oh: a few ounces…a few karats."

And then Rebecca's eyes widened, as Tracy brought her left hand out from behind her back. Then Rebecca's mouth dropped, and then Rebecca Dietz screamed. "OH…MY…*GOD*!!!" And then she stood, came from behind her desk, gave Tracy a quick hug, and grabbed Tracy's left hand. All that was missing was a jeweler's magnifier loupe. "Good Lord, Tracy," she said in awe. "What is this, 20 karats?"

"Shh," Tracy said. "It's not too much is it; too over the top?"

"Tracy it's beautiful." Rebecca hugged her. "Congratulations! I'm so excited! When's the big day?"

"Well, I want to talk to my mother first. I want to know if she'd rather have the wedding at the church near her, or if the Cathedral on Charles is okay. That's where I'm officially registered."

"Gotcha. So you haven't told her yet?"

"Uh, no. Brian and I already have a meeting scheduled for Friday; I'll tell her then."

"So you don't know—"

"I don't care what she thinks, Beck. I know in my gut, in my heart that this is right. My mother will just have to get used to it if she has a problem. But I think, at the end of the day, she's going to be really happy."

"Tracy, I am so happy for you. I'm thrilled, actually."

"Thanks, Beck." And then Rebecca gave Tracy another squeeze.

"Hey you two, what's going on?" Neal asked as the office entrance door closed behind him. They turned to look at him. They stared at him without answering. Suddenly he looked at his zipper; it was closed as it should be. That just started the two ladies laughing again. Neal was getting irritated. "Look you two, what's going on?"

"Neal," Tracy started. "Rebecca and I have something to confess, a secret we've kept from you for far too long. It's a story of..." But Tracy couldn't finish her fiction. They were both laughing again. Neal was not.

"Fine. You don't want to tell me? That's fine. I'll be in my office *working.*"

"Oh stop it," Rebecca scolded. "Look at Tracy's finger."

"What, the middle one?" he said testily. Tracy showed him the goods.

"Sweet mother of mercy!" he shouted. "What on earth is going on here?"

"I'm marrying a former client of ours. He said he couldn't pay my bill so I told him he had to marry me."

Neal blinked. It didn't take him long to do the math. "When did you start seeing Brian Shane again?"

"Friday."

"Wait a minute: you mean, the Friday that just passed us last....Friday?"

"Our Neal is pretty good at this, isn't he Tracy?" Rebecca teased. "I think you should really keep him around."

"You know Beck I sense a lot of typing coming your way," Neal shot back. "*A lot.*"

Tracy started laughing again. "Okay you two. Let's not start that." Tracy moved toward Neal. "Take some deep breaths, Neal. Feel the Chi."

"The what? Never mind. Tracy, are sure you're not rushing into things here?"

"Beck: get me a young priest and an old priest; I think my mother has possessed an employee of mine."

"Oh you're cute," Neal quipped.

"Hey, that's my line. And call the larceny cops while you're at it Beck."

"Tracy, seriously; you just started up with him again. Don't you think a little more time is in order? Didn't you see *Frozen?*"

Tracy rolled her eyes. "We're not getting married *tomorrow* Neal. It probably won't be until 2016—sometime in May, I think. I've always liked the idea of a May wedding: not too hot, but the weather is usually nice."

"It rains a lot in May."

"April. *April* showers bring May flowers."

"Now we're back to the poetry thing, huh?"

"Neal, stop raining on my Easter parade," Tracy said, starting to get annoyed.

     A Tracy Brubaker Mystery

"Tracy: I appreciate how you must feel—"

"You haven't the slightest clue how I feel! I'm done talking to you Mr. Man. If you can't be happy for me then just shut it."

Neal blinked. "Alright Tracy, I'll shut it. You'll let me know when I can open it again, won't you?" And then he turned and went to his office space.

"Sorry Tracy," Rebecca said. "You know that he's just looking out for you."

Tracy sighed. "Yeah, I know. But he's not my father or my big brother. Why couldn't he just be happy for me?"

Rebecca nodded sympathetically. Then Tracy's cell phone started buzzing. The smile returned to her face. "The hell with him; I'm going to take this call in my office."

"You bet."

Tracy hurried to the back and then closed her door. "Hi Brian," she answered quietly.

"Hi Tracy. How are you this morning?"

"My eyes are tired but the rest of me is buzzing."

He laughed. "We didn't get out of the jewelers until almost midnight. I thought you might sleep in."

"No; I'm not sure if I got much sleep last night. This ring has thrown me all off balance."

More laughter from the other end; "Well, I guess you could put it under your pillow at night so you could sleep."

"Are you kiddin'? This thing ain't leaving my finger any time soon." She paused while he finished his chuckling. "Brian, I think maybe I overdid it here. Maybe we should—"

"Tracy, you promised me when we agreed on the ring you wouldn't do this."

"I know I did but—"

"No 'buts.' It's perfect for you. And you're worth every penny of it. Now, can I see you tonight?"

"Oh, no Brian. Remember I told you about my meeting?"

"Oh right—you did tell me about that didn't you? Well, maybe during the day then."

"I'm not sure. I'm going to be pretty busy; may have to leave the office a couple of times."

"Not fair."

"I'm sorry."

"I understand. Well, call me at some point, even if it's after your late meeting."

"It's only one night, Brian. The office is closed on Friday and I'm not scheduling anything for tomorrow after 5:00. How about tomorrow we go to the Holy Thursday service together and then grab some late dinner?"

"That sounds perfect. I'm there."

"Supreme. I'll call you later."

"Right. I love you Tracy."

"I suspected as much. Love you too. 'Bye Brian."

"Bye Tracy." And that was all there was to say for now.

Tracy put her phone on the right side of her desk near her laptop and sighed. "Might as well get this over with," she thought. She didn't have much of a choice. She wanted to meet with Neal and be brought up to speed on his research. She had just stood up when there came a gentle rapping at her chamber door. "Come in."

Neal entered fitfully. "Pretend I'm waving a white flag," he said.

She smiled. "Oh come on in, Neal, and let's get this over with." There was a quick hug exchange.

"Congratulations Tracy. I'm happy that you're happy."

"I guess that will do for now," she said not sounding agitated.

"I thought you'd probably want to go through what I've found thus far. Obviously I just got some of the names yesterday so most of that's still in process."

"Sure Neal. Just let me know what you've found." Neal and Tracy took their customary positions at the latter's desk.

"Well, there's not much to tell on Timothy Pane. He was born August 19, 1987, the day Jackson Richmond was killed."

"I don't suppose you have an exact time of death for me, do you?"

"No, I'd have to talk to someone very close to him to find that out. But both his parents are still alive. They live in Pasadena. I bet the mother remembers."

"I was just wondering. I mean, what if it turns out he was born hours *before* the murder? That would pretty much end this whole reincarnation malarkey wouldn't it?"

"Only if you could show Richmond *knew* that."

"Yeah, you have a point there Neal. Okay — sorry to have interrupted; onward."

"Pane works at a printing company in Baltimore County but he lives in the city; has an apartment there where he's resided for almost six years now, ever since he graduated from college. Deggman's Printers and More. They do wedding invitations, if you're interested."

"Pass. What did he do at the printers?"

"Not sure; just know that he works there. I think he was in PR though. I saw his name listed in a brochure for the company; it had him listed as a contact if your business wanted to learn more about their services."

"Do you know how long he worked there?"

"I think since he graduated. Deggman's has been around about 25 years or so. Maybe Pane worked there during college."

"Okay; maybe his boss will talk to one of us. Anything else of interest on him: money problems, sudden wealth?"

     A Tracy Brubaker Mystery

"Nope. But he would be what you call a paycheck-to-paycheck guy. Lived alone, did his job. I couldn't find anything that said troublemaker."

Tracy shook her head. "I never thought he was a troublemaker. He got into this thing innocently, I believe. Heck, maybe whoever killed him never had to pay him or do whatever it was that was promised in return. Just some poor guy with the wrong birthday I'm thinking."

Neal shook his head. "That's doubly awful if you're right. Poor guy."

"Anything else to report?"

"Not on Pane right now. Anything more on him will require some legwork."

"How about our client?"

"Nothing that hasn't been covered in your interviews with him. I read the summary you emailed me yesterday."

Tracy smiled. "Okay. So he's lived a pretty straight and narrow life since he was released."

"Yup. His company has great ratings with the Better Business Bureau; his partner is just shy of sainthood—Jon Carruthers is on the board of directors of a children's hospital for crying out loud."

"Wow. I'm meeting with him tonight; him and his wife, Janie."

"I haven't checked too much into them yet. I'll do that now and see if there's anything you should know before tonight. Then I'll move on to the other names you gave me."

"Great Neal; good work as always. Thanks."

"Sure Tracy. Well, I'll get back to it then." He rose and headed toward the door. "Tracy: I gotta ask because Sara is going to ask me: how many karats is that thing?"

Tracy blushed. "I don't remember exactly."

"Oh come on…"

"I don't want to talk about that."

"Well, you better come up with a better answer than 'I don't remember' because NOBODY is going to believe you." Then he smiled at her and exited her chamber.

She shook her head. "I knew this thing was just too much," she mumbled aloud. But her fiancé had made it clear about not wanting to hear anything else regarding the ring: "Quoth the Brian: Nevermore!"

"I'm sorry Tracy," State's Attorney Arthur Pankow said. "There's no way Colin Richmond's getting released."

Tracy was standing in front of Pankow's desk at the Office of the State's Attorney for Baltimore City. "Why not?" she asked. "I mean, how can you be so drop-dead inflexible about it?"

"He's a flight risk."

"He doesn't have a passport. I checked."

"He has no real ties to the area Tracy; no family. He could just up and go."

"He's been a solid businessman for 10 years Art. That's something."

"But it's not just that Tracy. And I think you know what I'm talking about."

"Art, it's not fair to—"

"Tracy, you know fairness isn't a factor here; save your breath."

"Come on Art!"

"He killed a guy he hardly knew, Tracy! If that's not the definition of a danger to others I don't know what is!"

Tracy grunted. "So you're part of this then?"

"Part of what?"

"You want Colin in jail because you guys think he got away with murder before. You're massaging each other's bruised egos."

Pankow frowned. "Tracy: he's behind bars because he meets the textbook requirements for keeping someone there. I'm not part of anything."

Tracy sighed. "What would it take to at least get another hearing?"

Pankow shook his head. "It's not happening Tracy."

"Art—"

"You want him out of there? Start hoping someone walks into BPD and confesses to the murder of Tim Pane. Otherwise, as they say, see you in court."

Tracy shook her head. "This isn't right Art."

"Says you."

"I guess you want me to go then huh?"

Pankow squinted. "Well, unless you want to tell me what's wrong with your hand, I guess there is nothing else to say."

"My hand?"

"You've been keeping it behind your back this whole time. Did you fall on it or something?"

"No."

"Oh."

"Goodbye Art." And she moved quickly out the door without letting Pankow in on her little secret. She wasn't in the mood to share her good news with someone who seemed so determined to make her client's life—and thus hers—miserable. She'd let him wonder about it for a while, fair or not.

Jonathan and Janie Carruthers lived in a single family home in Howard County. The area was a planned community of homes, apartments, and shopping villages that was situated equidistantly between Baltimore City and Washington, D.C. It was one of the more expensive areas in Maryland and one that Tracy had thought about someday moving to. She arrived promptly for her Wednesday evening appointment and pulled into the driveway of the Carruthers' perfectly maintained home; at least it appeared so from the outside. There was a colorful, cardboard Easter bunny

 A Tracy Brubaker Mystery

decoration attached to the front door which made Tracy smile. She rang the doorbell. A woman opened the door soon afterwards; she smiled at her visitor.

"You must be Tracy; I'm Janie. Come on in."

"Thanks," Tracy said entering the abode.

"Let me take your coat." Tracy let her. "Jon's upstairs trying to settle the boys down. I let it slip a guest was coming over and they're very curious."

Tracy laughed. "I didn't realize I was a celebrity. I'll give autographs."

Janie chuckled. "I'll keep that in mind. Would you like anything to drink?"

"I'm fine; thanks though."

"Well, let's go sit down in the dining room. Jon shouldn't be too much longer." Tracy followed her hostess. She couldn't help notice how lovely a woman Janie Carruthers was; she had to be close to six feet tall. Thin, blonde, and a warm demeanor; she probably looked just like this in high school—teen boy's dream girl. Janie clicked the chandelier to life as the two women sat down at the dark oak table. Then Janie's eyes widened. "Oh my word," she said looking at Tracy's left hand. "Do you mind if I look?"

Tracy blushed. "Uh, sure; okay."

Janie took her guest's hand. "Wow. This is beautiful."

"Thank you."

"When's the big day?"

"Hopefully May of next year some time; still working that out." Both women turned to face the person who just entered the room. "Honey, look at this thing," Janie told her husband.

"Holy Toledo," Jon Carruthers said. "That's quite a briefcase you have there."

Tracy started laughing. Janie just looked at her husband and shook her head. "A real romantic this one," she said teasingly. "Seriously though Jon, isn't it gorgeous?"

Jon nodded. "Yes, it is." Then he offered Tracy his hand. "Jon Carruthers. It's very nice to meet you."

Tracy stood. "Nice to meet you too, Jon."

"Janie treating you okay?"

"You bet."

"Should I stay or do you want to talk just to Jon?" Janie asked.

"Oh: to the both of you, actually. You've both known Colin for a long time."

"Sure," Janie said.

"What can we tell you, Tracy? How can we help Colin?" Jon asked.

Tracy was taking her notebook and pen out. "Well, for starters: did either of you meet this Timothy Pane person, the one the police are saying Colin killed?"

They both shook their heads. "Colin told me about him," Jon offered. "He was telling me some of the things about this guy that reminded him of his father. It was really weird."

"Yeah, that's a good word for it," Janie agreed. "Jon told me what Colin told him. I thought he was pulling my leg."

Tracy nodded. "Jon: how did Colin seem to feel about it?"

"Well, he had just met the guy. They were just hanging out. He didn't know what to make of it yet."

"So he wasn't telling you that he thought his father had come back or anything like that?"

Jon laughed while shaking his head. "No, he didn't say anything like that."

"How about at some point in the past? The police apparently have some witness or witnesses who say Colin believed his father would be back someday or something like that."

"That was just talk," Jon said. "Colin would get a few drinks in him and he'd say the strangest things sometimes. His father's death is still very much a part of him. But I think it's been years since he expressed any thoughts about vengeance from the grave."

"Really? He used those words?"

"Uh, yeah, kind of. He said justice would be served one day. If the cops didn't serve it then his own father might return and do so."

"Colin likes those horror movies," Janie offered. "You know: all those zombies coming out of the grave."

Jon chuckled. "And he has those *Tales from the Crypt* comic book reprints. A lot of those stories are about corpses seeking retribution. I think maybe he just read one too many of them one night and got imaginative."

"I don't like that stuff," Janie said.

"I know," Jon said patting his wife's hand.

"I'm with you Janie," Tracy said. "Never cared for the gloppy stuff either."

Janie smiled. "Are you sure I can't offer you some coffee or something, Tracy? It's no trouble."

"I'm good, Janie. Thanks. Uh, speaking of horror movies, I understand Colin's a big fan of *The Lost Boys*."

Jon went a little pale. "Yeah. I guess you already know that's what he was seeing when his dad was killed."

"Yes," Tracy said softly. "Can either of you tell me anything about that night; anything at all?"

Once again they were both shaking their heads. "I didn't hang with Colin that night. Janie and I were out with her family."

"It was my grandparents' 45th wedding anniversary dinner that night, so Jon and I were together the whole night."

"And then when I got home my mom told me what happened," Jon said sadly. "I couldn't believe it."

  A Tracy Brubaker Mystery

Tracy nodded. "What can you tell me about Colin's dad? Was he hard on Colin?"

Janie looked at her lap. Jon looked at his wife and then at Tracy. "It didn't get bad until Colin's mother left. Then his dad was always yelling about something. Colin just got fed up with it and started doing his own thing. Colin wasn't a bad kid or anything."

Tracy studied Janie. She felt Jon's spouse may not fully agree with her husband's assessment. "Jon: could I trouble you for a glass of water?" Tracy asked.

"Oh sure. Do you want anything hon?"

"No, I'm fine," Janie answered.

"Okay. I'll be right back."

Tracy met Janie's eyes. "So was Colin an okay kid before his mom left?"

Janie turned in the direction her husband just followed; then she turned back. "Colin was lazy, didn't want to do anything but goof off. He was a bright guy so he did okay in school without studying much but he could have done better, you know?" Tracy nodded. "He was always trying to get Jon to blow off his homework and hang out. Luckily Jon usually did the right thing. But Jon's right in that it really got bad when Colin's mother left."

Jon Carruthers re-entered the dining room. "Here you are Tracy," he said putting a glass of ice water in front of her.

"Thanks so much," she said before taking a large gulp.

"What'd I miss?" he asked.

"Well, I was just about to ask a rather uncomfortable question."

"Really?" Jon asked.

"It's about Colin's mother. I didn't want to go into specifics with Colin, at least not yet. I don't know if it has anything to do with anything, but…"

"What is it?" Janie asked.

"Was Colin's mother having an affair with someone? Did the subject ever come up? I know it's a tough question."

The Carruthers stared at her. "Why would you think that?" Janie asked.

"I think the *police* think that, and that's why they stopped looking for her."

Jon nodded. "Colin's mother slept around."

"Jon!" Janie scolded.

"What Janie? You know it. I know it. Colin knows it. And his dad knew it."

Tracy felt a bit embarrassed by creating the tension that now joined the trio. "I'm sorry. Please don't get upset on my account."

Janie shook her head. "No, Jon's right. I just don't like talking about people behind their backs."

There was some silence. Tracy asked, "So no one's heard anything from Colin's mother since her disappearance a couple of years before the father's murder?"

"No," Jon said. "I guess she finally found what she was looking for and took off."

"She saw a lot of guys while she was married?"

"I really don't know if it was two or 200," Jon said quietly. "I got the impression though that she liked men and men liked her. Colin's dad worked two jobs for a lot of years to make ends meet. When Colin got older he was only home to eat and sleep. His mom started going out at night while her husband was working his night job. I guess that's how it started."

"Huh," Tracy grunted. "It doesn't sound like she was necessarily looking for a new permanent relationship; just some fun."

Jon nodded. "Yeah, that's what I always thought."

Tracy thought some more. "Did Colin's mom have a close girlfriend or girlfriends, a person or people she might confide in? Maybe they went out with her some of those nights."

Jon furrowed his brow. He looked at his wife. "What was that woman's name who was at the house a lot? Do you remember her Janie? She was a bit overweight but she had a real pretty face, always had a smile?"

Janie thought. "Oh! Right—I think her name was Chrissy something."

"Christine Jacks!" Jon shouted. "That was her name: Christine Jacks. You could check with Colin on that but I'm sure I got the name right. I remember asking Colin who his mother's new friend was once and that was the name he gave me."

Tracy smiled. "This is great you two. Thank you both so much!"

The Carruthers were both smiling, although they weren't exactly sure why. Janie asked, "Do you really think Colin's mother has something to do with this new thing?"

Tracy thought before answering. "Well, since I really don't know anything for sure either way: could you keep all this between us for now?" They both nodded vigorously. "I don't think any of us here believe this reincarnation stuff is for real. So that means Colin was set up. Why? I think it's because he's still looking for his father's killer. So who killed his father and why? I have to wonder if it's tied to Amanda Richmond's disappearance. I mean, I know sometimes people can sever family ties. But this woman doesn't show her face, or send a card, or make a phone call or anything for almost 30 years. Not when her husband is murdered, or their son is accused of it; nothing. Now that's either one cold-hearted person, or a person who's cold for a completely different reason."

The Carruthers' collective faces went pale. Janie looked at her husband. "My God," she whispered. She turned to Tracy. "Do you think something happened to Colin's mom?"

"I really don't know, Janie. I'm just trying to take a fresh look at everything, trying to figure out the whys behind all of this. I'm not certain of anything yet."

"And you just met Colin this past Monday?" Jon asked.

Tracy nodded. "Yes, that's true."

Jon gulped. "Well, if you need anything, don't you dare hesitate to ask me? If you're right about this then Colin's going to be hurting even worse than he is now."

Tracy nodded. "Please just keep what I told you between us for now. Once I know something for certain I'll talk to Colin about it."

They both nodded. "I promise I won't say anything," Janie said.

"Me too," Jon added. "Is there anything else we can tell you?"

"Not right now, Jon. Thanks. Thank you both so much for talking with me and helping me with Colin's case."

"No, Tracy," Jon corrected. "*We* should be thanking *you*. You let us know if you need to talk to us again."

Tracy smiled as she stood. She took a long sip from the water glass and then started toward the front door. There were handshakes, more thank yous, and some Happy Easter wishes too as Tracy left the Carruthers for the night. She was sitting in her car still parked in the Carruthers' driveway when she made her call.

"Hi Tracy," Brian answered.

"I know it's pretty late but can I come over?"

"I don't know Tracy; I mean you were here last night," Brian answered playfully. "I have a surprise waiting for you."

Tracy grinned. "I don't know if I can handle any more surprises this week."

"You can handle this one; I promise."

"Well, I'm in Columbia so I'll see you in about half an hour maybe."

"I'll be here."

"Okay. Love you!"

"Love you back." And then he went to prepare for his beloved's arrival.

Tracy was pacing back and forth as she was trying to tell Brian about her case without really telling him anything that may be privileged. It frustrated her because she wanted him to fully share in her excitement. It exasperated him because he hadn't the slightest idea of what she was talking about.

"Tracy: why don't you sit down for a moment? I think you're going to collapse if you keep this up; or at least ruin my carpet."

"Huh? Oh, okay. But you see what I'm getting at don't you?"

"Uh, kind of. There's a guy, accused of killing another guy. But many years ago the one guy—the first guy—was accused of killing yet another guy. But the real reason for all of this may have to do with a missing gal."

"Exactly."

"I have no idea what I just said."

Tracy looked at him quizzically; then she started laughing. "Oh, I'm sorry. I just need to share what I think may be the key to the case. Maybe."

"But you have certain rules to follow."

"Yeah; not that I think you'd go blabbing to somebody or anything."

"I understand, Tracy."

"You know, I should put you on the payroll. Then I can talk to you about this stuff since you'd be an employee of the firm."

"I don't think—"

"We could be like Nick and Nora, with me as Nick and you as Nora of course."

"Nick and Nora?"

"Don't you remember all those *Thin Man* movies I showed you; the ones with the husband and wife detective team and the cute little dog?"

"Oh, yeah; sure. They were pretty good from what I remember."

"Thank you Roger Ebert for that incisive review. But wouldn't it be cool if we could do something like that?"

"Tracy: you're a lawyer not a detective, private or otherwise."

Tracy scowled. "Now why did you have to bring that technicality up? I'm just sayin'."

Brian laughed. "Look: it's almost 11:00; time for your surprise." Brian got up from the sofa and went to his refrigerator. "Close your eyes," he ordered. She sat up straight and obeyed. He placed something in front of her. "Okay, you can open them." Again she complied. And it was a grand sight: a perfectly prepared lemon meringue pie was in front her, and it was beautiful.

"Fork please," was all Tracy said. Brian was soon cutting her a generous-sized piece, loading it onto a plate, and pouring her a glass of milk to go with it. A fork was provided. He did the same for himself and then joined her at the small dining table.

"How is it?" he asked her, intentionally waiting until her mouth was full. She gave a 'thumbs up' with her left hand. He chuckled. "I lucked out that there's a really good bakery close by; family run, been around for quite a while. I love family run businesses, especially food ones."

Tracy was nodding at Brian's comments. She took a drink of her milk. "Delish, Brian. Absolutely, totally nummy."

"Can I get a kiss then?" She leaned over and obliged.

"Mmm…meringue lips," she cooed afterwards.

Brian was now looking at her; there was something about her playfulness, the way she would grin at him that would start the rapid rise of his desire. He couldn't help himself. They had parted last night without any hanky-panky; it had been so late. Tracy was looking at him, and apparently reading his mind.

"Look Brian I should go. Two late nights like this in a row are bad for me. Tomorrow is going to be busy."

     A Tracy Brubaker Mystery

His disappointment was obvious; Brian never had a poker face. "Okay," he said. "I guess you're right."

"Thanks for the treat. It was very sweet of you."

"Uh-huh."

Tracy made a pouty face. "Brian: now keep your chin up. Besides, it's Holy Week. I wouldn't feel right about…well, besides…I mean…"

Brian finally smiled. "It's okay Tracy; I get it. I'm afraid I've become the cliché horny boyfriend that I always tried not to be."

She touched his cheek. "There will be time for more of that later. I love you."

He nodded. "I love you more."

"I'm not going to get into that back and forth mister," she told him as she arose. "Walk me to the door sweetie."

"Can't we just sit and hold each for a while; there's nothing wrong with that is there?" he asked quietly. "Please Tracy; just for 10 minutes or so. I've missed being with you so much."

She moved toward him, kissed him, and then took his hand and led him to the loveseat. They sat down together and she rested her head on his chest while he put his arm around her. She closed her eyes; warmth, and comfort, and love—that's what she felt when she was with him like this; memories of times gone by now being gladly revisited. She smiled. She felt him kiss the top of her head. "I love you," he whispered. The 10 minutes turned into 60. It turned out to be another late night after all.

Chapter 6

"I really want to talk to Christine Jacks," Tracy was telling Neal Thursday morning. "She may or may not be a tough one to find. But please find her."

"Sure Tracy," Neal said.

"I got some stuff from Colin's former attorney this morning. He did some interviews with the restaurant staff, and he had some copies of some of the initial police reports. There really didn't seem to be much there."

"Don't take this the wrong way, Tracy," Neal commented, "but he was doing what most attorneys should be doing."

Tracy sighed. She didn't feel like a verbal tussle with Neal over her unique approach to defense work. "I think I'm just going to do my own interviews. Besides, I've never been to a Denzinger's. I could grab a bite and get some sound bites all at the same time."

Neal gently laughed. "I wonder what the food budget on one of your cases is. I'm going to have to look at that at some point."

Tracy narrowed her eyes a bit. "I wouldn't advise that. You have better things to do with your time, what time you have left anyway."

"Alright," he said.

"I'll bring you back something; some mints maybe if they have a bowl of them."

"Tracy: your thoughtfulness and generosity once again overwhelm me."

"Hah. Any luck with the defunct carpet company?"

"A little bit. I searched some business records and found they forfeited their Maryland business charter in 1992. They may have actually closed shop before then. I'm still looking."

"Linda Schumacher?"

"Forty-seven years old; lives near Patterson Park. She has a couple of DUIs; works as a receptionist at a trucking company, Eastman's Transport. She has a son from her first marriage; 24 years old; Ken Vinton is his name."

"Do you know where *he* is these days?"

"I can try to find out."

"Okay. I guess I stole any thunder you had for Amanda Richmond."

"What I had didn't amount to a storm cloud. Again, her disappearance predated the internet takeover. I could order some articles from the *Sun's* archives I guess but they probably won't say anything."

"I'm going to have to follow up with El on this I'm afraid. But that will have to wait until next week unfortunately." Tracy paused. "Look Neal, why don't you see what you can find on Christine Jacks and Linda Schumacher's kid; just email me what you come up with. Then go home and start your long weekend."

Neal smiled. "Thanks, Tracy; that's awfully swell of you. What are your plans?"

"I'm going to see if I can meet with Mike Denzinger or this hostess, Peggy Osher, who Nick Fallston talked to. I want to know just how big this fight was, and if the version being told now matches what was told a few weeks ago."

"Gotcha. You're probably going to have to call and find out which location that Denzinger fellow is hanging out at today. I understand he rotates from store to store."

"Oh yeah? What do you know about him?"

"Not much; I know he had a nice write-up a few years ago in a magazine that profiles fine places to eat on a budget, or something like that. It had lots of pictures of the layout and such. And of course the steaks: big and juicy."

"Down boy..."

"Maybe I can even dig up the article. White collar food on a blue collar budget, I think is his motto. Sara knows how much I like steakhouses so she lets me know when she reads about one that gets good reviews."

"Huh. So these are really popular then?"

"Yeah; I think the weekends at those places are a madhouse."

"Now that is interesting."

"What do you mean?"

"I wonder how Pane was able to get a Friday reservation on such short notice. The two didn't meet until February 2, and they had that dinner on the 20th. I doubt Pane made the reservation on the second, so we're looking at less than three weeks time."

"Well: there's any number of possibilities; a cancellation, maybe he just got lucky—I mean: most couples would have gone out for Valentine's Day. So getting a reservation for two a week later may not have been so difficult."

"Perhaps. But thanks for the heads up. I'll make sure I call before I start visiting any of Denzinger's establishments."

"Okay. Well, if I don't see or talk to you beforehand have a nice Easter Tracy."

"Hey—that reminds me." Tracy leaned over and opened her large-sized bottom drawer. She removed four colorful, foil-wrapped chocolate rabbits and handed them to Neal. "Here—for your little and not so little ones."

Neal smiled. "Good Lord, Tracy. These things feel solid, not hollow."

"Solid."

"They'll love 'em; even Darlene. Her teen acne drama hasn't slowed down her chocolate consumption."

Tracy laughed. "Happy Easter, Neal."

"Thanks again, Tracy." He gathered his edible flock and headed back to the office. But at the doorway he turned. "I don't suppose you have fifth one in there, do you?"

She chuckled again. "Sorry; you'll have to ask your kids to share."

"What about Beck's daughter; she doesn't need to know."

"Will you stop? I already gave Beck her allotment."

"Oh, sure. Thanks again." Tracy had forgotten Neal had a sweet tooth himself; and she did kind of lie to him. She did have one more. But that was being saved for a certain Shandi Danbury, she who disliked lawyers. Bribery by chocolate was, as yet, not a chargeable offense in Maryland.

Michael Denzinger had agreed to meet Tracy at his Baltimore City location, where the argument between Timothy Pane and Colin Richmond had occurred. The owner was supposed to be in Anne Arundel County, but Tracy had explained her situation and had succeeded in getting him to change his plans. As if that weren't luck enough, Peggy Osher was going to be today's lunchtime hostess. Tracy would be able to knock out two interviews, have a tasty meal, and get an early start on her own holiday. Tracy entered Denzinger's Steaks and Chops at 11:15 a.m. She approached the lady at the greeting station. "Are you Peggy?" Tracy asked.

"Yes. You must be the woman who called earlier: Tracy, right?"

"Right. Is Mr. Denzinger here yet? He agreed to meet me here."

"Yes; he's been here about 15 minutes. Let me call the kitchen and let him know you're here." Peggy picked up the phone. "Tommy: tell Mr. Denzinger the lady he was expecting to see is here and can see him now. Thanks." She looked back at Tracy. "It shouldn't be long."

Tracy smiled. "That was some excitement the night of that argument huh?" she asked Peggy.

"Oh yeah. I've seen women walk out on their dates before, but I don't think I've seen a guy do that. I guess gay couples are like the rest of us."

"Is that what you think; that it was a lovers' quarrel?"

"Sure; I mean what else would it be, right?"

"Uh-huh. How long have you worked here Peggy?"

"Oh, about six years I guess."

"Nice work?"

"Mostly, yes. Most of the customers are nice. But you always get the complainers. You just have to smile and try to be understanding. It's not too bad though. Most people have reservations and the walk-ins know they're going to have a long wait." Tracy nodded. "Say, I couldn't help noticing your ring; it's beautiful."

　　　　　　　　A Tracy Brubaker Mystery

Tracy blushed. "Thanks."

"Those look real."

"Yes."

"You should be careful. During the day around here is no problem but we've had a mugging or two outside this place late at night."

"Oh. Thanks for the warning."

"Hello ladies," a friendly booming voice said.

"Hi Mr. Denzinger. This is Tracy."

He extended his right hand. "Mike Denzinger; glad to know ya."

"Nice to meet you too Mr. Denzinger; Tracy Brubaker." They shook hands. Denzinger was, quite frankly, a large fellow. He clearly enjoyed eating as much as he did serving. He stood about 5'9", and had dark curly hair and a boyish face. Tracy figured he was probably in his early 50s or so, even though he could pass for a mature 40.

"Let's go over here and sit down."

"Sure; thanks." Denzinger led Tracy to a booth.

"Want anything to drink? My treat."

"No thanks, Mr. Denzinger. I'm good."

"Forget the formal stuff; Mike's fine. Just don't call me Mikey. I hate that." And then he chuckled, and Tracy thought of a poem that included the line "a bowl full of jelly." He asked her, "So, you were telling me on the phone, you're this guy's new lawyer?"

"Yes. I'm sorry to be bothering you again with the same old questions."

"Don't worry about it. I must have told the cops the same story 20 times already. One more time isn't going to hurt anything."

"Thanks Mike. I'll still try to be quick. Now you were here the night of the argument."

"Yes."

"Where you back in the kitchen most of the night?"

"No; on the floor mostly. When I'm here I want the customers to see me; they like seeing the owner. I introduce myself, make sure people are happy with everything; I help out the staff too: bring food to people, refill drinks, take away dishes—really anything and everything. I want to see my customers smiling, enjoying themselves. If I think something's wrong I'll try to fix it. Like I said, customers really like that—lets them know we care."

Tracy was nodding as she was noting Denzinger's comments. "So what happened the night of the argument?"

"Well, I was talking with some of the other diners. Then I hear this yelling. I turn around, and see this one guy standing up, dressing down this other guy. I go over there right away and ask what the problem is. The standing guy says 'no problem' or something like that, and then he just turns and goes. Peggy helps him get his coat from the coat check in and then he leaves. Of course I try to get everybody back to enjoying their evening. Then a few minutes later—not even that—it's like nothing ever happened."

"What about the guy sitting down; what was he doing during all of this?"

"Not much really; just sitting there, taking it. It looked like he didn't know what the hell just happened." Denzinger shook his head. "After the other fellow leaves I ask the guy who's still sitting down what happened. He just shakes his head. Then *he* gets up and leaves. Wait, he hands me some twenties first, and then he leaves; more than covered the bill. It was just the damndest thing. First time for everything, I guess."

"What do you mean by that?"

"Huh? Well, I've seen plenty of women have a fight with their dates before. First time a guy walked out on his date."

"Oh, this was a date for the two of them?"

"Well, I thought it was after what happened. I mean: what friend walks out on his friend like that?"

"But you don't really know what the fight was about."

"No."

"Did you notice if anyone followed either of the two out when they left?"

"No, I don't think so. Why?"

"Well: it's interesting that both you and Peggy assumed they were on a romantic date. I was wondering if someone observing the incident made the same assumption and didn't like it."

"Hey: I don't tolerate that crap in my place; any of my places. Sure, you get some punks who have a few drinks and say some things. We've had some interracial couples in here get harassed. I give those jerks *one* warning to sit back down and leave my customers alone; otherwise they're out. People are here to relax and have a good meal and a good time. I don't put up with that at any of my places."

"Okay Mike; sorry if I offended you."

"No, you didn't offend me; thinking it about just gets me riled up. I try to be a happy guy."

Tracy smiled. "I hear you. So I take it neither of those guys were regulars."

"No; I know most, heck all probably, of my regulars. I'd never seen either of them before."

"How about the person who waited on the two; did you talk to the server?"

"Yeah—let me think. Raymond waited on them. I asked Raymond if he noticed anything was wrong and he said he didn't. He should be here by now. If he's late again…" Denzinger shook his head again. "Hey Peggy!" he called out. "You called Raymond right?"

 A Tracy Brubaker Mystery

"Yeah," she called back. "He said he'd come in even though he's off today."

"Oh. Well, let me know when he gets here." He returned his attentions to Tracy. "I had Peggy call him in since I figured you might want to talk to him. I didn't realize he was off today. But as many times as he's been late he owes me one anyway." And Denzinger started chuckling again.

"Thanks Mike. Hey: do you mind if we look at your reservation book from February? I'm curious when they made their reservation for their dinner."

"Sure; no problem. Sit tight while I ask Peggy to get it for me. Hey: you ever eaten at one of my places?"

"Not yet, Mike. But I'm going to, probably right after I'm done yapping."

He smiled and then left her briefly. When he came back he was holding something that was clearly not a reservation book. He sat down and put his initials on what turned out to be a gift coupon; he wrote 'None' on the expiration date line. "Here," he said handing Tracy the paper. "It's the best deal we have right now; equal or lesser value dinner entrée free with purchase. Get your fella to take you to dinner."

"Hey, thanks Mike. This is awfully nice of you."

He chuckled, jelly and all. "Well, look: you're an attorney, you take clients out to eat. If I get you to try my food I know you'll love it, so then maybe you bring your clients here once in a while, and then they bring their associates."

Tracy nodded. "Nothing wrong with that, Mike; nothing at all. Thanks just the same."

"Sure. Oh look here's Peggy." The hostess handed the ledger to Denzinger, and he handed it to Tracy. "Here, you can just flip right to, what was it, the 20th?"

"That's right," she answered. She found Pane's name; reservation for two. "Mike, it looks like the original reservation was whited-out and Pane's name written on top of it."

"Let me see," he said taking the book from her. "Yeah; it looks like we had a cancellation. That's what we usually do; just put some white out over the canceled one and write in a new one."

"Am I right in saying this Pane reservation was made on the 17th; is that what this 2/17 means?" Tracy turned the book 180 degrees.

"Yes; that's right."

"Do you recognize the writing here; can you tell who took the reservation?"

"Uh, it looks like Peggy's handwriting. But you can ask her. If you want to talk to her I can seat people."

"Wow, thanks Mike."

"Hey, you're going to be one of my best customers someday; I wanna keep my customers happy!"

"I'm sorry Tracy," Peggy said, now sitting where Denzinger had been just moments ago, "but I don't really remember taking that call. It is my handwriting though; so I must have."

"Well: could you tell me if you remember if the white-out was already in the book or if you whited-out the name?"

"Sorry, no. I just pick up the phone, look for the date they're asking for, and then write their name in if a slot is available. We had a space in the 7:00-to-9:00 slot so I just wrote the name in. I don't really remember names unless they become regulars. Then I have to remember them."

"I guess Pane just got lucky that you had an opening. I wonder if this was the first restaurant he called."

"I'm not sure. I don't remember anything about the call. And I guess it wasn't lucky after all. I mean it all ended rather badly."

"You have a point, Peggy," Tracy mused. "Hey Peggy, could I ask one more favor?"

"Sure."

"Could I look at the steak knives you have at this place; I don't care how many restaurants I've been too they all seem to have a different style of steak knife."

Peggy grinned. "Sure." She grabbed a place setting. "Well this is our standard knife," she said showing Tracy a nondescript silver bladed piece. "Now you can follow me to the back and I can show you what you get if you actually order a steak." Peggy led Tracy to an area behind the serving heaters. "These are the actual knives." Peggy picked up a thick, black-handled knife with a blade almost nine inches long. The letter D was close to the bottom of the wooden handle.

"Lethal," Tracy opined.

"I guess. The cops looked at one too. This wasn't the kind of knife used to kill that guy. The police told us that already."

"Mm; well, I guess that's it for the business stuff, Peggy. Thanks for your help."

"Sure. You ready for lunch then?"

"Oh, yeah. It's time for me to play the happy customer."

Peggy laughed. "Well, follow me then. I'll get you set up right proper."

"Awesome. And when Raymond shows up could you just bring him over?" Peggy nodded. And then Tracy proceeded to make good on her play date; she was a very happy customer indeed.

"I don't really remember any problems before the fight," Raymond was telling Tracy as she lunched on a small pork chop, mashed potatoes, broccoli, and homemade bread. "In fact every time I checked on them they seemed fine. They were laughing, and they were very polite customers, saying please and thank you. I mean, I just don't know what happened."

Tracy nodded. "Did you get the impression they were on a date, or was it more like two friends hanging out?"

Raymond twisted his lips. "Just seemed like two guys hangin'. I didn't see them hold hands or anything like that. I know Peggy and Mr. D think that it was some lover's fight or something. But I'm not sure."

"Have you ever seen either of them before?"

"I don't think so. But that doesn't mean anything. I've only been here a few months."

"Oh I see. That whole thing just sounds weird, doesn't it?"

Raymond nodded. "Yeah; I just don't understand it."

"Well, thanks for coming in on your day off Raymond. I really appreciate it."

"Sure. I could use some brownie points right about now." Raymond smiled as he rose from the table. "I'll see you later then."

"There's a good chance of that; you guys just picked up another loyal customer. This food is supreme." Raymond smiled at her and left Tracy to finish her meal.

Tracy left Denzinger's, her stomach filled, and made her way to her car that was parked on the street. There were a few minutes left on the meter. She called Rebecca after locking herself up safely in her auto. "How is it over there Beck?"

"Quiet. Neal said to tell you if you called that he emailed you some stuff; nothing head spinning though. He's still trying to track down Christine Jacks."

"Yeah, that's going to be tough. That might not even be her name anymore if she got married or divorced."

"Pretty slow here though."

"Then just close her up Beck. Put on the 'we're closed for the holiday' message, batten down the hatches, and go home."

"Thanks Tracy."

"Sure Beck. Have a great Easter."

"You too, Tracy. And thanks for Lucy's gift; if she doesn't want it I know two people related to her who will."

"Hah. See you Beck." And Tracy hung up. Her stomach was full, and her mood was fine. What now; start her mini-vacation early? No, she knew a certain bunny in her trunk that needed a new home. And Tracy started her engine hoping Shandi Danbury was in a good mood too.

"I'm very busy," Detective Danbury said after Tracy introduced herself.

"Well, I brought you this," Tracy responded, undaunted, as she handed the foiled chocolate treat to the detective.

"I...what is this?"

"It's a chocolate bunny; he's so cute, isn't he?"

"You brought this for me?" Danbury asked skeptically.

"Sure. I know the holidays can be difficult for people on the job; crime doesn't go on holiday — ever."

"You're right about that." Danbury studied this bunny-bearing visitor, not sure what to make of her. "Thanks," she finally said.

"My pleasure." Tracy was now studying Danbury. She was Tracy's height — 5'5" — thin with curly hair; African American. She was quite attractive; but she had a stern expression on her face which took away from some of that beauty. The job? Her divorce? Both? Not Tracy's business really. Here goes nothing. "Could we talk just a little bit about the Colin Richmond case? I'm just getting up to speed after being brought on board Monday. I won't bother you too long."

"Oh ho," Danbury said nodding. "The truth emerges."

"Hey: you keep the bunny whether or not you talk to me."

Danbury grinned, very slightly, but Tracy saw it. "I guess I can give you five minutes. Anything specific?"

"For now, just a quick run-down would be fine."

"Okay." Danbury reached over for a file folder on her desk while Tracy pulled out her small notebook. "Let's see," Danbury continued. "Victim is Timothy Pane; found stabbed to death Monday February 23 of this year. Multiple wounds; at least three."

"Yuck. Sounds bloody."

"Yeah, it was messy."

"Did you find Colin Richmond's bloody clothes?"

"He probably got rid of them. Moving on: time of death was between 7:00 and 9:00 that evening."

"That's interesting."

"What's interesting?"

"The range of the time of death is the reservation slot they had the night of the big argument."

Danbury stared a few moments and then continued. "Richmond claimed to be home during this time; but no one can corroborate that."

"I see. What do you think his motive was?"

"He was seeing that Pane fellow. They had a fight in a restaurant a few days earlier; they probably had another one."

"You think they were lovers?"

"Looks that way."

"But they just met a few weeks earlier. You think it got hot and heavy in that short a time?"

Danbury paused a bit. "It happens."

"Oh," Tracy said, understanding the implication. "I heard you guys were thinking something along the lines of — "

"That reincarnation thing?"

   A Tracy Brubaker Mystery

"Well, yes."

"That was my partner's screwy idea. I can't believe it made it out of this building."

"Sorry; I won't bring it up again."

"Good."

"Still, did you happen to check what time Pane was actually born?"

"Excuse me?"

"Well, I mean, was he born earlier in the day, or later?"

Danbury stared a moment, and then consulted her file. "Actually I do have that here. It says 8:02 p.m. as his time of birth. Huh."

Tracy widened her eyes a bit. "Spooky isn't it? I mean that kind of fits in with Colin's dad's time of death."

"What?"

"Wasn't Jackson Richmond killed in the evening, somewhere between 7:00 and 8:00 if I recall correctly."

Danbury stared at her. "Your five minutes is almost up."

Tracy quickly changed course. "Earlier today I was at the restaurant where the public argument happened."

"So?"

"So I was curious as to when the reservation was made, being how busy Denzinger's is and how short a time frame Pane had to make the reservation."

"Pane didn't make the reservation."

"What?" Tracy asked, turning a little pale.

"Richmond made it."

"But I saw the book and it said—"

"Richmond must have just given them Pane's name. It was Richmond who called Denzinger's."

"How do you know?"

"Because we did our job, Ms. Brubaker. We checked both Pane and Richmond's whereabouts in the days leading up to the murder. We checked Pane's cell, home, and business phone records and found no calls to Denzinger's. So we checked Richmond's: same result. But the day the reservation was made, Richmond and his partner were at a job site—an office building—setting up a new suite. There's a phone down near the building's café. That's where the call to Denzinger's was made, as well as two earlier calls to two other restaurants."

"I—"

"Your client called two other restaurants first and when he struck out with each of those he called Denzinger's. You see?"

"Yes, I see," she said softly.

"Now, why would he lie to us about that?"

"Do you have someone who witnessed the call?"

"Of course we don't. Who pays attention to stuff like that?"

"Richmond could have made the reservation using his own phone. Why do you think he used the building's phone?"

"Well, if he's in the closet, he might not want to be using his own phone to make such a rendezvous."

"But he had already told his best friend about Pane."

"Carruthers? He told him they were just friends. Of course Carruthers could be lying to cover for his friend."

"The Carruthers are good people," Tracy said mildly annoyed.

"Long time friends will sometimes cover for each other."

Tracy snuffed. "I know you have Richmond's prints on the knife. How about anywhere else in Pane's apartment?"

"No."

"Huh. What about the knife? Was it part of a set Pane had?"

"Pane had a drawer full of mismatched cutlery; there were no sets. That's not that unusual for a bachelor."

"Did you check Richmond's apartment for Pane's fingerprints?" Danbury turned her head away. "Oh, didn't find any did you?"

"They could have met elsewhere; hotels for example."

"Find any receipts?"

"If they're in the closet they could have paid cash and used false names."

"Then why did Pane or Richmond use a *real* name when making a reservation at Denzinger's if they're keeping things a secret? In all my years of eating out I have never, ever seen a host or hostess ask someone to prove their identity when claiming a reservation."

Danbury nodded slightly. "You're good; I'll give you that."

"What?"

"Arthur Pankow told me about you. He said you were good and not to let the sweet demeanor fool me."

"I…well…I'm just asking questions," Tracy stammered.

"Unfortunately I'm out of time answering. The SA still has some time before they have to turn everything over. You'll have everything then. Now I really have to get back to work."

"Oh, okay Detective Danbury. I guess I wore out my welcome."

Danbury gave a slight grin. "Look, Ms. Brubaker you seen like a nice person, so I'm going to give you some friendly advice."

"Really?"

"Yup: don't do it."

"What: defend Richmond?"

"No. Get married."

"Huh?"

"I see that ring on your finger. It really is something."

"Uh, thanks I guess."

 A Tracy Brubaker Mystery

"Don't do it. I don't care what he's saying and doing now, he'll change once it's legal."

"Brian's not like that."

"They're ALL like that. I see it in my work and elsewhere. I'll be interviewing a guy who you think is the perfect husband. Then I'll talk to his friends and learn what he's really saying about his wife behind her back; what he really thinks. Time and time again I see this."

"Well, Brian—"

"He rich, your man?"

"Huh?"

"That ring is either from a rich man or someone who now hasn't a penny to his name."

"Brian's well-off sure."

"Even worse. You'll just be property to him."

"Detective you don't even know Brian."

"And neither do you, really. You just *think* you do." Danbury leaned back in her chair and folded her arms. "Has he cried for you yet?"

"*What*?"

"That's a man's secret weapon sometimes when it comes to trapping his prey. It's the 21st century but men still don't cry too much; plenty of men still think that's a woman's thing. So if your guy cries for you, it's a big deal, right? It shows him being totally open, right?"

"Well, I—"

"I used to be married. First time I caught my husband cheating he cried. He cried a lot, saying he'd never done it before and would never do it again. I made the mistake of believing him."

Tracy was close to shaking. Tanner had warned her that Danbury was still bitter; but this? "Well, I'll think about what you said, Detective. And thanks again for your time. And enjoy the bunny. And Happy Easter." Then Tracy turned and moved quickly before Danbury could put any more ugly thoughts into her head.

So Pane didn't make the reservation; the police had circumstantial evidence Colin did. That in and of itself didn't prove anything, even if Richmond *did* make the call. But Tracy didn't like it; a lie from Richmond or part of the frame? Probably the latter. And what about the fact Pane was born at just the right time for the reincarnation angle? Who would know *that*? Tracy had been in pretty good spirits after lunch; now not so much. She parked her car in her reserved spot; home. It was almost 4:00 p.m.; not as much of an early start to the Easter holiday after all.

And what about Brian? Was there any truth to what Danbury said? He cries, and then asks her to marry him without missing a beat? "And I said yes!" she shouted aloud. She leaned her elbow on her car door and then rested her head on her hand. Then she felt agitated. "I can't believe this: one sit-down with Officer Doom and Gloom and I doubt myself; I doubt Brian. This is nuts. Brian will be coming over tonight once I call him. And I'm *going* to call him."

"Hi Tracy," he answered.

"Hi handsome. I just pulled in; still in my car as a matter of fact. Are we still on for tonight?"

"Absolutely. I can leave here at 5:00. I'll be over as soon as I can after that."

"Well, don't let me keep you then. I'll be waiting for you. I love you."

"I love you more."

Tracy smiled as she closed her phone. Then she started feeling irritated again. What did Danbury know about Brian and how he felt? Nothing, that's what! Besides, Tracy had bigger concerns. Tomorrow was Good Friday, the day she agreed to bring Brian over to her mother's; the day her mother would learn that Tracy had already decided on her future with Brian Shane. Violetta Brubaker would ultimately just have to accept it—and so would everyone else, from Neal to Danbury, not that Danbury mattered. Tracy knew what she wanted her future to be. Still, she wished she had an extra chocolate bunny somewhere; everything's better with chocolate bunnies—even certainty.

　　　　A Tracy Brubaker Mystery

Chapter 7

Tracy and Brian's trek to Aberdeen had suddenly grown quiet. They were on I-95 and Friday afternoon traffic was calm. Brian was looking at the lady driver; there was an expression on her face that was other than happy. He had seen it last night during their time together: from the time he arrived, through Mass, through dinner, and through their chaste evening. Now it was back again.

"Tracy is something the matter?" Brian finally asked. "You seem to have something on your mind."

She gave Brian a quick look. "I'm sorry; I don't know why I let people get to me sometimes. It's the stupidest thing. I'm sorry you noticed."

"Well, since I *have* noticed, in fact I noticed it last night, why don't you tell me what's wrong."

"You might take it the wrong way. I don't want you to worry about it."

"Tracy, you have to tell me. You know: no secrets and all of that."

Tracy licked her lips. "It's just this detective I talked to yesterday. She just went through an ugly divorce and she's down on men, and I mean *down* on men."

"Oh? Did the guy cheat on her?"

"Yes, but I don't know *all* of the details. I do know the guy was a divorce attorney by trade."

"Oh dear."

"Exactly. Well, she saw the ring and she started…let's say she offered unsolicited advice."

"Oh," Brian nodded. "Advice like: don't do it."

"Yup."

"Well, okay. But why would you let that bother you so much?"

"There were other things."

"Like what?"

She gave him another quick look. "Like a man's secret weapon."

"I beg your pardon."

"Not *that,* Don Juan; tears."

"Tears?"

"Yeah, crying."

Brian blinked a few times. "Oh, I see. So my display the other night was really a military strike."

Tracy smiled. "I guess that's one way of putting it."

"And now you're wondering—"

"No Brian, I'm *not* wondering. That's why I'm so irritated. I don't believe for a second that there was anything phony or manipulative or anything bad about you admitting to me about your feeling guilty. It really moved me, that you shared that with me. And this bitter…whatever has got her poison in me. I'm so mad…I cannot make it stop."

"Maybe you have some subconscious doubts that this detective helped bring to the surface, doubts you don't want to admit you have."

"No."

"It's okay Tracy. I bet every engaged couple has had doubts before the big day, couples who don't have the kind of history that we have. If you do have doubts let's talk about them."

"Brian, I don't doubt that you love me. I don't doubt that I love you. I want this; do you understand? I *want* this!"

Brian was smiling now. "Well, are there questions you still have, even if they seem trivial?"

She shook her head. "I can't think of any. The truth is, I've been wondering how today was going to go. Then, once this is all over with, I can breathe a little easier."

"I guess your mom isn't too fond of the guy who hurt her daughter like I did."

"That's in the past. She'll have to realize that. And besides, I'm still marrying you. I love you. I know you love me. I know that you've been in my heart for such a long time that it's the right thing for us to do."

Brian gulped. "I wish I could reach over and kiss you right now for saying that."

Tracy grinned. "Probably not a good idea given I'm going 65 miles an hour. But hold the thought for the first red light we come to."

They were both smiling now. "It's going to be a long wait," Brian said breaking the silence.

"It's not too much further to the red light silly."

"I wasn't talking about that. I was talking about the wedding."

"Oh; but I'm worth it, right?"

"Of course you are. I'm not asking you to forsake your dream of a May wedding. I was saying, well, what I said."

"I bet it will go by faster than you think."

"I highly doubt it. But I know I'm being selfish."

"You're being honest."

"I'm being honest about being selfish."

Tracy started laughing. "Oh Brian, let's just live in the moment; let's be happy for what we have now and not concentrate on what's not here yet."

"Huh? Is that more poetry?"

"Oh, I don't know. I just said it; I don't know if I stole it from somebody else."

"I love you Tracy; everything about you. It's going to be—"

"Not another word, Brian. You keep talking like that I'm going to lose my willpower and we're going to have an accident, and then it won't be a

            A Tracy Brubaker Mystery

wedding my mother's planning. There's poetry in silence too, you know."
She took her right hand off the steering wheel and reached for him. He
closed both of his hands over hers. They let the silence have its say.

"Ah Tracy, come in dear child," Violetta Brubaker said, greeting her
only offspring. She embraced Tracy firmly, lovingly and then stood aside
from her apartment's entrance so that her guests could enter. "Brian, how
are you?" she asked when seeing him.
"I'm well, Mrs. Brubaker. Thank you for having me."
"I remember how well-mannered you were. I'm glad to see *that* hasn't
changed. Now come and sit down."
The lovers sat beside each other on the small living room's couch. Vio-
letta sat on her easy chair. "Tracy, is something the matter with you arm?"
"What?"
"You're sitting on your hand there."
"No I'm not."
"Tracy: you are."
"Oh, I'm just cold."
Violetta eyes narrowed. "Difficult child; what happened to you hand?
Did you cut it or something?"
"It's fine."
"I want to see it."
"Later. I want to talk first."
"I won't be able to listen until I know what's wrong with your hand."
"You listen with your ears Mom, not with your hands."
"What does that mean?"
At this point Brian started laughing. He imagined that these two wom-
en could spend the rest of the evening doing this. "Tracy, just show her,"
he finally said.
"Show me what?"
Tracy stood up, put her left hand behind her back, and then moved to-
ward her mother. Then she brought her hand around. Three…two…one…
"Mary Mother of God!" Violetta shouted. "What's this?!"
"It's an engagement ring Mom. Brian asked me to marry him and I said
yes. With yes, you get ring. So I got ring. Do you like it?"
But Violetta wasn't looking at the ring. She was looking up at her
daughter, speechless. Tracy shrugged her shoulders and sat back down
next to Brian.
"Is this one of your jokes?"
"No Mom. I'm getting married."
"But you just started seeing each other again. You need time…"
"We had enough time together, we had a little break, and now we're
back as we should be."

"A *little* break?" Violetta asked incredulously.

"Call it what you want." She looked at Brian. "I love him and he loves me. Simple."

"Tracy: getting married isn't just about love. You have to have the same goals, want the same things out of life."

"We do."

"You've talked about all of this, have you?"

"Yes; we talked about it years ago. Little has changed."

"Tracy: marriage is a very serious thing; it's a sacrament."

"I know that Mom. I realize I'm not joining a health club here."

"A what?"

"Never mind; I am serious about it. Now enough; can I help you with dinner at all?"

Brian stood up. "Mrs. Brubaker, I realize that I hurt your daughter deeply and that in turn I hurt you. I made some very bad mistakes, to put it mildly, and I know we can't all pretend I didn't. But I do love your daughter, Mrs. Brubaker, totally and completely. And Tracy, with her beautiful heart, has forgiven me for the wrongs I did against her. I hope you too someday can do the same, even though I know it won't be easy.

"I made promises to Tracy and your husband many years ago. I want to keep those promises. I've righted my life thanks to Tracy believing in me. I'm my old self, the self I'm not ashamed of. I hope someday you can believe that too. I love Tracy; I want to spend my life with her, to have kids with her, and to grow old with her. It's what I've wanted for a long time. And I know Tracy wants that for us too. Please, Mrs. Brubaker, try to understand this, even if, you don't. Uh, I'll shut up now." And then he sat down.

Tracy was rubbing Brian's arm; he was looking at his lap. "Well, I see you're still good with the *words*," Violetta said not sounding impressed.

"*Mom!*"

"What? He talks good. He looks good. So then you should get married because of it?"

Tracy glared at her mother. "Well, he's damn good when he's not *talking*, either."

Violetta stood up. "Tracy! You think I don't know what you just meant!"

Tracy stood up. "I hope you *do* know; that's why I *said* it!"

"Oh you difficult child!"

"Oh you difficult mother!"

Brian covered his face. Oh these difficult women.

"Tracy: you were such a good girl," her mother said.

"I *am* a good girl Mom! But I'm *not* perfect. I've tried to do right by you and Dad all my life: I studied hard in school, I tried to take care of you any time you needed it, and I've tried to make time for you now. My job, my life is helping other people work through *their* problems." Tracy was close

 A Tracy Brubaker Mystery

to crying. "Now after all these years of being alone the man I love wants to marry me and take care of me. And you're there basically telling me that I'm an idiot. Well, you know what? Maybe I am. But I'm a happy idiot: I'm Tracy the Happy Idiot! So there!" She sat violently down on the sofa and folded her arms, sobbing. Brian put his arm around her, and then she leaned into him.

Violetta looked at the two of them. She shook her head briefly. "Well, I hope you know what you're doing Tracy. You want to get married to this man? I'm not going to stop you. Your father said he'd be good for you."

Tracy looked up. "Dad said that?"

"Oh, I have you attention now, huh? I bring your father up and you're listening to me, huh?"

"Did Dad say that?"

"Yes he did. He thought he knew everything, just like you."

"I don't know *everything*, Mom. But I do know how I feel and what I want." Brian handed Tracy his handkerchief and she wiped her eyes. "What else did Dad say about me and Brian?"

"Eh, not much. We met him only the one time." Violetta was now looking at Brian. "But he thought he was a nice young man." Brian smiled briefly.

"He is, s Mom."

Violetta sat back down. "So when are you getting married then?"

"Well, I'm hoping May next year. I wanted to ask you if you had a preference for the church. There's of course the one near here, or there's the church we went to when we lived near Little Italy when Dad was alive, or there's the Cathedral on Charles Street that I go to. It's very beautiful Mom. You've been there."

"I don't care which church you pick."

"I bet you have a feeling one way or the other Mom."

"It's *your* wedding, Tracy."

"So you don't want to be involved in it then?" Tracy asked, becoming agitated again.

"Why don't we talk about the church later?" Brian asked trying to sound cheerful. "I think your mom needs some more time to…process the news."

"I want to lock down a date with a church, because everything else springs from that," Tracy said firmly. "Mom: would the Cathedral be okay?"

Violetta smiled. "Yes Tracy. It will be fine."

Tracy smiled. "Good. I'll call next week and see what date I can get."

Violetta stood up again. "I need to check the fish."

"Can I help you with anything, Mrs. Brubaker?"

"No; you two sit there. I won't be long." The elder woman went to her kitchen.

Tracy turned to Brian and smiled. "That wasn't so bad."

"What?" Brian asked in disbelief.

"That went rather well, don't you think?"

"I…But you and the yelling and…"

"Oh that's par for the course with her. And it's over with now."

"So you're okay?"

"I'm perfect."

Brian leaned in and kissed her. "Okay Tracy, if you say so."

"So," she said.

The remainder of Tracy and Brian's Good Friday evening with Violetta Brubaker was a mostly quiet affair, aside from the praise for the food: tilapia, boiled potatoes, green beans, salad, and bread. Tracy was delighted though when her mother had a smile and hug for Brian as the couple prepared to leave. "We'll be here around 2:00 on Sunday to pick you up," Tracy said while hugging her mother. "I love you."

"I love you too dear child," Violetta said rubbing her daughter's back.

Shortly thereafter, in the car, Brian asked, "Do you want me to do any of the driving?"

"I'm fine Brian."

He cleared his throat. "So you really think your mom's okay with everything?"

"She will be if she isn't. In fact I bet she's on the phone now calling people. And when she's done calling the people she knows, she'll probably pick up the white pages and call random strangers just for the heck of it."

Brian chuckled. "Well, then I'm glad we came tonight. I wasn't so sure there for a while."

Tracy looked at her passenger quickly. "I'm sorry about all of the melodrama. I don't know why I let her get to me like that. Sometimes I feel like I'm four years when she starts in on me for something or other."

"I can empathize," Brian said quietly.

"Oh Brian, I'm sorry. That was insensitive of me wasn't it?"

"No Tracy. I didn't mean what I said as a jab at you. Your mother said what she said because she cares about you, because she wants to make sure you're not rushing into something. My dad got on me I swear because he enjoyed it."

"I'm sure that's not completely true. I think we're both victims of caring parents who don't know any other way to show they care other than treating us like we were still small. I try to remember that when Mom starts in but I don't always do a very good job of it."

Brian smiled. "I hope we have a daughter someday; I'd love to have a relationship with her like you had with your dad."

Tracy smiled. "I hope we have a son too. I think given everything that's happened to you that you would be a great father to a son. Of course I get

 A Tracy Brubaker Mystery

to play catch with him too; none of this men-only stuff when it comes to sports."

He smiled again. "I love you Tracy," he said.

"I love you more," she responded.

He reached for her hand. "So is this Sunday thing at the Paganinis' going to be like tonight at all?"

"Oh no," Tracy said reassuringly. "Max will love you, and so will his family. He's a dear man who I think is probably one of the happiest people alive right now. I think it will be a wonderful Easter."

"Tracy," Brian said quietly. "I know you don't feel right about us doing anything real physical because of Easter and all. But can I stay with you tonight? I promise I won't try anything…I mean, well, you know what I mean. I just want to be with you."

She took another quick look over at Brian. "Okay Brian. I guess that would be okay."

"Great. Thanks Tracy." She smiled; the truth was she wanted to be with him too.

Brian made good on his promise to behave; the lovers fell asleep beside each other at Tracy's condo. He went home Saturday morning after breakfast; he would return early Easter morning to attend the Sunday service with his fiancée and then later the Paganini dinner. Brian had promised his sister Crystal that he would spend some time with her this weekend, so Saturday was going to have to be the day. When he asked Tracy to join him, she declined. She was tired, and quite frankly she wanted a day without questions; and Crystal would have questions. She would see her old friend another day, that was a promise. "I'll call you later," Brian told her as he finally exited, after which Tracy lay down on her couch, still in pajamas. She fell back asleep quickly.

The Sunday activities came and went; as predicted the food and laughter were in plentiful supply at the Paganini homestead. In fact, Max Paganini appeared to be in great health as well as spirits, and he couldn't have been happier for Tracy. But Max being Max, he still had to play the protector.

"Listen young man," he told Brian. "I got three sons here who are like brothers to her. You treat her right—you know what I'm telling you?"

"Yes sir," Brian had answered seriously.

"What 'sir'? Call me Max!" And then Max put around his arm Brian and said nothing more about his big strong sons the rest of the day.

But Tracy's happiest realization came when she watched Brian's reaction to the drinking that was going on around him; and there *was* plenty of drinking. It didn't seem to bother him. He freely told people about his problem, and the Paganinis expressed their admiration and support for him. Maybe Brian *had* been right during their Good Friday drive that Tracy had some subconscious doubts. Maybe she *had* wondered how Brian would be in a social situation where alcohol was served. But after today, if she had had such doubts, they were gone. She left the Paganini party happier than ever.

Tracy, Brian, and Violetta were now in Tracy's car headed back to Aberdeen. There was gentle snoring coming from the back seat. Tracy chuckled. "I don't know when the last time it was that Mom had so much wine. We might have to carry her to her apartment. Are you up for it?"

Brian laughed. "I'm game."

Tracy cleared her throat. "Brian, can I ask you something?"

"You know you can."

"How was it today, seeing people drinking; having a good time while doing so?"

Brian looked over at her. "It was okay. I mean, I would have liked to have just a small glass. But I know I can't do that. It was okay."

"I was really proud of you. You were so open and honest with everybody. I can't believe that was easy."

Brian was silent a moment. "I find if you try to avoid the topic you get paranoid that people are talking about it behind your back. It's just easier to be upfront about it. Besides, like you told me, they're great people. I did like them all very much, just like you said I would. That made talking about it easier than it may have been otherwise. And then there's the Tracy factor."

"What?" she asked amused. "What's the Tracy factor?"

"I just meant you were there, being supportive and being affectionate—you know: the hand holding and quick pecks now and again. That means more than you can know."

"I see," she said smiling. "You know if you ever find yourself struggling you can talk to me about it, right?"

"Yes Tracy. That's another part of the Tracy factor. I know if it had gotten bad that I could have come to you and you would have done something for me." He paused. "I just don't want to take this all for granted; I don't want to blow this. You see, drinking isn't an option for me anymore. It just isn't."

Tracy didn't immediately respond. For a few moments, the only sound in the car was Violetta's heavy breathing. "Brian," Tracy said quietly.

"Yeah Tracy?"

"Remember how you told me that you would make sure I felt loved by everything you said and did?"

"I said that?"

"Something like that, yes."

"Right, I did, didn't I? After you told me I wouldn't get a third chance."

"Uh-huh."

     A Tracy Brubaker Mystery

"Yes, I remember."

"Well, I just wanted to tell you that you're doing a swell job of it." Then she looked over to give him a quick smile. He stared at the side of her face; for how long he didn't know.

"I love you more," he said.

Tracy chuckled. "Not fair, jumping ahead like that. What am I supposed to say now?"

"You don't have to say anything; your actions speak for themselves."

"There you go again, making me want to pull the car over."

"What would we do with your mother?"

Tracy started laughing so loudly that her mother snorted and rejoined the conscious world. "What happened?" she asked sleepily.

"Nothing Mom. I think I just saw the Easter Bunny driving by like a bat out of hell; almost took my front off." Now Brian was laughing too.

"What are you talking about?"

"Everything's okay, Mrs. Brubaker. Tracy and I are just talking."

"Uh-huh. You two think you're so funny."

"No Mom," Tracy corrected. "That's another reason why I should marry Brian: you're looking at the two least funny people on the face of the earth."

"Bah!" Violetta snorted while waving her hand dismissively. Then she closed her eyes and resumed her snooze.

"*Easter Bunny driving like a bat out of hell*?" Brian asked. "Tracy, where do you get this stuff?"

"I have bunnies on the brain I guess. Brian, if you see any chocolate Easter bunnies on clearance in your travels, pick up some will you? I don't know why I didn't get myself some already."

"Uh, sure Tracy; you bet." And then he started laughing again.

"I love you more than chocolate bunnies Brian."

"If you don't quit that *I'm* going to be the one who wakes your mother up this time, unfunny as you may be." Now there was mutual laughter wafting through the auto. Violetta however remained undisturbed.

"I know I need to leave but I don't want to," Brian said, once again preparing to depart Tracy's domicile. They were in an embrace, her head near his shoulder.

"It won't be like this for much longer," Tracy said smiling.

"So, you're going to call the church tomorrow?"

"Their office will probably be closed; they likely have Easter Monday off. But I'll call this week. Any day will work for you right?"

"Of course it will; my 2016 calendar is wide open."

She looked at him. "Don't forget to keep your eyes out for discounted bunnies."

He nodded. "I love you; I love you so much."

She kissed him. "You need to shoo."

"Can I come back if I find a store open that has bunnies?"

She laughed. "Sorry; no bunny bribery tonight."

He hugged her, then gave her yet another goodbye kiss, at least his third in the last five minutes, and started his lonely journey home. And she in turn watched him move down her hallway and board the elevator. The doors always seemed to close quicker when he was leaving for the night. Why were they in such a hurry?

So the Easter weekend was officially over for her. Her mother had been safely delivered home, Brian was on his way to his, and Tracy would now have to focus on Colin Richmond and his predicament. She really didn't have anything solid yet though; but she did have some leads to follow up on. She wasn't going to dwell on it tonight however; tomorrow, when she was dressed for business and in her office: that's when she'd think about Richmond. Now she wanted to sleep; almost midnight. It was looking like another night of six hours sleep maximum. Oh, the sacrifices one makes when in love.

Her phone rang; Brian already? That was too quick. She answered with a cheerful hello.

"Is this Tracy Brubaker?"

"Yes," she said to the unfamiliar voice.

"You're Colin Richmond's lawyer?"

"Yes," she answered apprehensively.

"I'm Officer Bounds. Ms. Brubaker, your client just tried to kill himself."

Chapter 8

It was 1:30 in the morning, Monday. Tracy was pacing the halls of the detention center's medical area, waiting to see her client. Finally someone approached her, and introduced himself as Dr. Stahl. "He tried to hang himself with his bed sheets," he told Tracy when she asked what happened. "We didn't realize he was a suicide risk."

"I'm no doctor but I realized he was down the two times I spoke with him," she said sharply.

"Forgive me ma'am but most people here *are* down. You won't find happy people here."

Tracy shook her head. "What brought this on?"

"I'm not sure."

"Did he get some bad news today or something? I didn't think you had visiting hours here on Sunday."

"I really can't say. When we asked him if he'd like us to call someone he said your name. That's really all I know."

Tracy gulped. "Will he be okay, physically I mean?"

"Yes; he must have been found shortly after he…well, he never really completely lost consciousness."

"I see. Can I talk to him for a few moments?"

"Yes. Follow me." Tracy followed the doctor to the guarded room where Richmond was now resting. There was already a chair next to the bed; Dr. Stahl motioned for her to sit there. "Not too long now," he whispered before leaving.

Colin Richmond was staring at the ceiling. If he realized Tracy was there he didn't acknowledge it. "Colin," Tracy said softly after sitting down. He slowly turned to face her.

"Hi Tracy; sorry to spoil your weekend," he said flatly. Then he turned his eyes back to the ceiling.

"Colin, what happened? I thought we had an understanding." She was smiling, not quite sure what to say.

"Oh, I'm sorry. This has nothing to do with you," he sighed. "I guess I just feel so hopeless."

"Colin, I know it looks bad right now but there are some things I'm looking into. I think there's reason to have hope."

He shook his head. "That's not what I'm talking about. I mean, first my mom leaves, then my dad gets killed and I get blamed for it, and now this. I mean, how much shit can happen in one person's life until you get the hint that maybe it's time to check out?"

Tracy squirmed in her chair. She thought about how she felt after she learned her father had been killed; how she felt when Brian walked out on her. She could empathize with his feelings of despair. She gave him a weak smile. "Oh Colin, I'm so sorry about all of this. I wish each person's life had a misery limit." She had both of her hands on the bed's sidebars.

"When did you get *that*?" he asked her, his eyes a little wider now.

"What?"

"The ring; you didn't have it the first two times I saw you."

"Oh," she responded blushing. "I got engaged a few days ago."

"Wow—that looks like some ring."

"Uh, yeah."

"Congratulations."

"Thanks Colin. But I'm really concerned about you."

"You don't have to be. I mean, I tried and I failed. I realize now how stupid it was, letting him get to me like that."

Tracy perked up. "Let *who* get to you?"

"Oh, that Pinkerton asshole."

"Who's *he*?"

"The detective who arrested me for my dad's murder."

Tracy felt her anger making an early debut for the work week. "When was he here?"

"Today. Not sure why, but he made it a point to see me."

"And what did he do to you; what did he say?"

"He didn't hit me if that's what you mean. He just taunted me; told me that there's no way I'd get away with it again, that he'd make sure everyone on the jury knew what I did, that I should get used to the bars, and other stuff like that. And he was smiling the whole time, laughing, saying it was his turn to laugh at me like I must have been laughing at him all those years ago. I mean: I had to listen to him; there was nowhere I could run to."

Tracy was officially furious. "You're right—that guy *is* an asshole. I'll make sure that doesn't happen again Colin; that shouldn't have happened to begin with."

"Thanks Tracy but I'm alright now; really. I just had a bad moment." He looked back at her. "I can't believe you came to see me; you could have waited until the morning."

"Well, I couldn't very well go to sleep after I learned what my favorite new client tried, now could I?"

Richmond laughed. "Favorite huh? You're a really nice person."

"Pinkerton's not going to think that when I get through with him."

"Oh Tracy don't get yourself in any trouble because of me. I'll be okay now."

"Pinkerton shouldn't have done that Colin. Period. Anyway, they'll keep you under observation for a few days, and have you have talk to a shrink probably."

        A Tracy Brubaker Mystery

"Whatever."

"They'll probably be kicking me out soon. Is there anything I can do for you Colin, anything at all?"

"Actually you already did; I mean, just coming here like you did. I'll be okay now."

She smiled at him. "Okay. But if anything like what happened earlier today happens again, you let me know *immediately*."

"Okay, I will."

"Goodnight Colin. Hang in there buddy." She stood up and made her way to the guard, who let her out of the hospital quarters. Then a few minutes later she was headed back to her condo, her fury building with each passing block. "Well," Tracy thought, "Colin's hit the no-bail trifecta now: a flight risk, a danger to others, and now a danger to himself. Art will find out about this as soon as he steps foot into his office in a few hours." Tracy shook her ahead. "Oh, Colin…"

She arrived at her building and made her way to the elevator. Upon reaching her floor, she nearly struck at the transport's doors when they opened too slowly for her liking. Finally she was making her way down the hallway to her unit. But she came to a screeching halt when she got to her door: there at the base of her entranceway were two 8.5 inch tall foil-wrapped Easter bunnies. She bent over to pick them up, a smile now on her face. "Oh Brian," she said aloud softly, "You dear, sweet man." She entered her abode and placed the gifts on her kitchen counter, trying her best to center them. She kicked off her shoes, sat on her couch, and drifted off to sleep, where the bunnies could keep watch over her the rest of the night.

Detective Tanner was usually happy to see Tracy when she visited him at his office at BPD. And while it was true he wasn't the actual target of her wrath, she had picked him for various reasons as the first person to see this Monday morning.

"Good morning Tracy," he said to her. "I hear congratulations are in order."

"What?" she asked without enthusiasm.

"Didn't you see Danbury last week? Well, apparently she mentioned to Arthur you were engaged after you talked to her and Arthur told me when I talked to him this morning."

"Oh — that. Yes, Brian and I are getting married."

"That's great Tracy."

"But that's not why I'm here."

"Oh. I thought you were here to tell me in person."

"No, sorry El. I'm too mad right now."

Tanner sat down. "Uh-oh. What happened?"

"Pinkerton happened."

"Huh?"

"Have you heard about Colin Richmond?"

Tanner looked at his desk. "Yes; I heard. That's why I was talking to Arthur this morning. I didn't realize you knew yet."

"They called me last night after they found him. Or rather, after he told them to contact me."

"Oh; I didn't know that."

"Do you know *why* he tried to kill himself?"

"No, I don't."

"Pinkerton came to see Colin yesterday. He verbally harassed him; a law enforcement person spoke with someone who was known to be repre-sented by counsel *without* contacting counsel. Do you know the shit-storm I can bring over something like that?"

Tracy rarely used profanity, so Tanner didn't have to guess just how angry she really was. "Tracy just calm down."

"I *won't* calm down! What are you going to do about Pinkerton?"

"Tracy: I'll talk to him and let him know in no uncertain terms what you just told me."

"Maybe I should see him."

"Uh, probably not a good idea right now."

Tracy sat down and made herself comfortable across from Tanner. "So, Pinkerton was the lead detective on Richmond's father's case."

"Yes."

"And he thinks Colin got away with murder."

"Not just him Tracy."

"Oh? Are there other people planning to pay Colin a visit and let him know *their* feelings?"

Tanner scowled. "Of course not."

"Then I don't care what other people thought. Why is Pinkerton so obsessed over this case?"

"I don't know that we can use the word obsessed here."

"No? He makes a special trip on Easter Sunday to speak with Colin, to taunt him. He had to have used his position and authority to gain entrance on a no-visitor's day to see a man he had no justifiable reason to see. What word would *you* use, El?"

Tanner took a deep breath. "No cop likes it when a murder goes unpun-ished — especially when you're sure you've got the killer dead to rights. But like I told you before, Richmond was a punk who dared us to arrest him, made the investigation more difficult than it had to be. Who knows: maybe if he hadn't been so busy playing the tough guy he could have been help-ful to us, put us on a different path. So Pinkerton took this to heart. You weren't there to see the grin on Richmond's face the day he walked out of court, the grin he made sure to show to all of us."

Tracy looked out the office's side window. She couldn't help but feel some empathy for Tanner and the rest of the officers involved in the Jack-

 A Tracy Brubaker Mystery

son Richmond murder case. She had great respect for law enforcement people as a rule; the father she adored was one after all. And she really wasn't holding grudges against anyone over the Brian Shane and Massimo Paganini cases. Still, the Pinkerton move was inexcusable. So Colin Richmond had been a total prick; yeah, she could believe that. Janie Carruthers had suggested as much. Tracy shook her head.

"I hear what you're saying El. But he was only 17 at the time so maybe he just handled the whole thing in the way he could best deal with it. I know I wouldn't want to be judged on things I did when I was 17."

"I don't think you have anything to worry about on that score, Tracy."

She ignored the compliment. "Well, Pinkerton needs to stay away from here on out. I'll let you deal with it diplomatically. If he stays away I won't feel the urge to have a face-to-face with him."

"You mean an in-your-face with him."

Tracy chuckled. "Whatever."

"I'll talk to him today."

"Good. When I can go through what you have on the Jackson Richmond murder?"

"How about Wednesday? Most everything is supposed to be here tomorrow so why don't you come here first thing Wednesday and I'll get you set up?"

"That'd be great El; thanks."

"Okay. And Tracy, I do appreciate you bringing this Pinkerton thing to me first instead of just blindsiding the guy. I doubt he really meant for Richmond to kill himself. But, like I said, I'll talk to him."

"Sure El. After all the crap I dealt with dealing with Lennon during the Paganini case, I'm not ready to make another enemy that wears a badge right now. You know I love all you guys."

Tanner smiled and nodded. "Yes Tracy. Like I said, thanks for coming to me."

"Okay. Can I ask you one more question before I'm off to spread sweetness and light elsewhere?"

Tanner chuckled. "Sure."

"Are you as sure Colin Richmond killed his father as you were sure Brian Shane killed his?" Tanner just stared at her. "You don't have to answer if you don't want to. But please think about it." And then she exited her chair, pulled open Tanner's office door, and left the detective to ponder her question.

When Tracy arrived at her office, Rebecca and Neal were already there. She recounted the events of the early Monday hours including her talk with Detective Tanner.

"So you didn't get any sleep, did you?" Rebecca asked.

"Not really; how *could* I sleep after what happened?"

"Well why don't you go home and grab some zzz's?" Neal asked. "Beck and I can handle things."

Tracy gave him a tired smile. "I may lie down on my couch back there if I feel the urge. But I think I'll stay here for now." Just then Tracy's office suite door was pulled open. Nick Fallston entered swiftly. Tracy turned her head away so he didn't see her roll her eyes; this couldn't be good.

"Can we talk Ms. Brubaker?" he asked immediately without as much as saying hello.

"About what?"

"Oh come on; it's all over the place about Richmond."

Without a word Tracy turned and moved toward her space in the back. Fallston followed and closed the door behind him. "I knew this would happen," he said shaking his head.

"What?" Tracy asked skeptically. "You *never* told me you thought he was depressed enough to do what he did."

"I told you not to get his hopes up."

"Are you trying to blame this on *me*?" She asked angrily, raising her voice.

"Of course not."

"Then why are you here?"

He sighed. "Maybe you should try for some mental defense."

"Oh you've got to be kidding."

"Why?"

"Because Colin isn't crazy."

"He certainly went crazy last night."

"That was Pinkerton's fault."

"Pinkerton? What's he got to do with anything?"

"You don't know? He was the primary investigating detective in Colin's father's case."

"Now why would I know that?"

"You didn't bother to look into that murder while working on the current one?"

"Why would I? That has nothing to do with what Colin's dealing with now."

"You're so sure, are you? Jesus Nick didn't you do any work on this thing? You really think there's no connection between these crimes?"

Fallston scowled. She had him on the defensive again. "What are you going on about? I'm a lawyer not a cop. I was trying to defend someone, not solve a crime; that's what the cops do."

Tracy rolled her eyes. But Fallston was right. He wasn't a detective and neither was she. Nevertheless, Tracy still felt the murders were tied together. "Be that as it may I think that looking into the old murder is part and parcel to the defense of the current one. So that's what I'm doing."

          A Tracy Brubaker Mystery

"I see." Fallston scratched the back of his head. "You still might consider having his competency evaluated though. What if he tries this again?"

"I'll worry about that Nick. He's *my* client now. I really wish you'd remember that."

"Yeah, well; I still feel a certain responsibility here."

Tracy looked at Fallston quizzically. "I'll tell Colin you were asking about him. Is there anything else?"

"You don't like me do you?"

Tracy sighed. "That's not true; I really don't know you very well."

"People I've talked to that know you seem to like *you*. I guess I'm curious."

"Curious?"

"Well, how do you manage to stay friends with people who you have to attack in court, or in depositions, or whatever?"

Tracy smiled. "Maybe because I try not to *attack*; I just ask my questions; raise my points; explain my position. Oh sure, I can get a little flip sometimes. But I realize that most people are doing their jobs the best they can; most of the witnesses I deal with are decent people. I try to remember that and try not to make it personal. Other than that I don't know what to tell you."

Fallston nodded. "I understand you. Okay. Look the truth is when I heard what happened I wanted to make sure Colin was okay. I thought you were probably the best person to talk to in that regard. I really wasn't here to blame you. I'm sorry if I gave that impression."

Tracy approached him. "Don't worry about it Nick. I think it's refreshing that even though Colin's not your client anymore that you care. If I seem testy it's only because I didn't really sleep last night."

"Fair enough. Look, maybe I can still help. I have a lot of contacts downtown. Keep that in mind."

"Sure Nick; thanks."

"Maybe we could grab lunch sometime."

She recalled the last time a fellow attorney started getting friendly. "Uh, I'm engaged Nick."

He laughed. "Oh I didn't mean *that*. I'm in a relationship. I meant as two professionals who may be seeing more of each other if you continue to be involved with criminal matters. You know, old fashioned networking."

"Oh," Tracy said, slightly embarrassed.

"I guess you get hit on all the time since you're so pretty."

Now she felt completely flushed. "I...I don't know what to say to that."

"Well, I'll get going. Thanks for talking to me Tracy."

"Sure Nick. Uh, Nick, before you scamper away, tell me: have you ever had any dealings with this Pinkerton I mentioned before?"

"Well, I do know a Lieutenant Alexander Pinkerton."

"That must be him. He'd be in his late 50s or early 60s."

"That's the one. I've had him on cross before."

"What can you tell me about him?"

Fallston scratched his chin. "Uh, well, he seems to be a good cop. He can be pretty intimidating when he wants to be. He makes a great witness for the State. Juries always seem to believe him; he has one of those authoritative voices, you know the type: filled with confidence. Other than that, I don't know what to tell you."

"Oh that's fine. I just wanted to get a peer's impression of him."

"I wish I could I tell you more."

"Oh don't sweat it Nick. I'll be seeing you." She offered Fallston her hand and the two shook. Then he left her office, just in time avoid Tracy indulging in a huge yawn. It was time for a strong cup of coffee, something to keep her up. She was starting to pour when Neal approached her.

"I found Christine Jacks," he said smiling. Suddenly Tracy didn't need that coffee anymore.

Christine Jacks Wellman lived in a three-bedroom home in Baltimore County, very close to the Carroll County line. Her house was just off of Liberty Road, hidden amongst the trees that could be seen from the main road. Chrissy, as she liked to be called, sounded friendly enough on the phone, and had agreed to talk to Tracy this very afternoon; right after lunch would be perfect. Tracy pulled into the driveway about 12:45 p.m. She had wanted to call Brian and tell him about her night after he left her, but that was now going to have to wait. Tracy needed to talk to Chrissy.

"Come on in dearie," Chrissy said smiling. "Want some tea? I just made some; nice and hot."

"Thanks Chrissy; sounds perfect."

"Back here…"

Tracy followed her hostess to the rear of the house where the kitchen was located.

"I always like a nice cup of tea after lunch. It just seems to hit the spot. And it's better for me than sweets." Chrissy chuckled at her own medical opinion. "Milk or sugar, hon?"

"Oh, make it straight Chrissy. Nice and strong."

"That a girl," and then she chuckled again. She put a flowery mug emitting steam in front of the attorney. "There's still some left in the pot if you want more; don't hesitate to ask."

Tracy blew and sipped; nice and strong. "Just perfect Chrissy. Thanks."

Chrissy chuckled. "So you're a lawyer?"

"Yes."

"I like the lawyer shows I see on TV. Is it anything like that?"

"No, not really. They always skip the boring parts and go right to the exciting ones."

 A Tracy Brubaker Mystery

"Yeah; I figured." Chrissy sipped from her own mug. "Do you work in a big firm? Is everybody sleeping with everybody else?"

Tracy couldn't help laughing. "No; there are only three of us where I am. And there's no *ménage a trois* arrangement."

Now Chrissy was laughing. "Oh, I figured that too. When my husband was alive we'd watch that stuff and he'd say how silly it all was."

"When did your husband pass Chrissy, if you don't mind my asking?"

"Oh, must be almost four years ago now. Heart attack, you know; he never took care of himself."

"I'm sorry Chrissy. How long were you married?"

"Almost 20 years. I didn't get married until I was in my 40s… oh my God would you look at *that!*" Chrissy was staring at the ring. "Honey: you must have found yourself a real keeper. May I?" Tracy offered Chrissy her hand. "Is your fellow a movie star or something?"

Tracy laughed. "Only in *my* movie."

Chrissy released the digits. "I don't think I've ever seen anything like it."

Tracy felt embarrassed — again. "Thanks Chrissy. Are you all by yourself out here?"

"Most of the time. My husband had kids from his first marriage so they stop by with their own kids once in a while. I go out a lot myself; still like being social."

"I get it," Tracy smiled. "When did you meet Amanda Richmond? Do you recall?"

"Mandy? Oh, sometime in the early 1980s I guess. She started coming to the same bar I hung out at. When I realized she might be a regular I went to check out the competition." Chrissy chuckled. "We became instant friends."

Tracy nodded. "So you gals drank, danced, and flirted a little; just having fun?"

Chrissy chuckled some more. "Yup; just like the song says, girls having fun or whatever. I mean, we were in our late 30s but we felt like we were in our teens. I didn't even realize she was married, much less had a kid, until months later."

"Really? She didn't wear her wedding ring in the bar?"

"Nah; maybe she had something like you got right there and didn't want to wear it in public."

"Do you remember how you found out about her family?"

"Sure: she invited me over one afternoon. It was obvious once I went into the apartment: pictures on the walls, school books on the kitchen table."

"I see. Did you ever meet her family?"

"Not that day, but eventually. He husband was a quiet one but her son seemed pretty nice."

"What, if anything, did she say how she felt about her son?"

"Oh, not too much. When we were together she just wanted to let loose, you know? But I think she really loved him a lot."

"Oh? Why?"

"Well, sometimes, she'd get a little down, and she'd tell me if it weren't for the boy she'd leave her husband. She said that a few times."

"Huh. Isn't that what happened though? I mean, she left her husband."

Chrissy paused and moved her hands over her hot mug. "I don't really know," she finally answered. "She wasn't looking for anything long-term; at least that was the impression I had. There were some guys who wanted her, you know, for their own. She was a pretty lady, with a great personality. Guys liked her."

"But she never indicated she felt enough about someone to run away with them, leave her son."

Chrissy shook her head. "No, not that I remember. I mean, there weren't a lot of people she could have shared that stuff with. I was the only person she really hung out with that I remember. I was surprised when she stopped coming to the bar, and more surprised when I found out she ran off with someone."

"The police talked to you then?"

"The cops?"

"Sure, when they investigated the disappearance."

"Well, if they asked me questions while I was at the bar I might not remember," Chrissy laughed. "I really don't remember."

"Oh, I see. How about the guys who wanted more from her; do you remember any of those?"

"Well, let me think about that. She was into real short-term type things, you know. Sometimes she'd see a guy for a while, but she usually didn't get into names, you know? Usually she'd come up with some nickname for him."

"Gotcha. Remember any of those nicknames?"

"Um, let me think a bit." Then Chrissy started laughing, and then she waved at Tracy with the smallest finger on her right hand."

Tracy laughed nervously. "Uh, I don't get it Chrissy."

"I'm waving goodbye to you." And there was more laughter.

"Oh, should I go?"

Chrissy shook her head. "No no no. That's what Mandy did when she broke up with Pinky." And Chrissy waved her right pinky some more.

"Ooooh…I see. She broke up with a guy she called Pinky."

"Right! When I asked her how it was going with him one time she started doing that; waving bye-bye with her pinky. Cute, huh?"

"Yes, Chrissy; cute. Do you know anything else about Pinky: his real name, what he did, how they met?"

     A Tracy Brubaker Mystery

"Oh no I…Wait, I think he may have been a cop."

"A *cop*?" Tracy asked eagerly. "Why do you think that?"

"Because I remember she said she probably shouldn't have broken up with him because he could have fixed her tickets, or something like that."

"A cop with the nickname Pinky."

"Yup; I think so, if this old memory of mine is right."

And then, in spite of the hot tea, Tracy went cold; pale and cold. A cop with the nickname Pinky: Pinkerton. "Sweet Jesus," Tracy thought. "Pinkerton was having an affair with Amanda Richmond and then investigated her husband's murder."

"Are you all right sweetie? You look sick."

"I'm fine," Tracy answered quickly. "Do you remember any other boyfriends, nicknames, or anything?"

"I can try to remember; no promises though."

Tracy reached into her briefcase. "Here Chrissy; here's my business card. If you think of anything else about Mandy could you call me?"

Chrissy took the card. "Sure." She stood up and put the card on her refrigerator door, holding it with a magnet shaped like a sliced cake piece.

"Thanks Chrissy. Oh, would you recognize Pinky if you saw him again, assuming you saw him in the first place, that is?"

"Well, I don't know. If you have a picture of him I can look at it."

"Okay; I'll get back to you on that. Thank you Chrissy, for the tea and more importantly for talking to me."

"Hey, it was fun. I sure do like talking about Mandy. I really wish I knew what happened to her. I keep hoping I'll hear from her again someday."

Tracy smiled as Chrissy followed her to the door. The attorney turned to give her hostess another smile and then made her way to her car. She quickly entered and returned Chrissy's goodbye wave through the windshield as she backed out of the driveway. She didn't share with Chrissy the thought she had: Tracy didn't think anyone was ever going to hear from Amanda Richmond again.

Chapter 9

It was all starting to make sense, even though Tracy hated thinking about it. But how could she not? The drive back to the office would be lengthy enough so that she could start to work things out in her head.

Pinky and Amanda having an affair.
She tells him that she doesn't care.
First come threats
Then comes killing
And then poor Jackson
With his own blood spilling.

"Real cute Tracy," she scolded herself. But it did make sense now. Pinkerton and Amanda fight; Pinkerton kills her, maybe on purpose, maybe by accident. He succeeds in covering up the crime; he is a cop after all. Then what? Did Jackson Richmond not believe his wife took off, that she was a victim of foul play? Chrissy said she met the husband; did he question her at the bar and find out about Pinky? Rats—she forgot to ask Chrissy if Jackson talked to her after the disappearance. She would have to follow up on that. If Jackson did find something out, did Pinky find out Jackson found out? Pinky shows up dressed like Colin that fateful night; he kills the father and implicates the son. Gets himself assigned to the case and targets Colin from the beginning. But the son doesn't go away for it; he's still out there looking for his father's killer in much the same way Jackson was looking for his wife's. Okay: so Colin starts getting close, or gets close to getting close. Jackson finds out about the reincarnation thing. How though? Well, sometimes cops moonlight as bartenders. Maybe at least one bartender at Ritchie's Digs is a cop or former cop. Who else, after all, but a cop could have found someone with a birth date that matched up with the murder date? Neal didn't turn up any criminal record on Timothy Pane, not that Pinkerton would have wanted someone with a record anyway. How did Pinkerton get Pane to go along with it? Money? Cops don't make a lot of money. If Pinkerton is bad maybe he's got something on the side that *does* make money. Plus, Pinkerton could have found a way to transfer Colin's prints to the knife; she knew that could be done. Maybe Pinkerton accesses the old evidence in the Jackson murder; lifts Colin's prints from something in there—the trophy perhaps—and puts them on the knife. Bottom line: Pinkerton sets up Colin *again*, this time trying to taunt him, get him to feel hopelessness and despair. It almost works too.

     A Tracy Brubaker Mystery

Tracy shuddered; she hated thinking like this. But it made sense, right? Still, there was the biggest question: how would Tracy go about proving such a thing, any of it? She shook her head. "You're going to hate me El," she thought. "After what I tell you, you're really going to hate me."

"I don't believe it," Tanner said firmly after hearing Tracy's summary. "Lieutenant Alex Pinkerton is *not* a killer Tracy. He's known in the department as someone who's never fired his gun for crying out loud. Do you understand that?"

"Well, Jackson Richmond was struck and Timothy Pane was stabbed; no guns involved. But forget that. What about the coincidence of a boyfriend named Pinky?"

"Even if I grant you the affair, which I'm not saying I am, that doesn't mean he killed her."

"Okay; what if he thought the husband did it and killed him for revenge, to avenge his lover's death?"

Tanner shook his head. "And framed the kid?"

"Maybe he didn't frame him; maybe it just worked out that way. Maybe he was even relieved when Colin walked."

"Uh-huh. And what about Pane then?"

"A scared man who thinks he's going to be found out might do desperate things El after so much time."

"And come up with the idea of using reincarnation, or belief therein, as a motive? Come on Tracy, that's pretty fanciful. Cops don't tend to be fanciful; we're more practical."

"Well that works both ways El. Being fanciful, as you just pointed out, makes a cop look *less* likely, you see?"

"Tracy: you are reaching so far you're about to fall out of the tree."

"How could a layperson find out about Pane's birth date? Tell me that."

"You are assuming Tracy that I don't think Colin did this. It could be just a horrible, unfortunate coincidence about the dates."

"A bunch of coincidences, you mean: the birth date, the limp, the arbitrary meetings, etc."

Tanner sighed. "Alright Tracy, I'll put it to you this way: you are going to have to bring me some damn compelling evidence before I go after a cop. And you're *nowhere* near to having any."

Tracy scowled. "What do think I'm going to be able to find 30 years after the fact, El? How can you put this on *me*?"

Tanner scowled back. "Because *you're* the one making the accusation, based on nothing but a nickname, which doesn't *prove* anything."

Tracy turned her head. "How about the visit to Colin? You don't think that tilts things in my favor a bit?"

Tanner didn't answer. "I haven't talked to Pinkerton about that yet."

"Why not?"

"I'm going to see him tomorrow."

"How about me seeing the evidence in the Jackson Richmond murder?"

"I told you: Wednesday."

"How about the report that was prepped for Amanda Richmond's disappearance; can I get a look at that?"

Tanner sighed. "I suppose I can see if that's anywhere to be found. But as you pointed out, that's a 30-year-old case."

"But technically it's still open; she was never found."

"True."

"Okay. Look El, I don't want us to fight over this and get upset with each other. I just ask you to keep an open mind when speaking with Pinkerton. There are just too many coincidences in this case to look the other way on Pinkerton, despite his record."

Tanner gave a half smile. "Okay Tracy; fair enough. But if I do that for you then you need to think about something too, something that is likely to be offered if Pinkerton goes on the offensive."

"What are you talking about?"

"If you're right about the affair, maybe Amanda Richmond was going to leave her family. Maybe Colin came home when she was packing, and there was a fight; Amanda gets killed."

"*Colin killed his mother?*"

"Maybe the father finds out, maybe he's known the whole time. Colin eventually kills him. Pinkerton comes to the right conclusion, and makes sure justice is done, or tries to anyway."

"El, that's nuts."

"No more nutty than your theory, Tracy."

"I talked with an old friend of Amanda's who swears Amanda wouldn't leave her son."

"Whom did you talk to?"

"I'm not saying; I want to protect my potential witness for now."

"Oh Tracy come on!"

"I'm serious, El. I'll tell you about this person at some point but not now."

Tanner put his hands up. "Fine Tracy."

"Okay; I guess that's it for now. I'll call you tomorrow afternoon to confirm Wednesday."

"Alright Tracy." Tracy stood up and quickly went to the door. They didn't even say goodbye to each other.

     A Tracy Brubaker Mystery

"Are you going to tell me what's wrong, Tracy?" Brian asked. It was the dinner hour and he and Tracy were sitting at her condo's dining room table. She was twirling her spaghetti without actually eating any of it.

"Huh? Oh, I'm just not that hungry."

"You not hungry? What's wrong Tracy, or can't you tell me because is it's all confidential?"

"Uh, well, I guess technically it's not privileged since I didn't get the stuff directly from a client. On the other hand, it *is* part of my case."

"Oh, I see I guess."

"Hey, do you remember all those years ago when we were driving back after you met my parents?"

Brian was chewing his salad so he just nodded.

"Do you remember what you told me when I asked what you and Dad talked about in secret?"

Brian wiped his lips. "Uh, I think so."

"You said something like he told you he knew all the ways he could hide a body without it ever being found."

Brian started chuckling. "Oh yeah; right. I didn't think you thought it was that funny."

"Yeah, well, whatever…I think I may have that here."

"What? You think someone got rid of a body?"

"Maybe. I think a cop may have killed somebody and hid the body so that it hasn't yet been found; probably never will be at this point."

Brian had a look of horror on his face. "A cop? Oh Jesus Tracy what have you gotten yourself into *this* time?"

"What do you mean?"

"Don't play dumb. You told me all about those thugs and those feds involved in Max's case. And now you're involved in a case with a crooked, murderous cop?!"

"I don't know that for a fact Brian. I'm just exploring the possibility."

"Oh Tracy; you need to stop getting involved in things like this."

"Hey, it's not my fault!" she cried out defensively. "I don't know these things when I *take* a case. I find it out later and by then it's, well, too late to turn back."

Brian, visibly upset, stood up. "You need to tell your cop friend Tanner about this and let him take it from here."

"Uh, actually I did: it was the last stop I made before I came home."

"Oh good," Brian said sounding relieved and sitting back down. "What'd he say?"

"He didn't believe me."

Brian's relief was short lived. "Oh Tracy. This just isn't right."

"I know Brian; none of it is."

"What are you going to do?"

"I don't know yet. Dig around a little more—stealthily dig. This cop doesn't know what I'm thinking yet."

"But he'll find out Tracy."

"No he won't; not yet anyway. The only person I talked to about this is El and he won't bring my name into it."

"You're so sure huh?"

"Yes, I am. Even if he doesn't believe me 100% I've still put a bee in his bonnet. In fact I bet he's at dinner with Rita right now and the buzz is loud."

Brian gave her a weak smile. "Tracy, you know now I'm going to worry about you until *this* case is done." He was close to tears. "I mean, I just got you back Tracy."

She reached for his hand and squeezed. "Brian, I'll be fine. Please don't let yourself get worked up with worry. If I'm wrong, I'm fine. If I'm right El will be right there. I'm not worried; why should you be?"

Brian shook his head. "If you're not worried then why aren't you eating?"

"That's not worry; that's just me thinking."

"Uh-huh. Sorry Tracy; I think you're serving me baloney now."

Tracy smiled and laughed gently. "Brian, stop. Now finish your dinner or you get no dessert."

"What's for dessert?"

"Finish up and I'll tell you."

Brian managed a grin. "I love when you tease."

"Just eat; I'll do the same." And they did. Tracy grabbed the dishes and placed them in the sink. Then she brought dessert to the table. "Here we go: Biff and Bonnie Bunny."

Brian was now staring at the two bunnies he had left at Tracy's door the night before. He tried not to hide his disappointment. "Oh, you named them."

"Yup; *someone* left them at my doorstep so I adopted them." She grinned.

"Uh-huh. How did you determine gender?" Brian leered slightly.

Tracy blushed a bit. "Will you stop that kind of talk? They've kept their foil on; although, a bunch of mini chocolate bunnies running around isn't really such a bad idea."

Brian sighed. "Tracy, is everything okay between us?"

Tracy looked confused. "Sure. Why do you ask me that?"

"Well, we haven't fooled around for a while."

"Oh Brian; there are reasons for that."

"Holy Week."

"Yeah. And I really didn't get any sleep last night so I'm really, really tired."

"Ah."

"And, the truth is, we should probably be careful anyway. I mean, maybe even wait until we get married."

Brian's eyes widened. "You're not kidding, are you?"

Tracy sighed. "I just want us to be like we were before we started having sex; for a while, anyway. You used to just hold me, and let me fall asleep on your shoulder. I loved that. Now it's like since we've been intimate, there's this mentality that we have to be or there's disappointment. Do you see what I mean?"

"Tracy, I never tried to get you to do something you didn't want to do."

"I know that, Brian. And I'm not suggesting for a moment that you did. In fact: I was the one who got a little crazy a couple of weekends ago. I don't know what came over me. I guess I was just, I don't know, feeling lusty, maybe."

"You were incredible."

More blushing from Tracy: "Well, you were too."

"So that weekend was what then, us just getting something out of our systems?"

Tracy frowned. "I don't know. Putting it like that sounds a little cold, even if there is some truth to it." She sighed. "I'm sorry if I unintentionally made you think things were going to be like that all the time."

"No, no…I don't mean to sound whiny. I just, well, I don't know how else to say it: I want you, I want you totally."

"I'm not saying any of this because I don't want you, Brian. I *do* want you too. But, we do have to think about the consequences."

"I can wear something."

"I don't feel right about that either."

"Huh?"

"Brian, can we not talk about this right now. I'm really tired."

"Okay, Tracy. I didn't mean to be a jerk about it."

"You're not being a jerk; we're talking openly and honestly. That's a good thing, right?"

Brian smiled. "Okay. In that spirit then let's go over to the couch and sit down, and you can fall asleep with my arm around you, like you used to do."

Tracy smiled. "We haven't had our rabbits yet."

"They can wait for another day."

"Okay. I want to get into my pajamas first though."

Brian chuckled. "Sure. Let me wash the dishes while you get changed."

"Now you're turning me on."

Brian looked at her. "Don't tease, Tracy."

"Sorry Brian. But this is exactly what I'm talking about. I used to be able to do that and you thought it was okay."

"That was before we made love."

"Right. But why does that fact mean we can't have some verbal fun like we used to?"

"Alright; I see what you're saying. Get changed and I'll wash."

"I love you Brian."

"And I love you Tracy."

She kissed him softly on the lips and went to her bedroom. Brian sighed, wishing he was following her in there. He started on the soiled dinnerware and had it sparkling in short order. Tracy sat down on her sofa, looked over, and smiled at him, a tired smile that nevertheless had him hurrying over to attend to her. He sat down and she laid her head on his lap. He ran his fingers through her hair, occasionally rubbing the side of her head. She was asleep almost instantly.

He leaned his head back on the sofa, and closed his eyes. He smiled briefly remembering how many nights long ago she would do the same thing after studying most of the night for a test, afraid if she put her head on an actual pillow she would oversleep. So she'd snuggle with Brian as they both sat on her dormitory bed. Eventually she would be asleep in his lap; warm memories; happy memories.

Then Brian thought of the mystery killer cop, the one he wasn't supposed to be worrying about, and the smile left him. He decided he would stay with her all night if she didn't wake up and send him away. Nobody was going to take her away from him; nobody. Maybe he should get a gun for protection; she probably wouldn't like that though. For someone who once wanted to be a detective like her father she had a pretty contradictory stance on firearms: she didn't like them. She no doubt wouldn't ever want one in their home. How was he going to protect her then? For now he would stay here.

Around 1:00 a.m. someone was calling his name. "Huh?" he finally asked.

"Brian, you should head home now. It's very late, or very early depending."

"Oh, I guess I dozed off."

Tracy smiled. "It's okay Brian. But don't you want to go home and make sure you get enough sleep?"

"The truth? I'd rather stay here."

"Brian, I'm going to bed."

"I can stay here on the couch."

"Brian, you need to shoo."

He stood up, not happy he was being shooed. "Alright then. You're going to bolt and lock everything right?"

 A Tracy Brubaker Mystery

She laughed gently. "Yes. I'll follow you to the door and lock it up tight."

He removed his coat from her closet and stood by her door. He leaned over to kiss her and they exchanged an intense smooch, which then had him pulling her as close as he could manage. When she pulled away she looked up at him, and they studied each other eyes. She gulped.

"Goodnight Brian. See you tomorrow. I'll call when I'm leaving the office or to let you know if it's going to be a late night."

Brian nodded. "You look so beautiful Tracy, even tired and all."

She smiled. "I love you."

"I love you too. See you tomorrow then." He turned and left and Tracy quickly locked up. Usually she'd have watched him get on the elevator. But tonight she had barely escaped. "Whew, that was close," she thought. "If he had been here any longer he would have been here a lot longer." She made her way to her bedroom to resume her rest. But her pillow didn't provide the comfort that Brian's lap had.

Tracy brought Neal up to speed on Lt. Alex Pinkerton and the tale told by Chrissy Jacks Wellman. Neal looked almost as upset as Brian. "Here we go again," he finally said.

"Neal: let's not get all worked up *quite* yet. El's looking into things. You know we can trust *him*."

"I still don't like it, Tracy."

She sighed. "You said earlier you found Ken Vinton, Linda Schumacher's boy."

"Yeah; he lives in an apartment near Park Heights Avenue."

"I guess he works during the day."

"He works at a department store, Lonny's Discount near his apartment."

"I'll stop by Eastman's Transport and see if Linda will talk to me. Then I'll see if it's worth talking to her son."

"Okay."

"Hopefully first thing tomorrow I can stop by BPD and see what they have from the Jackson Richmond case; El should also have the file on Amanda's disappearance."

"Are you going to try to talk to Pinkerton too?"

"Not yet. I'm going to cool my jets on that. It's a touchy subject obviously, and El was obviously not liking what I was saying."

"Tracy, are getting mellow in your—"

"You better choose your next word carefully."

"—your *young* age. That's what I was going to say, honest."

"No is the answer to your question. If I think Pinkerton is involved I'll go after him full throttle. But it would be easier if El believes me, in part anyway."

"Right."

"I'm off to Eastman's now; then I'll check in."

"Okay; I've got things under control here."

"Supreme!" she said, and then moments later Tracy was out the door.

"I never even met this fella, this Pane guy," Linda Schumacher was telling Tracy, sounding slightly annoyed. "I can't help you. Besides, I just got off a break; boss will have my ass in a sling if I'm out here gabbing with you instead of working."

"Oh," Tracy said. "You do more than answer the phones then."

"No."

"Well can I just talk to you in between calls? I'll be quick."

Linda looked at Tracy skeptically. "What do you want to know again?"

"Just about Colin. You guys dated for a while."

"Yeah."

"How long?"

"Oh, who knows? Uh, maybe six months; a little more maybe."

"Nice guy?"

"What do you think I'm gonna say to that; he dumped me."

"Oh, it was a bad breakup then?"

"What is it with you? You heard of a *good* breakup?"

Tracy was beginning to feel like Linda Schumacher did not like her. "Well, some people agree to go their separate ways, stay friends even."

"Not here."

"Okay. What did you guys like to do: movies, dinner, sporting events?"

Linda chuckled. "We drank and we got it on. I ain't looking for romance."

Whew boy. "Where did you drink?"

"A bar called Richie's Digs."

"Oh sure."

"You know it?"

"Colin told me about."

"Oh. You two screwin' then?"

The question caught Tracy off guard, so much so that her face changed to a nice shade of scarlet. "No, Linda; Colin's just a client."

"Whatever you say."

"Were there regulars at Richie's you guys may have talked to; maybe had a favorite bartender you chatted with?"

"Yeah, I'd see some familiar faces. Don't remember names though, if that's what you're hoping. I haven't been back there since Colin sent me away; what a prick."

Tracy blinked. "How about the bartender, do you remember anyone in particular?"

"Nah, I don't get chummy with cops or ex cops."

"What does that mean?"

"They got cops working there: bartenders, a bouncer. Assholes pull me over and give me tickets over nothing; I can handle myself after a few drinks."

"Can I ask how you know they were cops?"

"Ain't no secret. You go there enough you hear the people talking. People drink, people talk."

"I see. Did Colin ever talk about his father?"

"Don't think so; don't really remember."

"I know this will sound like a strange question, but did Colin ever talk about reincarnation at all?"

"Huh?"

"Reincarnation; when somebody comes—"

"I know what it is. I never talked about that with anybody that I remember."

"Okay. Back to the cops: do you by chance recognize the name Pinkerton?"

"Who?"

"Pinkerton: he's a cop too."

"Work at Richie's?"

"No, but maybe he was friends with some people there."

"Can't say one way or the other."

"Okay," Tracy said disappointed. "Did anyone ever give either of you a hard time at Richie's, or anywhere else for that matter?"

"What do you mean? I ain't no troublemaker."

"I didn't mean it like that; plenty of nice people get bothered by not so nice people."

"You think I'm nice? Boy you got a way about you, I'll give you that."

"Well, I don't know that you're *not* nice, Linda."

"Oh, don't get your panties in a bunch honey. No, nothing like that ever happened. Like I said, lots of people know cops are in the place so things are pretty calm there, for a bar I mean. People get rowdy when they're having a good time sure. But we never got hassled."

"Okay. So, where did the two of you go when you wanted your privacy?"

Linda pursed her lips. "What business of that is yours?"

"I just meant did you go back to your place or did you go to Colin's? Maybe Colin struck up a friendship with a neighbor of yours or something; maybe your son."

"My *son*? What's he got to do with this? How do you even know about him?"

"I don't think he does have anything to do with this. I'm just looking for the names of other people that I might be able to talk to about Colin."

Linda's face muscles relaxed. "Oh. Well, my son only met Colin once or twice. He doesn't live with me. Sometimes he'd come over for a free meal; Colin was there for dinner a couple of times when Kenny stopped by."

"Did they talk at all?"

"You kidding? My son knows what's going on. He don't like any of the guys of mine he meets. I tell to him to call before he visits but he just comes on over when he feels like it; probably checking on me, thinks he's being protective. Lots of weirdoes out there, you know. One time he comes over and me and my guy are doing it right there on the living room floor; not a stitch on either of us." Linda started laughing. "You think he'd have learned his lesson then. Poor Kenny; probably scarred him for life."

Tracy looked at her notepad. "Was that Colin he saw on the floor with you?"

"Nah; that was a couple of years ago. Don't even remember the guy's name. Ain't that something?"

"Well, you seem mad at Colin. But, after talking to him, I get the sense he liked you. I think he wanted a more serious relationship with you."

Linda shook her head. "Eh, I don't want that anymore. Tried it twice, didn't work out either time. Not interested in getting screwed over a third time. And it's not like I'm having any more kids at my age."

"Okay. Well, I think that's all Linda. Thanks for your time."

"Yeah, okay. You think Colin will be alright? I mean I can't see him killing anybody."

"I don't think he killed anybody."

"Good. I'd hate to think I screwed a psycho killer or something."

Tracy made no additional comment; she smiled, rose, and made for the exit. Between Linda Schumacher and Detective Shandi Danbury Tracy had felt the romance being sucked right out of the air around her. But Linda had confirmed what Tracy thought a possibility: there were cops at Richie's. She'd want to talk to some of them, ostensibly about Colin. But the real person she was interested in once went by the nickname Pinky. Tracy made her way back to her car, amused by the fact the phone hadn't rung once the whole time she was at Eastman's Transport.

Tracy was in her blue Audi, having decided on her next move. So Ken Vinton had met Colin Richmond and didn't care for her mother's choice in men? That's a potential motive to hurt Colin. But kill Tim Pane and frame the ex-lover? Colin had broken it off with Linda *before* Pane even entered the picture. Vinton had no criminal record; no reports filed of assaults on unwanted, temporary step-fathers; at least, no one had pressed charges if anything like that had happened. Still, Tracy was curious. 10:15 a.m.: a little early for lunch. She pulled into the parking lot of Lonny's Discount.

"Can you direct me to Ken Vinton?" Tracy asked the smiling gentleman at the customer service desk.

 A Tracy Brubaker Mystery

"Uh, he's probably on the floor somewhere helping a customer or re-stocking something."

"Oh. You see I don't know what he looks like so I thought I could maybe get some help."

He smiled at her. "I'll page him for you."

"Thank you!" And then a booming voice asking for Kenny Vinton to report to the customer service desk could be heard throughout the store.

"What's up Paul?" a skinny but somewhat handsome young man asked his caller.

"This lady wants to talk to you. You can thank me later," Paul winked.

Vinton looked at Tracy. "Do I know you?" he asked eagerly.

"No Kenny. My name is Tracy. Can we talk briefly somewhere?"

"Sure! Right over here." She followed him to a deserted part of the store which led to the bathrooms. "So what did I do to deserve a visit from *you*?" he flirted.

Tracy grinned and handed him a business card. "I'm an attorney representing Colin Richmond."

"Who's he?" Vinton asked confused.

"Your mother used to go out with him."

The friendly face of Kenny Vinton vanished, and was replaced by a stern visage that was no longer eager to speak with Tracy. "Oh," he grunted. "I didn't recognize the name."

"They dated until about last January, maybe a little before that. They had been going out six months. Your mother said you had dinner with him a couple of times."

"Oh yeah; I know who you mean now." His tone was still not what one would call friendly. "You talked to my mother?"

"Yes."

"Why?"

"I was trying to get some general information on Colin. Since you met him too I wonder if you could tell something about him."

"Like what?"

"Anything that you remember could potentially be helpful."

"Helpful how?"

Good grief. "I'm trying to see if Colin had any, well, let's say enemies."

Vinton reclined his head slightly and tilted it to the side. "Oh, you mean like people who don't like their mother's boyfriends?"

Tracy sighed. "If that's how you felt about him, then I guess I'd have to say yes to that."

Vinton shook his head. "God," he snorted. "Look: what my mother does is *her* business. She goes through guys like an addict through heroin. Why should I care one way or the other?"

"So you didn't feel any more or less strongly about Colin than anyone else?"

"No. The fact is he hardly made an impression. He was quiet; hardly said anything during those dinners. Truth is he probably couldn't wait for me to leave so he could get my mom into bed."

Tracy cleared her throat. "Do you know if your mom liked him any more or less than her other boyfriends?"

"What does that mean exactly?"

"Do you know if she was very upset over the breakup with Colin? She seemed a little angry about it even now."

"Lady: I don't know what to tell you. You think my mother would confide in me about how she felt? She was used to getting the heave-ho. I mean, if she found out a guy wanted to get serious with her, he didn't have much longer. She'd dump him or vice versa. See what I mean?"

"Sure," Tracy nodded.

"She didn't go on and on about it. It's not like a hell hath no fury thing, you know?"

Tracy blinked. "Right," she nodded. Tracy's mind drifted.

Vinton looked at her quizzically. "You okay? You have a funny look on your face."

"What? Oh, no; I'm fine. So you only saw Colin those couple of times. Did you see him anytime outside your mother's apartment, like maybe in the hall or parking lot talking to anybody?"

"No. Now look, I need to—"

"Thanks for your time Kenny. I guess you need to get back to work. I won't keep you any longer." And then Tracy turned and left the open-mouthed and confused Ken Vinton standing there by the water fountain scratching his head.

"Chrissy, it's Tracy," she said into her cell phone. Tracy was seated in her car in Lonny's Discount parking lot.

"Oh hi! How are you?"

"I'm fine, Chrissy. Can I ask you some quick follow-up questions?"

"Oh sure."

"Thanks. Did Jackson Richmond ever talk to you about his wife's disappearance; maybe try to get some details about the men she was seeing?"

There was silence. "I know I talked to him once or twice after Mandy went missing. But I didn't know too many of Mandy's men's names. Truth is: I wasn't comfortable talking to him."

"So you didn't mention Pinky to him?"

"Oh no. I didn't know Pinky's real name. I didn't think just telling him a nickname would be helpful. I guess too I didn't want to get involved."

"I understand."

"Anything else?"

"Yes, actually; do you know if any of the wives or girlfriends of any of the men Mandy was seeing ever confronted her? Maybe they came into the

 A Tracy Brubaker Mystery

bar to confront her, or maybe she told you about someone calling her or even stopping by her apartment. Anything like that ring a bell?"

There was more silence. "I can't think of anyone. But that doesn't mean nothing like that ever happened. I mean, I don't remember Mandy ever saying she was being harassed by a woman. Guys she broke up with sure; but not a woman."

"Oh; okay."

"You think a lady hurt Mandy?"

"Well, hell hath no fury like a woman scorned, as they say."

Chrissy chuckled. "Oh yeah, I've heard that one before."

"Thanks again Chrissy. And remember to call me if you think of something. Bye Chrissy."

"Sure will. Bye Tracy."

Could a significant other of one of Amanda's lovers have killed her? Tracy was suddenly thinking it was a real possibility. She kills Mandy and what, gets her husband or boyfriend to help dispose of the body? Or does she manage to dispose of it on her own? Now Tracy started speculating wildly. Does the guy find out what his gal did? Does Jackson find out what the gal did? Does the gal's guy go and take care of Jackson? Geez—how many people may be involved in this? Tracy snorted and looked at her watch: approaching the lunch hour. And Tracy already had an idea of where she wanted to dine this afternoon.

Richie's Digs was a cozy looking pub located just off Charles Street in the city. Tracy lucked out with street parking and found the bar open for business. There were some tables along the wall and in the back to seat those interested in lunch or dinner, as well as the bar itself, which offered plenty of room for those who just wanted to drink and maybe watch what was on one of the two monitors that bookended the counter. Tracy had arrived just after they had opened for the day—11:00 a.m.—and there were already several people making themselves at home, bottles in hand. Tracy was making *herself* comfortable on the chair-like stool when the bartender approached her.

"Good morning!" he said cheerfully. "Thanks for hangin' with us at Richie's. What can I get you little lady?"

Tracy chuckled; what a friendly place this is. "How about a ginger ale with three lumps?"

"You bet." He grabbed a laminated card wedged between the napkin holder and condiments. "Here's our lunch menu. Take a look while I get your drink." Then he smiled and left her. She perused it; there were some tempting choices. Her host returned with her beverage. "Here ya go young lady. Want to order anything?"

"It all looks great. Uh: I'll try your stuffed mushroom caps and then your mini burger, medium well, with all the trimmings."

"Sure," he said smiling. "Let me go put that order in right now." He was punching away at his keypad when Tracy spoke.

"What's your name there barkeep?"

He answered without looking at her. "Bobby."

"Can we talk a bit Bobby?"

Now he looked over at her. "About what?"

She smiled and motioned with her hand for him to come over. "My name's Tracy. I have a few questions concerning Colin Richmond."

The smile left Bobby's face. "How do you know Colin?"

"I'm his lawyer."

Bobby started nodding. "Oh, I see."

"Do you know Colin at all?"

"Sure. He's a regular. Of course I usually see him when I'm working nights."

"He's been coming here a while I understand."

"Yeah, for years; nice guy."

"I agree. I'm trying to help him. I don't think he killed anybody."

"Sure."

"He used to come here with a girl named Linda. Do you remember her?"

"Oh sure. Linda was a trip."

"Really? How so?"

"Hey Bobby I'm dry over here!" A voice called out.

"Be right back, Tracy." When Bobby returned he had Tracy's appetizer. "Here you go Tracy," he said putting the plate in front of her.

"Thanks Bobby. They look and smell supreme. I'll try one as you tell me about Linda."

He grinned. "Not much to tell. She came in with Colin for a few months. She had a great big mouth and swore like a sailor, as they say. She'd get a little loud but she was fine. She wore a little too much makeup if you ask me; probably trying to make herself look younger."

"Your 'shrooms are *awesome*," Tracy said. "So Colin and Linda were good customers, no problems?"

"Nope."

"Did you know Tim Pane, the victim?"

"Let me check on my customers and see if your burger's ready while I'm at it. Be right back."

Tracy finished her mushrooms, and then made her notes. Bobby was back with her burger. He didn't need prompting. "I saw that Pane fellow couple of times. But he wasn't what I'd call a regular."

"He just showed up one day."

"Pretty much."

"And then he started hanging out with Colin."

"Yeah, they did start hanging out. They'd watch some of the games, have some beers."

"But you never saw them argue, did you?"

"No. Colin's a pretty mellow guy; sad almost."

"Sad?"

"Yeah. You can tell when you start talking to people on a regular basis if something's bothering them, or if something's going on in their life. Colin seemed down a lot."

"I see. So you talked to him now and then?"

"Yup."

"Did he talk to you about his father?"

"Yeah, once in a while. They never got the guy who killed him, he told me. Colin was trying to play detective, follow up leads if he found any."

"He told you all this?"

"Yup."

"Bobby: did Colin ever talk about reincarnation?"

Bobby started laughing. "As a matter of fact he did, at least he used to. It's been a couple of years though. But it was just somebody who had too much to drink talking. Eventually he started laughing about it."

Tracy nodded, finishing a bite of burger. "The sandwich is really good too."

"Yeah, our food's really good here. Take another bite while I help the people who just sat down."

"Oh, sure; no problem." So Tracy busied herself with her food while Bobby did his duty. Upon his return she asked, "Do you have any trouble-makers around here, in or outside?"

Bobby laughed. "Not really."

"I know sometimes police officers work at bars to make ends meet."

"You do huh?"

"My father was a detective with BPD."

Bobby stood straight up and looked at her seriously. "He was?"

"His name was Peter Brubaker. He was killed in the line of duty when I was 20."

Bobby blinked. "I'm really sorry to hear that." He gulped. "Do you want another ginger ale?"

"No thanks."

Bobby licked his lips. "Yeah, we have cops around here all the time. Some work as bartenders part time. Our weekend bouncer used to be one. And plenty of our customers are cops; they come in for a quick bite or after shift for a drink or two."

"I see. Do you know a lieutenant by the name of Alex Pinkerton?"

Bobby blinked. "The name is not familiar; if you showed me a picture I might recognize him though."

"That's okay Bobby; no big deal." Tracy was done with her meal. She reached in her coat pocket for a business card and then handed it to her server. "If you think of anything else about Colin or Pane or Linda or anything could you call me, Bobby? I'd really appreciate it."

He took the card. "Tracy Brubaker," he said out loud. "Didn't I read about you a month or so ago? Didn't you have something to do with that real estate guy getting arrested?"

Tracy smiled. "I got some press; no big deal though."

Bobby started nodding. "Sure; sure I'll call you if I remember anything. In fact, why don't you give me another card?"

Tracy obliged while asking, "Why? Is there someone else here you think could help?"

"Oh no. I was just going to put your card in for our drawing."

"Your drawing?"

"Sure. Over by the seating post there is a fish bowl where you put in your business card for a chance to win our legendary beer-battered onion rings and special sauce appetizer."

Tracy laughed. "Oh, I get it. Maybe I should give you all of them."

Bobby laughed. "If you put them in yourself I won't tell."

"Thanks Bobby. You've been great. Can you ring me up please?"

He looked at her. "Forget about it."

"What?"

"I forgot to mention: my dad was a cop too. He got gunned down during a drug bust when I was 10."

Tracy looked at Bobby, shock and horror on her face. "Oh Bobby—I'm so, so sorry."

"That's part of why I'm here; I like serving cops, taking care of them. They put their lives on the line every day. People like you and me really understand that, don't we?"

Tracy nodded. "Yes. Still, I'd—"

"Forget it. If Colin didn't do this thing, then get back to helping him."

"Okay. Thanks again Bobby."

"No sweat." Tracy readied herself to leave, and as soon as Bobby left to tend his thirsty patrons she put a $20 bill on the counter, and then quickly exited. She wondered what Bobby would say if she had told him the reason she wanted to know about Pinkerton.

Tracy finished telling Neal about her morning. "Did Shakespeare write that?" he asked her.

"Huh?"

"The thing about women scorned."

"Actually no," Tracy told him. "I believe the author most often given credit for that is William Congreve."

"Who?"

"He's also responsible for the quote of not kissing and telling if I'm not mistaken."

Neal stared at her. "How do you know all this?"

"Oh, I loved poetry in high school. I had a lot of time to read. And given I am a woman who has been scorned, I looked up the quote one day."

"Oh; well, I guess we shouldn't get into that."

"You catch on quick."

"Gulp. So: what next? I guess maybe we should talk to some of Pane's co-workers," Neal commented.

"Yes, I agree. He may have said something to one of them that can link Pane to Pinkerton, or someone."

"Still got Pinkerton on the brain huh?"

"Until a better suspect comes along, you bet."

"*Deggman's Printers and More* was where Pane worked. Want the address?"

"Yup."

Neal handed her a sticky note with the requested information contained thereon. "Here you go. They're in Baltimore County."

"Right. I guess that's where I'm going to be this afternoon."

"You've barely been in the office this week," Neal grinned.

"Yeah," she smiled. "I'm just trying to find *something*. I don't like Colin being locked up. If I could get a lead, something solid, maybe I could at least get another bail review hearing, in spite of Art's stubbornness on the matter."

"If you *do* find something you may get more than that."

"Grrr. Between you, Tanner, and Brian I think I'll be fine."

Neal smiled weakly. "Just be careful whom you talk to and what you say."

"Sure Neal. Now tomorrow first thing I'm going to go to BPD to review the evidence in the older cases. So I'll be tardy. I've already reminded Beck."

"Sure Tracy."

"Well then, I'm off to look at wedding invitations."

"What?" Neal asked her, a puzzled expression on his puss. Then he smiled. "Oh right, Deggman's does invitations."

"Uh-huh. Might as well see what's out there. See ya!" And then she was once again on the move. Neal followed her and watched her say adios to Rebecca and then whiz out the door.

"She's a regular Tasmanian Devil," Neal said to Rebecca.

The secretary laughed. "More like a bloodhound; she has the scent."

"Well," Neal said ruefully. "I'll agree with you that this case is starting to stink." And then he went back to his desk.

"Your ring is really something," Janice Grant told Tracy. "When is the big day?"

"May next year I hope. I still have to firm up the date; just one of the many things on my to-do list."

Janice smiled and nodded. "Oh, believe me, I hear you."

"Uh, Janice, before we start looking at some of your lovely offerings, I have a confession to make."

"Oh?"

"Yes. I'm Colin Richmond's attorney."

"Colin Richmond?"

"He's accused of killing your co-worker, Tim Pane."

Janice gulped. "Oh, I see. And you want to talk to me about Timmy."

"Yes, if you'd be willing to. I don't believe Colin killed Timmy but I'm starting to get an idea of who may have. I'd *really* appreciate it if you or someone else here could talk to me."

Janice looked at her own hands that were holding her invitation sample book. "I suppose that would be okay."

"Thanks Janice. For starters, what can you tell me about Tim—general things?"

"He was a nice guy; funny and sweet. Everybody liked him."

"Was he particularly close to anyone here?"

"Uh, you may be talking to her."

"Oh. Were you and Tim involved?"

"No; I mean, well its tough dating someone you work with, especially in such a small place like this."

"Sure. So you guys liked each other."

"Yeah; we'd go out to lunch sometimes, go out for drinks after work on a Friday sometimes. But it never went beyond that." Janice turned away from Tracy. "And now it never will."

Tracy reached for Janice's hand. "I'm sorry Janice. Tim sounds like a great guy."

"He was."

"Good sense of humor?"

"The best; he was always cracking jokes. If he thought you were down, he'd come over and tell you just the worst joke ever. And you'd cheer right up."

Tracy shook her head. "Did he like practical jokes too?"

Janice looked at Tracy. "Huh?"

"Like hand buzzers, or whoopee cushions—that kind of stuff."

Janice laughed gently. "Well, not exactly. But he could keep a gag running."

Tracy smiled. "What do you mean Janice?"

"Well, last year I think it was, we had a guy who worked here and he was a bit of a butthead. It was pretty clear this wasn't his thing, trying to come up with designs for stationery and memo sheets, stuff like that. So

                    A Tracy Brubaker Mystery

one day Tim goes over to this guy's waste basket and takes out this design Henry—that was the guy's name—was working on and then threw away. Timmy puts it back on Henry's desk when he's at lunch. So Henry comes back, sees it, and throws it away again, mumbling to himself that he was sure he already threw it out." Janice started chuckling. "Well, Timmy takes it out of the basket *again* later, and puts it back on Henry's desk when he's away." Now Tracy started laughing, understanding where this was going. "So now Henry comes back, sees it, and starts looking around. Now you have to understand that Timmy had a great poker face, but the rest of us, not so much. So we're all trying not to laugh and Timmy's just sitting there. Anyway Henry grunts or something and throws it away again. Well, after Henry leaves for the day Timmy takes the trash *again*. Then he tells me to come over to his desk and I see him write on the paper 'Henry, don't you love anymore me?' and then he buries it on Henry's desk. So the next day, I'm waiting for Henry to find this thing, and suddenly I hear him yell, 'What the hell?' real loud. And the whole office starts laughing, I mean we were all in tears practically; except of course for Timmy who's just sitting there. Henry rips that paper to shreds, he got so mad."

Tracy was near tears now too, imagining the scenario. Suddenly she liked Timothy Pane very much; he would have fit right in at *her* office. "My goodness, that's great!" she finally told Janice.

"Yeah; it's kind of a legend around the office now." Janice stopped laughing, her expression turning sad again.

"Did this Henry guy ever find out who was behind it?"

Janice shook her head. "No; nobody told him. A month or so later Henry was gone; quit with no notice. What a jerk."

"Did Tim ever get mad at anyone that you saw, give somebody a real what for?"

"No—never. That's what I don't understand about all of this. I've worked here three years and I never, ever saw Tim yell at *anybody*. I heard about the fight he was supposed to have had and I just don't understand it. Tim could get irritated like anyone, but yelling just wasn't his style."

"Hmm. What if it were part of a gag?"

"Huh? Oh, you mean like *pretending* to be mad? Well, I guess so."

Tracy was feeling the excitement she always felt when her suspicions were being confirmed. "Do you know if Tim was recently involved in some prank or something?"

"I'm not sure."

"Well, do you know why he started limping then? Did he hurt himself recently?"

"Limping?"

"Yes, Colin had said he had a limp."

Janice's eyes flew open. "You know, now that you mention it, I did see him limping one day; maybe it was around the Christmas holidays. I asked him what happened and he told me nothing, that he was, I think he said, rehearsing. Then he just smiled. I guess I just forgot all about it until now."

"Janice: anything else you can tell me about Timmy, anything at all?"

"Uh…"

"Like what did he do for fun: sports, movies…?"

"Oh. He liked photography, I know that. He liked to go out to eat; I'm not sure he ever ate at home."

"Have you heard of Richie's Digs? It's a pub in the city."

She shook her head. "No, I'm sorry. There's a bar not too far from here we would go to. Not sure of the name; it just says 'Bar' over the door."

Tracy smiled. "Okay."

Janice smiled in return. "You don't really want to look at these invitations, do you?"

Busted. "No Janice, I was really here about Timmy. I guess I lied a little bit."

Janice smiled. "That's okay. It was nice talking about him, remembering what he did to Henry." She paused. "So you think this argument was part of some elaborate joke, maybe the limp too?"

Tracy just continued smiling. "Maybe. I want to thank you again. Can I leave you my card in case you remember something else?"

"Oh sure; that'd be fine. And I'll ask some of the others around here if they can remember something. We all want whoever did this to Timmy to hang for it — in a manner of speaking, of course."

"Hey, I understand." Tracy paused and smiled sympathetically. "You loved him, didn't you Janice?"

Janice blinked, and some tears escaped. "Yes; I guess I did."

Tracy put a card on Janice's desk. "Thanks again Janice. You've been super nice and helpful. And I promise to bring my fiancé with me next time to look at your invitations. You'll have to point out to me the ones you designed."

Janice smiled. "Sure, okay." Tracy rose to make her exit, turning to give Janice another quick smile. Janice was just staring at the invitation sample book.

Tracy was in her car, sympathy and anger simultaneously consuming her emotions. So here was yet another victim to add to the pile: Amanda, Jackson, and Colin Richmond; Timothy Pane; and now Janice Grant. Sweet Janice, a woman secretly in love with a man who seemed, from all Tracy had heard, to be the kind of person Tracy would have liked as a friend; a friend she would now never have. She ached for Janice. She suddenly felt she had another client in this case, an unofficial client that she wanted to help regardless. And the only way she could do that was to make sure Timothy Pane's killer was brought to justice.

     A Tracy Brubaker Mystery

Tracy called the office to see if anything needed her attention; nothing that Neal and Rebecca weren't able to handle. She would see them tomorrow after her visit with Tanner. Next she called—and ended up leaving a message for—Brian. He could come over anytime after work. Seeing him every evening was becoming important to her. No real explanation for it, except perhaps for the very simple reason that she loved him.

Tracy had changed into more casual attire as she awaited Brian's arrival. He hadn't called her back but she wasn't worried; she kind of liked not knowing exactly when he would get there; anticipating the surprise. It was silly but exciting nonetheless. When the bell rang just after 6:00 she opened the door immediately.

The problem was, however, that it wasn't Brian on the other side. She didn't know who this person was. He was tall and distinguished looking, salt and pepper hair and clean shaven. He had a slight grin on his face. Was this a new neighbor? "Are you Tracy?" he asked her.

"Yes," she answered slowly.

"I'm Lt. Alex Pinkerton. I believe you want to talk to me."

Chapter 10

The smile, by now, had left Tracy's face. She suddenly felt cold. She stared at her uninvited visitor. He must have seen the panic in her face.

"You don't have to be afraid of me Tracy," he said soothingly. "I'm just here to talk." He pulled apart his sport jacket. "You see? I'm not armed."

"My fiancé will be here any moment," she sputtered. "I thought that it was him at the door; that's why I answered so fast."

"Well why don't we talk while you wait for him? I'm here now so why not take advantage of it?"

Tracy gulped. "Well, okay. Come in."

"Great! Thank you."

Tracy stepped away so Pinkerton could enter. Before she closed the door she peeked out to see if Brian was making his way down the hall. He was nowhere to be seen.

"Shall we sit at your lovely table here?" Pinkerton called out.

Tracy closed her door. "That would be fine lieutenant. Can I offer you something to drink?" she asked, trying not to sound nervous.

"No—I'm fine. Come and sit down and we can talk."

Tracy approached and sat across from Pinkerton. He was still smiling.

"I understand your father was a detective, in fact partner to Detective Tanner."

"Yes," she said softly.

"Horrible what happened to him; you have my sympathies."

"Thank you."

"Tanner's a real good man too. I don't know why he never took the sergeant's exam. He should be a lieutenant himself."

"He doesn't want a desk job; he likes the investigating," Tracy said flatly.

"Yes; some people have no interest in the administrative side, dealing with the headaches."

"Uh-huh."

"So Tracy, why don't you ask me those questions you must have?"

"Lieutenant: I really don't understand why you're here or what questions you think I have for you." And then she thought, "Brian, where are you?"

"I had a talk with Detective Tanner a few hours ago. He told me all about Colin's suicide attempt, and that his lawyer was concerned that I spoke to him on Sunday."

Tracy sighed; might as well have a chat. "*Colin* said you spoke to him."

"Well, I did."

"Lieutenant you of all people should know you should have gone through me—his attorney—before speaking to him."

"Oh, technicalities. Besides, I didn't talk to him about any case specifically. I just told him that it all had finally caught up to him."

The nervousness was leaving her; she wasn't going to be intimidated. "You taunted him."

"That's an extreme way of putting it."

"Given what he tried to do to himself I don't think it is an extreme way of putting it."

"Well, I feel just awful about that. I didn't want him to do that, to take the easy way out."

"The easy way out?" she asked incredulously.

"I want him to go on trial, so that it all comes out. He had so much fun thumbing his nose at us the last time. I realize that sounds petty, but well, I guess I'm guilty of pettiness. But that's *all* I'm guilty of."

"Why are you so sure he killed his father?"

"My instincts as a cop and the evidence."

"What evidence: fingerprints on a trophy that belonged to Colin? Some fights with his dad that fathers and sons have all the time? An eyewitness who didn't see the killer's face?"

Pinkerton's smile was now more like a grin. "My, you've really been looking into the old murder haven't you?"

"It's going to be a factor in this new murder, whether it's admissible in court or not."

"Mm... And I guess you know all about fathers and sons and murders right?"

"What?"

"Isn't your fiancé Brian Shane, the man who was accused of murdering his father? Some eerie similarities to this case—fingerprints on the weapon, a history of antagonism."

Tracy gulped. "Brian was proved innocent."

"Oh I realize that. But not everyone is innocent like your lover. Colin killed his father."

"And why do you think he killed Tim Pane then?"

The smile was back on Pinkerton's face. "Well, I understand Colin was under the impression that this Pane fellow was his father reincarnated. Or maybe they just had a fight and Colin behaved true to form."

"Well, I don't think Colin killed anybody."

"You hardly know him. At least with your fiancé you had a legitimate reason to support him, given that you knew *him*. That is: you knew him until he became a drunk."

Tracy scowled. "You sure do know an awful lot about me, don't you, Lieutenant?"

Pinkerton laughed. "No, not really. I do know though about the Massimo Paganini case. You did some fine work there. Your father would have been proud."

"Is there anything else you want, Lieutenant? Given that you're so sure the world is flat, I don't see the point of trying to convince you it's round."

Pinkerton laughed. "Well, I guess I just wanted to give you some friendly advice."

"Advice?"

"Yes. If you start digging around in the Jackson Richmond murder you may end up hurting people."

"What are you talking about?"

"Well, there are things that came to light during the case, things that are not part of anything public; for example, you won't find everything in the court transcript."

"I still don't understand."

"We learned things that we didn't feel were germane to the case that were therefore never entered into evidence; things that could hurt innocent people."

"Why don't you stop talking in riddles and give me a for instance."

"Very well. Did you know, for instance, that Colin and his best friend's girlfriend at the time, Janie, had an affair?" Tracy's mildly shocked expression told him she didn't. "It's true. In fact Jonathan married the girl, didn't he? They have a family, don't they? I wonder if Colin ever told Jon about it. I can still remember Janie, that sweet girl, begging me not to say anything; that it was a mistake, it was over, blah blah blah…The things lying women say before they start your blubbering."

"You son of a bitch," she thought. So this was his game. But Tracy put up a brave front. "You think after all of this time Jon Carruthers would even care?"

"He might. It could add tension to the business relationship anyway."

"Uh-huh. And you'll make sure that comes out if I push too hard."

"Oh, my dear Tracy, of course not. I would never intentionally let something like that come out. I mean: that couple had rock solid alibis from what I remember. So they weren't suspects. That's why I was able to keep the secret; and look how nicely it turned out for them. Do you understand?"

"Sure, I understand."

"Good. You know: Tanner speaks very highly of you. He said you were very upset over what Colin tried to do to himself; that you're a very caring person. So I wanted to make sure that, being a caring person, you realize that other people could get hurt if you try to involve Colin's father's murder in this. That's all."

Tracy wasn't buying what Pinkerton was selling; he sure had that used car salesman's smirk. "Well: I appreciate what you're saying, Lieutenant. I just want to see if there's anything about Jackson Richmond's murder that can help with the Pane killing. I'm not trying to hurt anybody."

"Of course you're not. You're not trying to hurt witnesses or cops or anyone else, *are* you?"

Tracy gulped again. And then there was a knock at her door. "That would be Brian," she said firmly.

"Of course: the fiancé. You must introduce me."

"Sure," Tracy said as she moved quickly toward her door. She opened it and stepped back. "Come in Brian. I have a guest I want you to meet." Brian gave her a confused look as he entered, and then he saw Pinkerton standing, smiling from ear to ear. "Brian, this is Lieutenant Alex Pinkerton. Lieutenant, this is Brian Shane, my fiancé."

"A pleasure young man," Pinkerton said, offering his hand as he moved toward the new arrival.

"Nice to meet you too," Brian said while shaking.

"Well, I'll be on my way, and let you two get to your evening together." Pinkerton gave Tracy another smile, and then he let himself out as Tracy and Brian, now standing side by side, watched Pinkerton leave. He closed the door behind him.

Brian turned to Tracy; anger was his mask. "That was him, wasn't it Tracy?"

"What?"

"The cop that can make bodies vanish."

"Brian, don't—"

"Are you going to deny it? I see the look on your face. I see the tension in your body language. I know your body pretty well, remember."

Tracy turned and went to sit down on the couch. Brian didn't move. "Yes, Brian; that was him."

"The one who you said didn't even know about you?" he shouted.

"Brian, please don't."

"Please don't *what*, Tracy? Tell you I told you so? Not to start worrying? What?" When she didn't answer he went over to her, sat down, and put his arms around her. "Alright; I'm sorry. I shouldn't be yelling at you." He leaned his head on her shoulder. "So how did he find out?"

"Well: El mentioned Colin's attorney complained and Pinkerton just took it from there."

"Oh."

"Pinkerton knew things about me that I'm sure El wouldn't have told him. He must have spent his afternoon finding out about me."

Brian sighed, trying not to get angry. "Did he threaten you in any way?"

"Oh no. He made veiled threats that he might leak long-held secrets, secrets that might be hurtful to some people involved in the case. But he's a lieutenant, Brian. He's not about to come out and say anything directly."

Brian nodded. "What are you going to do now?"

"I'm going to tell El about this of course. And I'm going to look at the evidence I requested from the old cases. Then I'll go from there."

"Tracy, this sounds dangerous to me. If this guy is digging around looking for things on you he means business."

"Brian: don't you think I know that? Like I said, I'm going to tell El about the conversation. I may even just tell him everything about everything. What else can I do?"

"Tell your client to get a new lawyer."

"Absolutely not," she said quickly and firmly. "That's not happening."

"Even if *I* asked you to?"

Tracy stood up while Brian remained seated. She faced him. "Now look Brian, maybe we should have this discussion now. I'm going to make this clear: do not ever ask me, order me, or in any other way try to get me to drop a case. I love you. And I know that your love for me is where your request is coming from. But you have to understand you have no say in what cases I take, unless I specifically ask you. Do you get me?"

Brian pouted. "Yeah, Tracy, I get you. I hear you loud and clear." Brian arose and started moving toward the door.

"Where are you going?" she asked mildly alarmed.

"I have to go back to work. The reason I wasn't here sooner was because we had a server crash, and I had to help out. And I told them I'd be back, that I just needed to take care of something. And, well, I just need to get back."

Tracy gulped. "You're mad at me."

"Well: you've just basically shut me out of part of your life."

"That's not fair; my work requires confidentiality."

"It doesn't require you to put your life on the line for every damn client!"

"It *doesn't* put my life on the line for every damn client."

"Oh really? Tell that to, what was his name, Larry Waters was it? Or that thug Brandice? Do *you* get *me*?"

"Brian, please stop yelling at me."

"What if we had a kid Tracy? What if you had a baby and a Pinkerton type showed up, made veiled threats that he'd hurt *our* baby? What would you say *then* Tracy? Would you tell me I have *no* say in *our* baby's safety?"

"I...you're being unfair."

"No, you're the one being unfair. Tracy, if we get married, and if we have a family, then we—your family—are going to have to be number one, not your clients. Is that so difficult a concept to grasp?!"

"*If* we get married?" Tracy said, starting to tear up.

"Poor choice of words; I'm sorry. I just meant that you can't just shut me out of anything in your life given we're supposed to be sharing our lives."

     A Tracy Brubaker Mystery

"So if I don't drop this case you won't marry me?"

Brian shook his head. "Tracy: I *want* to marry you; you know I do. And no, I'm not giving you an ultimatum. I'm sorry if it sounded like I was."

"Then why are you in such a hurry to leave?"

"I told you."

"I bet you could stay longer if you really wanted to." Tracy sat down on the couch and started crying, feeling like she was being abandoned at a time she most needed support. Brian felt the guilt wave wash over him. Nice going, Brian. He went over to her.

"Oh Tracy I'm sorry. I'm really sorry. I overreacted and I hurt you, after I promised not to do that." He put his arms around her again. "I just got upset and scared and I…I'm really sorry Tracy. I love you so much and I just freaked out."

Tracy looked at him. There were tears on her cheeks but a smile was struggling to make an appearance. "I'm sorry too Brian. I shouldn't have been so dictatorial about my job. I just wanted to make a point and I over-did it. I didn't mean to suggest you have no role in that part of my life. I hurt you first. I'm sorry."

Now they were smiling at each other, and Brian was using his thumbs to clear her face of water. "It's okay Tracy. I understand. You can't drop a case anytime someone makes threat. You'd become known for that and then no one would hire you."

She nodded. "Something like that, yeah. But honestly Brian: if I really thought my family was in danger I'd do whatever I could to protect them. In fact, I've kind of done that already."

"Really?"

"I don't want to talk about that right now. If you need to get back to work, I should make you something to eat."

Brian laughed. "You know who you sound like?"

"Don't you *dare*." That just made Brian laugh harder.

"Look, you know what one of the silver linings of having a fight is right?"

Tracy grinned. "Making up?"

"Yes. Shouldn't we be making up right now?"

"I thought we did."

"Not officially."

"Officially?" Tracy asked chuckling. "Is there a book of official relation-ship rules I don't have?"

"No, but I can give you a live demonstration." And then Brian kissed her, and kept on kissing her. She returned the gesture.

"Brian," Tracy said when her lips were free, "I think I get the point. And I think you should tell your pointer that that's enough for now."

Brian buried his head in her chest and let out a loud sigh. "You're kill-ing me."

His comment started her laughing. "Come on, let me make you a quick something, so you don't die of starvation."

He looked up at her, and then kissed her again. "I love you; I'm crazy about you. You know this right?"

She smiled warmly. "Of course I do. And I love you and am crazy about you too. *You* know that right?"

"Sure."

"Then let me show you by filling your tummy."

"There's a dirty joke in here somewhere."

Tracy laughed as she made her way to the kitchen. "Hold that thought."

"And there's a dirty joke there too."

Now Tracy was laughing harder. "Behave yourself before I put you on time out."

"I'm *already* on time out."

"Brian, let's not go into that now. Sit down and let me feed you."

He shrugged his shoulders. "Sorry. I was hoping we could have another fight so we could make out—I mean make up—again."

Tracy went over to him, put her arms on his shoulders and kissed him. "Okay, that was cute. Now you're going to eat." And in 15 minutes Brian and Tracy were enjoying spaghetti and sauce.

"I guess I really should be heading back," Brian said. "I'm surprised they haven't called."

Tracy was hugging him at the door. "Did you tell them where you were going for dinner?"

"Uh, yeah."

She looked at him. "Well, they're probably expecting you *not* to be on time."

Brian smiled. "And I'd hate to disappoint them." He kissed her.

"Call me if you get out at a decent hour. I have to be up early tomorrow so I'll probably be in bed around 10:00 or so."

"That's only a couple of hours away. I doubt I'll be done that quickly."

Tracy made a sad face. "Then I'll call you tomorrow."

Brian nodded. "Thanks for dinner."

"You bet."

"And I'm sorry about earlier, really."

"It's forgotten, really."

"You're wonderful. I hate leaving."

"I hate when you leave too."

"Then why don't I move in? I can sleep on the couch."

Tracy chuckled. "Nice try."

"I'm serious."

"I know you are. But my answer is 'no' for now. Okay?"

Brian frowned. "Okay. I love you."

   A Tracy Brubaker Mystery

"And I love you too." He gave her the smile and goodbye kiss, and then left her abode. She watched him board the elevator.

She cleaned up the dishes and changed for bed. She was tired, but she pulled out her notebook and flipped through its scribbled-upon pages while sitting on her sofa. Pinkerton: that slimy, toad-like…She couldn't finish her thought. Did he know about the bar visit yet? Bobby might mention it to someone who'll mention it to Pinkerton. But it really didn't matter at this point. He had made his intentions known if she made too much noise about Jackson Richmond's death. She suddenly realized she never called Tanner to confirm tomorrow. But that didn't matter; if there had been a problem he would have let her know. She closed her notebook. It was quiet in her unit. She turned her head and looked at the empty couch. She started stroking the empty cushion next to her. She thought, "I'll call the church tomorrow and see about a date. Maybe they'll have something as early as October." She sighed. "I'm not going to be able to do this for another year." She rose slowly and made her way to the bedroom. "I hate when you leave," she said to the couch. Then she turned and closed the door.

Before she arrived at BPD Wednesday morning Tracy debated with herself what she wanted to tackle first: the evidence on the old cases or Pinkerton's recent visit. She should have known herself better by now; no way could she keep her mouth shut about the latter.

"Are you exaggerating any of this?" Tanner asked after hearing the details of Pinkerton's trip.

"No," she said flatly.

"He said he'd tell Jon Carruthers about his wife's relationship with Colin."

"No, El. He said secrets like that might come out. I mean: Jon and Janie were just dating at that point anyway. Maybe Janie told Jon about it already."

"So that's not really much of a threat then, is it?"

Tracy glared. "I can't believe you're being so nonchalant about this."

"Tracy, I admit that his visit is a little curious. He didn't tell me he was going to see you."

"Did you mention my name?"

"Not initially. When I mentioned Colin Richmond's attorney he immediately said your name, so he knew about you already."

"That didn't seem weird to you?"

"No. He probably heard about Richmond's suicide attempt and made some calls. He probably found out who Colin asked to see."

"I think there's more to it than that."

"He was honest about why he went to see Richmond; admitted he was being, what did he say, petty?"

"That might not be the real reason."

Tanner should his head. "Tracy, if I had any real reason to believe Pinkerton is the bad guy you say he is I'd look into it. But as soon as I started doing such a thing he'd find out about it. There is nothing in his record, to my knowledge anyway, that says he's bad. Can you appreciate my position?"

Tracy nodded. "Sure El. He's a superior officer above reproach. If you went after him your career would be over."

"Right on all counts."

Tracy sighed. "Well, can we go to the evidence box now?"

"It's right in here. I have to stay with you, you understand."

"Sure El. I want you to stay here anyway in case I have some questions."

Tanner arose from his chair and went to the Bankers Box that was in the corner. On the top of it was a thin file folder. He had already cleared a space on his small table so he rested the items there. "The folder on top is the missing persons report on Amanda Richmond."

"Uh-huh. Not very thick is it?"

"No."

Tracy started flipping through it. There was Christine Jacks' name: mentioned Amanda had many men friends, but no mention of Pinkerton or any other name. Amanda's husband was questioned, but there was no sign of foul play and he could account for his day. Notes were made that the husband was cooperative and seemed upset. So was Colin, upset that is. He didn't have much to say to the police, but he was home before his father was and his mother was already gone. The disappearance was in May 1985 and Colin was in school for the day; the husband at work. Last known contact: a neighbor named Betsy Riggs: she saw Amanda Richmond bringing trash from the unit at approximately 11:00 in the morning. More notes: husband realized a suitcase was missing, as was his wife's purse and some clothes and toiletry items. Airports, bus terminals, hospitals, etcetera were all checked; nothing found. Amanda Richmond had simply vanished. But with no obvious signs of a crime scene, and no clear suspects, the investigation had stalled.

"There were no pictures listed as missing," Tracy said aloud.

"What?" Tanner asked, now seated at his desk.

"There's a detailed list of items here made by Jackson Richmond of what he wife allegedly took with her. There are no pictures listed."

"I'm not following you."

"The person I spoke with about Amanda, as I mentioned before, said she loved her son. You'd think she might grab some pictures of him on the way out."

"Maybe she did and the husband didn't realize it, or maybe she had plenty in her wallet or purse."

 A Tracy Brubaker Mystery

"She didn't take any shoes with her, other than the ones she was wearing, I mean."

"What is it now?"

"She packed several outfits but didn't pack any extra shoes. That doesn't sound odd to you?"

Tanner stood up. "Well maybe the husband didn't realize it. I couldn't tell you how many pairs Rita has."

"Or maybe he did realize it."

Tanner was now next to her. "May I?" he asked, motioning for the report folder. She gave it to him.

Tanner skimmed through it and frowned. He looked at Tracy. "You'd think they would try to follow up with some of the lovers this Jacks woman alluded to."

"Even if she couldn't remember names?"

"Well they could check credit card receipts maybe, talked with other people."

"Curious isn't it?"

Tanner looked at her. "You think she was murdered don't you?"

"Yes, I do."

"And that her husband may have found something, more than two years later."

"A distinct possibility."

"And you think Pinkerton killed them."

Tracy paused. "I will say only that I believe he was having an affair with Amanda Richmond, and that she broke it off."

"Uh-huh. Alright, let's look in the box then."

Tracy removed the tape that had sealed the carton. The first thing she noticed was the trophy, wrapped in a plastic bag. It was a medium-sized Little League trophy with a thick marble base. "Do you remember how many times Jackson was hit with this?"

"A few," Tanner said softly. "Somebody beat him until they cracked his skull with it."

Tracy breathed in heavily, shaking her head. She found a list of contents and pulled it out: she started reading aloud. "Medical Examiner's report, witness statements, fingerprint tests, clothes analysis, first officer reports… You were one of the first officers El?"

"Yes; I and my partner, Antoine Mahalwe, took the 911 call by a neighbor and found Richmond there."

"Huh," Tracy grunted.

"What?"

"Here's Colin's ticket to *The Lost Boys* that night."

"That doesn't prove anything Tracy. He could have torn the ticket himself or snuck out. He had already seen the movie before — many times before."

"I was just talking out loud El. I wasn't suggesting it proved anything one way or the other."

Tanner sighed. "I'm sorry Tracy. I guess I'm getting feisty given every-thing."

"No worries El." Tracy continued scanning the list. "This is weird," she said.

"What's weird?"

"Thumb tacks."

"Thumb tacks? I think I may have heard there were some tacks under or near the body. I don't really remember though. That would have been the lab's area of expertise. Not really much to go on anyway."

Tracy rummaged around the box until she came upon the bag of tacks. Then the color drained from her face.

"What's wrong Tracy?" Tanner asked.

She showed him the bag. "These aren't thumb tacks, El." He looked at the bag. "They're carpet tacks."

Tanner took the bag. He looked at her, a look of surprise on his face. "You're right. Someone mislabeled them I guess."

"No El, you don't understand. Two or so years ago Colin ran into an old neighbor of his who remembered a carpet company van was there the night Jackson Richmond was killed."

Tanner rolled his eyes. "Oh dear God: no."

"Waverly Carpet Installers or something; they're out of business now."

"I don't believe this."

"Neal went over the trial transcripts; there was no mention of tacks — thumb, carpet or otherwise. Yet here they are in the box; why?"

"Tracy I—"

"Face it El: you have to face the facts, or the tacks rather. There's some-thing very wrong here. Maybe Pinkerton didn't kill Richmond; maybe someone who worked for that carpet company did. But who else but a cop could make sure these tacks never made it into evidence during the inves-tigation and yet have put them here after the fact?"

Tanner turned and moved toward his chair, seating himself slowly.

"What are you going to do El?" Tracy asked him.

Tanner shook his head. "I'm not sure yet."

"I want you to call Pinkerton. I want him here ASAP and then you and I are going to talk to him. Or I'm going to start talking to other people, the kind that print sensationalistic stories first and then bury retractions in small print in the back later. You know I'll do it too."

Tanner nodded and then he dialed his phone. "Hi Alex; it's Elias. I need you come to my office, and I need it to be right now."

 A Tracy Brubaker Mystery

Chapter 11

Tanner said, "It's about time you're honest with me, Alex. I'm afraid the floodgates are about to open and I want to be prepared for the showers."

"You have no right talking to me like this, Elias; summoning me like you did. And she should not be here."

"I'm here whether you like it or not," Tracy said defiantly. "Where's that smile of yours now, Lieutenant? Or do you only use that when you're trying to intimidate someone?"

"You better watch yourself young lady," Pinkerton snapped.

"I have a witness who knows about your affair, *Pinky*."

Pinkerton went white, not having been prepared for Tracy's out of left field comment. "You're lying."

"I am? Then how did I know about your nickname? How do I know that Amanda used her pinky finger to wave goodbye to you? Once I show this person your picture, you're going to be toast."

Pinkerton swallowed. He turned to look at Tanner. Tanner spoke. "I have convinced Tracy—and you have no idea how hard that was to do—to sit on this for now. She said she'd be willing to do so only if she were here when we talked. She's convinced Amanda Richmond's disappearance is connected not only to Jackson Richmond's murder but the current murder as well."

"I wouldn't want an innocent person or persons to get hurt by my investigation," Tracy added sarcastically. "Would *you*, Lieutenant?"

Pinkerton took a deep breath, shook his head, and sat down. He cleared his throat. "First of all, I didn't kill anybody. And if you try to suggest otherwise Ms. Brubaker I'll make sure you never set foot in a courtroom again."

"Yawn," Tracy said aloud.

Tanner spoke quickly. "Look, both of you stop whatever this is going on between you. Alright Alex, let's hear it."

Pinkerton shook his head, sighed, and began. "Okay, yes: Mandy Richmond and I had something for a while. But we were both married, and we eventually broke it off."

"But you still loved her, didn't you?" Tracy asked him, no hostility now in her voice.

"I cared about her. Love her though? I'm not sure."

"What do you know about her disappearance?" Tracy asked.

"I didn't have anything to do with it."

"Well: what did you do when you found out she vanished?"

Pinkerton twisted his lips. "My partner knew about me and Mandy. So I asked him to keep an eye on things when the investigation started. When they started pursuing old lovers I got a little nervous. My partner helped keep me out of it."

"What was your partner's name?" Tracy asked.

"He's got nothing to do with any crime, and I'm not dragging him into it."

"Alright lieutenant," Tracy said. "But didn't you think it was a possibility that one of her lovers didn't break up with her as gracefully as you did?"

"Sure, of course. But I wasn't in missing persons and I couldn't just start looking into things without calling attention to myself. All I could do was try to keep abreast of the investigation. But there was really nothing I could do officially. or unofficially for that matter."

"You might have been able to help if you came clean."

"I could have lost my job and family, lady."

"Oh I see. I guess the killer got lucky then, huh?"

"Tracy," Tanner scolded.

Tracy snuffed. "So what happened when you heard about Jackson Richmond?"

Pinkerton took a deep breath. "I heard the address come over the call. I recognized it. I just took it, telling—I don't even remember who was up for cases that night. Well, I just said I'd take this and then went to the scene. I wasn't even sure who was dead. I thought maybe Mandy had come back and her husband fought with her. I don't know. Anyway we show up and there's Richmond with his brains bashed in. We start talking to the kid and we all agree he did it."

"All? How many was that?"

"What?"

"Your mock jury that convicted Colin on the spot?"

"Listen, that kid was a punk. Ask your friend Tanner; he agreed with that assessment."

"How many of you decided Colin was guilty on the spot?" Tracy asked again.

"Me and my partner, and Elias and his partner."

"Why? What was it about this kid whose father just got killed that told you all he was guilty?"

"Evidence: the witness, the prints, our experience."

"And the tacks?"

"The what?"

"The carpet tacks, or thumb tacks as they were labeled. They were in the evidence box but were never introduced at trial."

Pinkerton blinked. "They have nothing to do with this."

"WRONG!"

"Easy Tracy," Tanner interjected.

"Lieutenant: there were some carpet installers in the building that day. Yet I don't see any interviews with carpet installers in the evidence box."

"What carpet installers? Nobody told us about that."

"Well then you didn't talk to all of the witnesses because my client found someone who remembered the carpet installers the day of the murder. And that's why Colin was set up this time."

"You're lying!"

"No lieutenant. *I'm* not the liar here!"

Tanner looked at Pinkerton. "Why didn't those carpet tacks make it to trial, Alex?"

Pinkerton shifted in his chair, not able to look at Tanner.

"You pulled them, didn't you Alex? You removed them from the evidence log didn't you?"

"We knew the kid was guilty Elias, all of us. Those damn tacks would have just confused matters."

"Oh my God!" Tracy yelled, throwing her arms up.

"Look: I didn't know about carpet installers being there that day. So what if they were? It didn't mean the kid *didn't* do it!"

"You arrogant prick! You didn't know about the carpet people because you decided Colin was guilty and that was that. You did a piss poor investigation, and you withheld potentially exculpatory evidence. It's a miracle they ended up in the evidence box. What happened: did your partner maybe get a case of the guilts? Maybe he wanted to make sure the tacks didn't disappear since Colin wasn't convicted. I mean: I can't imagine *you* put them back in there, and El didn't know about them really. That leaves only your partner as the one who could have put them back."

Pinkerton was quiet for a moment. "Colin Richmond killed his father."

"No, he didn't. Or are you next going to tell me that, at 15, he killed his mother?"

"One doesn't necessarily have to do with the other."

"I think it does. And before you say you don't care what I think, you better *start* caring. You better start hoping I believe you're innocent of murder so that this doesn't all come out in a courtroom or someplace else. And I'm still debating on whether or not to lodge an official complaint about your visit to my client on Sunday. If I didn't have such respect for the police since my father was one, I wouldn't hesitate to do so."

Pinkerton sighed. "You're real sure of yourself aren't you? You're more arrogant than I ever was."

"I would NEVER falsify evidence to win my case, even if I believed I was right about my client! And that's EXACTLY what you did!"

Tanner rose. "Alright; that's enough for now. I think Lieutenant Pinkerton was honest here."

"Well it's about damn time!"

"Tracy, please! Now are you going to keep your word and let me look into some things before letting this all come out?"

Tracy sighed. "Yes, El. I'll let the department handle things if I end up believing Pinky here isn't a killer." Pinkerton shook his head. "But I am going to have to ask one more question."

"And that is?" Pinkerton asked snidely.

"I need to know the name of your partner who helped you on the Richmond murder."

"I told you: I'm not dragging him into this."

"Sorry, lieutenant; you're going to have to."

"Why? For what possible reason?"

"Because if you didn't kill Timothy Pane then another cop may have."

"WHAT?! What the HELL are talking about?!"

"It is my belief," Tracy said calmly, "that Colin was set up, and the person who set him up was looking for someone like Tim Pane whose birthday was the day Jackson Richmond was murdered. Now who would have access to such information, be able to look through a list of birthdates and then track someone down?"

Pinkerton shook his head. "You're out of your mind lady."

"I may very well be; doesn't mean I'm wrong though."

"What you're suggesting, that my partner set this all up to cover his own ass, is impossible."

"Why?'

"Because he's *dead*, that's why! He's been dead for 15 years now. You get it now lady?" Pinkerton eyes moistened.

"I'm sorry," Tracy said quietly. "I didn't realize that; all of us here know that pain, don't we El?"

Tanner nodded. "I'm sorry Alex. Tracy really didn't know."

"How did your partner die?"

Pinkerton swallowed. "He got killed during a drug raid. Those assholes must have been tipped off we were coming, because they were ready for us. Bobby didn't stand a chance."

Tracy's head shot up. "Your partner's name was Bobby?"

"Yeah."

"Does he have a son?"

Pinkerton's eyes narrowed. "Don't you even—"

"There's a mid-20ish bartender at Richie's Digs with the name Bobby whose father was a cop killed during a drug bust. This bartender said this happened when he was 10; that would make him 25 now. So I ask you again lieutenant: does your partner have a 25-year-old son named Bobby too?"

"I don't care what you do to me; you leave him out of this!" And then Pinkerton stood up and marched out of Tanner's office, slamming the door behind him.

　　　　A Tracy Brubaker Mystery

"A cop protecting his fallen partner's child: I can certainly empathize with that," Tanner said softly.

"I'm sorry El. You know I have to talk to Bobby about this. It can't be a coincidence that he works at Colin's favorite hang out, can it?"

"Why not? You know Tracy, there are such things as coincidences—that's why we have such a word."

"Cute El, but that's not good enough."

"I know; I don't know why I even wasted the words."

"You think I *want* to hurt your colleagues and their families?"

"Of course not Tracy; of course not."

"I met Bobby just yesterday. I liked him. I hope he's not involved, El. But when I brought up the name Pinkerton, Bobby said he didn't know him. And I believed him when he told me that. But now I know he was lying. You see?"

Tanner nodded. "When are you going to see him again then?"

"Well: would you like to go with me now to his house or other job? You can vouch for me; assure him that I'm not there to hurt him."

"Okay Tracy. I'll drive you. He still lives with his mother. She'll know where he is if he's not home."

"Thanks El."

"Well, it's the least I can do. I admit it Tracy: you were right, right about everything so far. I hope you know I had nothing to do with burying that tack evidence."

Tracy smiled. "Of course not El; I could never believe something like that of you."

"But I thought Colin was guilty; I sang with *that* chorus."

"And what now El? What tune are you singing?"

Tanner smiled. "Something about mea culpa maybe. Let's go see Bobby Sugarman. I hope to God he's not involved in this."

"I hope not too, El. And I really mean that." And then Tracy followed Tanner out his office door as they made their way to the parking lot.

"I'm sorry I lied to you Tracy," Bobby Sugarman told Tracy. Tanner, Tracy, and Bobby where seated at a small kitchen table in his mother's house. "It's just that Uncle Alex said I should never admit to knowing him; it might be risky for me with all the enemies he's made putting people away. I guess I just lied out of habit."

Tracy laughed gently. "You know, when I was younger I called El here Uncle Elias. I guess that might be normal."

"I don't know."

"Well, let's forget about your little fib. How is it you came to work at Richie's Digs?"

"Uncle Alex got me the job through his buddies that work there. He wanted me to keep an eye on Colin."

Tracy rolled her eyes. "Your 'uncle' knew Colin was a regular there?"

"Yeah, I guess. He said Colin got away with a murder, maybe two, a long time ago and that he and my father vowed to get him someday. Since my dad was dead, that left me to take care of it."

"Oh Bobby, I'm sorry. That wasn't fair of him."

"I didn't mind at first. But then I got to know Colin; I mean, if he killed his dad, why was he talking about finding his dad's killer all the time?"

"How long have you been working at Richie's?

"Since I was 21 pretty much."

"Is it safe to say you like Colin now?"

Bobby nodded. "Yeah; I mean, I just don't think he killed anyone. Truth is: if did kill anyone it would probably be himself."

Tracy looked at Tanner, who had said very little except to make Bobby comfortable with talking to Tracy. "Bobby: did you and Pinkerton have any kind of falling out over what he was asking you to do? Did you tell him that you thought Colin was a good guy?"

Bobby shook his head. "I never told Uncle Alex that I felt that way. He really hasn't bothered me about Colin for a while come to think of it."

"Anybody else bad mouth Colin? Other cops? Other patrons?"

"No, not that I recall; it's a nice bar and people tend be friendly; very little trouble."

Tracy nodded. "Okay, Bobby. I don't have any more questions for you right now. Thanks for speaking with me."

"I'm sorry I lied to you before."

"Don't worry about it Bobby; really."

He smiled as he, Tracy, and Tanner stood. "Goodbye Detective, goodbye Tracy," Bobby said at the door. They smiled at him and left, headed back to BPD.

"What do think, Tracy?" Tanner asked her while en route.

"I think what Pinkerton did, asking Bobby to spy, using his father's name to do it, was reprehensible."

"Did you hear what Bobby said about Pinkerton thinking Colin got away with two murders?"

"Yup. It seems to me Pinkerton *did* think Colin killed his mother; that may be why he went so out of control. He wanted Colin convicted not so much for his father but for his mother."

"Yeah, I agree."

"You did bring that possibility up earlier after all."

"Yes; but to tell you the truth, I didn't really believe it."

Tracy chuckled. "And what do you believe now El, off the record and all that?"

Tanner sighed. "Off the record?"

"Sure."

          A Tracy Brubaker Mystery

"I think I'm leaning toward your way of thinking. Yeah, Tracy: you made me a believer."

Tracy beamed. "So now I need your help on the biggest mystery of this whole case."

"And that is?"

"How did the killer find out about Tim Pane? He works for a small printing company, miles from Richie's Digs; in fact he and a coworker visited a bar much closer to their office. How did the killer know about Colin's drunken ramblings about reincarnation? How did the killer find out about Tim's birth date?"

"You want me to find out if anybody I know was asked to look up birthdays?"

"Something like that; yes. Unless you can think of something else."

"Not at this time."

"No one connected with the DMV seems to be involved in this case. Maybe the killer has access to hospital records. I wonder where Pane was born."

"I'll see what I can find."

"You'll do that for me El?"

"As long as I don't cross swords with Detective Danbury."

"Oh, sure."

"I heard you brought her a chocolate bunny."

Tracy chuckled. "I figured it couldn't hurt."

"She came to see me."

"Really?"

"Yup; she apparently asked who in the department knew you best and I lost the lottery."

"Lost? Oh, you're cute."

Tanner laughed. "She asked me if you were for real."

"What does that mean exactly? I looked like a mannequin or something?"

"That whether or not your sweet routine was all an act."

"Oh. What'd you tell her?"

"How does that nursery rhyme go? 'When she was good, she was very, very good. And when she was bad, she was horrid.' I think that's close."

Tracy laughed heartily. "Oh El, how can you suggest I've been horrid?"

"Do you want examples?"

"Pass."

Now Tanner was laughing. "I thought not." He cleared his throat. "How are things with you and Brian Shane, if you don't mind my asking?"

She smiled. "They're good El. I...I can't wait until we're married. You *are* going to walk me down the aisle, right El?"

"Of course Tracy; it will be my honor to do so. And a relief."

Tracy started laughing again. "Everybody wants to be rid of me!" she jokingly cried, putting her forearm against her forehead. "Woe is me; I'm so woe."

"Let Brian deal with you from now on," Tanner agreed chuckling.

"I'm really happy though El. I can't wait."

Tanner was smiling. "That's great to hear Tracy. You deserve it; to be happy I mean."

"Gosh you're a sweetie when you wanna be. How are Elias, Jr. and Marleena doing? I keep meaning to call her for lunch."

"They're doing just fine, Tracy. I may have two weddings to deal with soon."

"*That* good? Well I think it's wonderful. I always liked El, Jr."

"You know: your dad and I would talk about the thought of you two getting married someday."

"Really? Dad never said anything."

"I didn't either to anyone but your father. But your personalities never really clicked."

"Well, that doesn't mean *we* wouldn't have. I mean, opposites attract right?"

"There are opposites, and then there are you two."

Tracy laughed. "I guess the point is moot now anyway."

"Yeah, it would appear so."

Tracy looked at Tanner. "Thanks for today El. All of this couldn't have been good for you. I mean, it must have been tough."

"You're welcome Tracy. And it would have been, except for those damn carpet tacks. I mean: once it was clear someone buried evidence, it took everything not to give Pinkerton a good punch to the gut. He involved at least one other cop in his cover up: Robert Sugarman Sr. I'm just furious over that. Now I have to start wondering about all of the cases Pinkerton has been involved in. It's a damn shame is what it is."

"You El: punch someone? When El was good, he was very, very good. But when he was mad, watch out!"

"What's next then, Tracy?" Neal asked her after getting all the day's juicy tidbits.

"El is pulling out all of the stops looking into Waverly Carpet Installers. Technically he's looking into Jackson Richmond's cold case, the carpet tacks being the justification. At some point though, he's going to have to bring Detective Danbury in on this too."

"I still can't believe Pinkerton would do that. He has such a good reputation."

"He didn't want the jury 'confused' by some meaningless tacks," Tracy said contemptuously.

                    A Tracy Brubaker Mystery

"You think his old partner was the one who logged them in the evidence box then?"

"I bet it was. Maybe Sugarman had second thoughts about Colin's guilt, and when the case was going to be filed away, he made sure the tacks got back in there. But he stayed quiet, loyal to his partner."

"And then he got killed."

"Sadly yes; and then Pinkerton got the son involved." Tracy furrowed her brow.

"What is it Tracy?" Neal asked noticing the change on her face.

"I wonder if I'm looking for the same killer as 27 years ago."

"Huh?"

"Well, Pinkerton bringing his partner's son into this has me pondering something. I mean: let's assume that the same person killed both of Colin's parents. That was a long time ago. Maybe the killer is dead, or in jail for another crime, or hospitalized. But what if 'killer one' has a child, a niece, a nephew: somebody that knows what happened, found out via a deathbed confession or a night of drunken confessions. And then Colin Richmond starts poking around."

"And so this person—killer two—sets Colin up in order to protect his or her murderous relative."

"Possibly. The thing is though I keep coming back to how Pane's killer found him and chose him. Other than the cops involved in this case, nobody else would seem to have the means to find out Pane's birthday. If we could find somebody who works at the DMV or a hospital even…"

Neal blinked. "Jon Carruthers."

"What? He works at…wait, that's right. You told me he was on the board of a children's hospital, didn't you?"

"Yes," Neal nodded.

"But why would he want to kill Pane and set up Colin?"

"What about the affair with Janie?" Neal asked her.

Tracy shook her head. "I can't believe after all of this time anyone would kill another over something like *that,* unless in the heat of passion or something. I mean, this Pane murder was carefully planned. Besides it's not like Jon and Janie were married at the time; they were kids."

"Still Tracy: there could be more to it than that. Jon and Colin have been best friends for years; they work together. Then one day Jon finds out. You don't think he might be just the little bit pissed off?"

"Enough to kill? I don't know, Neal."

"Well, let me consult my notes and get the name of the hospital. If it turns out that's where Pane was born…"

"Okay—if it turns out to be the same I may owe you an apology. I hope it isn't though. I don't relish the thought of dealing with this."

"I hear you."

"Do you mind taking another look into the Waverly thing? With both you and El on it we might find something quicker. I need to get Colin out of that place yesterday. He's there because they were able to bring up his past at the bail hearing, and now we know that whole trial was tainted. But I'm not sure that's enough to get him out on bail."

"Roger that. I'll put on my extra super-duper thinking cap."

Tracy smiled. "That's the spirit!"

"Anything else?"

"Yes; see if you can find Betsy Riggs, the witness I mentioned who saw Amanda Richmond the day she disappeared. I want to talk to her."

"Sure."

"Supreme! Now off with you my good man." And Neal was off. Tracy drummed her fingers on her desk and then dragged her hand down her face. Her phone buzzed.

"Negative on the hospital," Neal said over the speaker. "Carruthers' is more of a research facility that wasn't even constructed until the 1990s."

"Thanks Neal. That's good news as far as I'm concerned."

"Sure. Bye then."

Tracy sighed. Now she was debating with herself. She had that personal phone call she wanted to make. But how could she be thinking about her wedding when Colin Richmond was still in jail? There had to be something she could be doing to help him. Of course: how come she hadn't thought to see him and get the name of the person who saw the carpet people? Her call would have to wait. She wanted to see Colin Richmond.

"Jesse Alton," Colin told her. "He lived on the floor above us."

"And you said you saw him about two years ago?"

"Something like that. Where was I when I saw him?" Colin wiggled his nose. "Oh: at a Target near my office while I was getting some supplies. I look over and I recognize him and he recognizes me, even after all those years."

"Did he tell you where he was living?"

"I know he lived near that Target. He said he went there all the time."

"So how old is this Jesse fellow?"

"Oh, in his 60s I think. Nice guy though. We start talking about stuff and I tell him what I did for a living. He got confused and thought I put carpets in offices, and that's when he mentioned the carpet people being at the building that day."

"Was he absolutely sure it was the *same* day, and not the day before or the day after?"

"I didn't really push him on that. I was so amazed that he remembered the name of the company that I was just happy for *that*."

"Yeah; I can certainly understand that. Did he say if the police talked to him?"

     A Tracy Brubaker Mystery

"They didn't; but then again he was in and out a lot. He was staying over his girlfriend's most of the time. I think that's why I remembered *him,* because of *her.* She was a knockout."

Tracy smiled. "Do you remember her name?"

"Only her first name: Brandy. Can you beat that? He was always telling me how he was getting drunk on Brandy." Colin smiled. "I asked about her, but they broke up a long time ago."

Tracy nodded. "Colin: I don't want to go into too many details or get your hopes up prematurely, but things are happening with your case. I'm going to head out and see if I can talk to Jesse Alton; I hope he's still in the area. So I need you to keep a positive attitude."

"Yeah, sure. I'm not thinking of trying anything again. I really meant it when I said I know how stupid it was."

"Good. Do you need anything, other than the obvious?"

"No. Just knowing you're out there…Well, that's enough."

She smiled. "Okay. I'll be in touch."

Neal worked his magic. Tracy had called in and told him to look for any Jesse Altons that lived near the Target closest to Colin's office building. Now she had an address, and the White Pages indicated Alton was still there. It was a small single family home with a fenced-in small yard—low maintenance. Tracy opened the gate and heard a dog barking as she approached the front door.

"Stop that racket Crenshaw or you're going in the cage!" a voice shouted.

Tracy climbed the steps and the front door soon opened. The screen door, however, remained shut.

"I ain't interested lady," the occupant told her. "I ain't got no money."

Tracy giggled. The resident was a small guy, maybe 5'2", wearing a baseball cap, white undershirt, jeans, and white socks. Gray stubble covered most of his face. Tracy could smell the beer. "Oh I'm not selling anything, Mr. Alton. I was hoping to talk to you briefly."

"How do you know my name? Do I know you? You ain't gonnna tell my you're a long lost kid of mine are ya?" And then he started chuckling.

"No, nothing like that. I'm a friend of Colin Richmond. He knew you from the 1980s; you lived on the floor above him."

Alton scrunched his face. "Oh yeah! Colin! Sure, that kid who killed his father."

"Well, I don't know about the last part."

"How do you know Colin?"

"I'm his attorney. Could I talk to you Mr. Alton?"

"Oh, sure I guess." Alton opened the screen door and stood aside so Tracy could enter. "The dog won't hurt you none. He's just loud, aren't you Crenshaw?" The dog's tail started wagging upon hearing his name.

"What kind of dog is Crenshaw?" Tracy asked smiling at the four-legged onlooker.

"Weimaraner," Alton told her. "Crenshaw's 13 years old, and as ornery as ever. You like dogs?"

"Yes, I do. I don't have one myself though; I'm not at my place a lot and I think it would be unfair to leave a dog alone so much."

"Yeah. I didn't used to like them myself much."

"Oh; why not?"

"I used to work for the post office. Damn things would make so much noise if you got too close to the house; I knew of at least two people that had been bitten. Besides, like you, I wasn't home much."

"You never got married?"

"Nope; man's best friend is a dog, right? Ain't that right Crenshaw, you filthy bastard?"

Crenshaw ignored his owner's question and continued to study Tracy as he sat by Alton's side. Then he yawned and walked away slowly.

"Well, why don't you sit down? You say you're Colin's attorney?"

"Yes," she answered as she rested on a yellow-ish recliner. "He told me you remembered seeing a truck or van outside the building the night Colin's father was murdered. The vehicle had the name Waverly Carpet Installers or Installation on it."

Alton blinked. "Oh right. Waverly Carpet Installers, Inc.: that's what it said on the side. The damn thing almost hit me when I got home that night. I thought about calling the company and complaining. But I never did; what would have been the use?"

"What time did you get home that night?"

"Uh…maybe 7:30. Not really sure. But I was gone not long after that."

"Really? Why?"

"I had to change out of my work clothes; I was running late and I was supposed to pick up my girl for dinner. Man, she bitched at me even though I was only a couple minutes late."

"Her name was Brandy, right?"

Alton chuckled. "Yeah, that's her. Colin told you about her, huh?"

"A little."

"Yeah, those boys in the building used to drool all over her. I knew what they were thinking: Colin, that friend of his, a couple of others. I was a teenager myself once."

Tracy grinned. "The friend of Colin's: that was Jon Carruthers."

"Uh, yeah—sounds right anyway. He had a girlfriend himself as I remember it; she was a looker too. But that didn't stop him from peeking at the menu." Then Alton started chuckling again.

"Did you see anyone else that night that you recall, especially if they were unfamiliar to you?"

"Nah—I don't think so."

  A Tracy Brubaker Mystery

"Did you at least get a look at the driver?"

"Nope, just made sure I got the name right that was on the side of the van."

"You didn't notice any commotion going on when you were there?"

"I don't recall any. I guess I just missed everything. There we were, me and Brandy, watching the news, well kind of watching the news, and all of a sudden my building's on the TV."

"But the police never talked to you."

"Nope."

"And you didn't try to contact them yourself."

"Are you kidding lady? I've got no love for cops."

"Oh."

"They've tried to take Crenshaw away from me. And before that, they hassled my Brandy."

"Why did they do that?"

"They were prejudiced."

"Why? I mean what was it about Brandy that made them prejudiced?"

"Her job."

Tracy blinked. "Oh. Brandy was a professional person."

"Huh? She was a whore."

Tracy closed her eyes and rubbed her forehead. "Yes, I…Well, I guess you treated her nice though."

"Sure I did. I had her exclusive for a while. I knew it wouldn't last forever. But I didn't care."

Tracy sighed. "Do you remember anything else about the carpet van: a bumper sticker, body damage, or anything like that?"

Alton pondered her question. "Nope. Sorry." Alton's eyes flew open. "Jesus H. Christ!"

"What?!" Tracy asked excitedly.

"What the hell is that on your finger there? I mean: Jesus!"

Tracy gulped, and then she turned red. This ring thing was getting annoying. "It's fake; it's nothing," she mumbled.

"Like hell it is!"

"Thanks for your time Mr. Alton. I really must be going."

"Huh? Oh, okay." He started to get up, which started Crenshaw barking. "Will you shut up you? The lady ain't gonna hurt nothing."

Tracy smiled again. "Nice doggie," she said while waving. And then Crenshaw barked louder.

"Don't worry about him," Alton said staring at his roommate. "I swear I'll put you in that cage!" Crenshaw looked at his master and then at Tracy, and then stopped barking. Tracy moved hurriedly to the screen door and pushed it open.

"Oh Mr. Alton: one more question. Did you ever see that carpet van at your building before the night of the murder?"

"Uh, maybe. I'm not sure."

"Did Jackson Richmond ever talk to you about the day his wife disappeared; ask you if you saw anything?"

"Hmm," he said, scratching his stubble. "Well, I know he was asking people if they knew anything about his wife leaving. But I couldn't really tell him anything."

"Okay. Thanks again Mr. Alton!" And then Tracy made her way quickly to her car before Crenshaw had another reason to start his yelping. She didn't want to hear another peep from the mutt.

"I have an idea El," Tracy said over her mobile phone.

"What's that?"

"DMV records; the witness who saw the carpet van didn't see the driver. But that got me thinking that even if Waverly went out of business, could the DMV still have how many vans Waverly had registered, and who owned them, in their records somewhere?"

"I can look into it."

"Supreme. If we can find the owner or owners we might be able to at least get a list of employees, or people they used."

"Okay. Anything else?"

"Not for now El. I owe Neal a call so I'm going to do that next."

"Alright; bye Tracy."

"See ya El." Tracy did a quick scroll of her stored phone numbers and pushed Neal's name. "Hi, Neal: you called while I was with Alton."

"Yup. I found the Waverly brothers."

Tracy's eyes popped open so that they almost rolled out of their sockets. "You're incredible!"

"I don't know why I didn't think of it before. Going out of business usually means bankruptcy so I did some legwork this afternoon regarding 1992 bankruptcy filings. I found a listing for Owen and Stewart Waverly, doing business as Waverly Carpet Installers."

"Neal, great work! So where are the Waverly boys now?"

"I'm still looking."

"Okay, look: call El and give him everything you found. I wished I had called you first but I just talked to El about looking into vehicle registrations. If you two work together we should be able to track down the brothers."

"Okay Tracy; I'll do just that after we're done."

"Any other great news?"

"Well, Betsy Riggs still lives at the same building she did 30 years ago."

"More great news! I want to talk to her. Anything else?"

"Nope; just wanted to share that."

     A Tracy Brubaker Mystery

"Great share! Now don't let me hold you up; call El and I'll see you back at the office. I'm going to stop at Colin's old place and see if I can talk to Betsy. Then I'll be heading back."

Tracy couldn't help smiling. Carpet tacks found at the crime scene and a witness who remembers almost getting hit by a van whose business was carpeting; no way in hell *that* was a coincidence. And the timing was right too. Alton said 7:30 p.m.; the librarian thought the time of the crime was around 7:20 p.m. if Tracy remembered Neal's transcript notes correctly. Tracy wanted to let out a howl. Had she, she might have made Crenshaw sound like a baby chick in comparison.

Chapter 12

Betsy Riggs looked skeptically at the young lady standing outside her door. "You have some ID or something?" she asked Tracy. Tracy handed her a business card and offered to show her driver's license. "Nah, you don't have to do that. Come on in."

"Thanks Mrs. Riggs," Tracy said as she was offered a seat. "How long have you lived in the building?"

"Oh, let's see. I got married in 1962, when I was 25. I guess me and Darren moved in here in 1969."

"Wow! I didn't realize the building dated back to the 1960s."

"Well, it was brand spanking new when we moved in. We never had any kids so we had no reason to look elsewhere."

"Is your husband here?"

"Oh he's out golfing with his buddies. He's been golfing something awful since he retired."

"What did he do?"

"Worked for BGE for 40 some odd years."

Tracy looked around. "Well the apartment looks really nice and cozy."

Betsy smiled. "So when are you getting hitched?"

"What? Oh, the ring gave me away again," Tracy said looking at her finger.

"Well, it's hard to miss."

"It will be next spring; not exactly sure when yet."

"Well good luck. Me and my Darren have been married 53 years. I hope you are as lucky as we have been."

Tracy smiled, thankful for a positive look at coupling for a change. "Thanks Betsy."

"So: you're Colin's attorney you said."

"Yes. I understand you may have been the last person to see Amanda Richmond the day she disappeared."

"Oh dear. That was such a long time ago."

"Yes; 30 years. But I was reading a statement you gave the police when they were investigating the disappearance. You said you saw her while she was taking trash to the Dumpster or something."

"Hm. Yeah, that's right. She was coming down the stairs and I was walking up the stairs. She had a bag of garbage in her hand; yeah. I just assumed she was taking it out. There's a place on the side of the building where you put it." Betsy chuckled. "Of course I'm too old now to go up and down the steps. Just use the elevator these days, although Darren takes it out most of the time now."

"Oh, you had just come back from dumping your trash."

"Yup. Almost got hit doing it too."

"What? What happened?"

"Oh sometimes those hot shot kids, who should have been in school, would tear through the alley where the Dumpster was. I was coming out and this something or other almost nicked me."

"What kind of car was it? Do you remember?"

"Oh a little sporty thing, red with two doors I think."

"I see."

"I guess he would rather have hit me than the van."

Tracy's eyes once again bulged. "Van? What van?"

"The one parked on the other side of the alleyway, across from the Dumpster. I guess that hot shot had to turn suddenly to avoid hitting it and almost hit me instead."

Tracy asked excitedly, "What kind of van was it? Do you remember? Did you notice any writing on it?"

Betsy closed her eyes for a moment. "I don't really remember."

"Oh," Tracy said disappointedly.

"I think it may have been carpet people."

"What? Why do you think that?" The excitement had quickly returned.

"Well, the back was open and I remember seeing carpets sticking out of it."

Jackpot! Score! Blackjack! "Do you remember if you told the police about this?"

Betsy sighed. "I don't think so. They kind of lost interest after I said I didn't see anything or anyone I thought was strange."

"I see. I guess seeing a van in the alley really wouldn't have seemed unusual."

"Nope. In fact the only other person I probably have talked to about this was Jackie Richmond; before he was killed of course."

"You told Jackson Richmond about the van?"

"Yup." Betsy shook her head. "And then a month or so later he's dead too."

Royal straight flush! "You didn't compare notes with Jesse Alton, did you? He used to live in the building."

Betsy thought. "I honestly don't remember; sorry."

"No apology necessary, Betsy; you've been more help than you could possibly know. I want to thank you so much."

"My pleasure," Betsy said obviously pleased with herself. "Any more questions?"

"Not right now; no." racy hurriedly left the kind Betsy Riggs and head-ed to her auto. She had it now; there could no longer be any doubt. Amanda comes out to dump her trash and someone is there. He follows her back to the apartment; they keep things quiet—she because she doesn't want neighbors to see her Mr. Right Now and he…and then something happens and he kills her. The van is used to take the body and suitcase away. Betsy Riggs and Jesse Alton: witnesses by luck, chance, or some divine force whose mission is to right the wrongs of this world? Tracy didn't care how she got so fortunate. She was rushing back to her office. The poor Richmond couple may no longer be among the living, but their murder cases were very much alive.

"What do you mean they're both dead?" Tracy asked her associate, devastated.

"Well they were in their mid-50s when they closed shop. Owen died in 1999 of lung cancer, and his brother Stewart died in 2005 of a heart attack."

Tracy started lightly banging her head on her desk. "No no no no no!" she muttered.

"I'm sorry Tracy. I got your hopes up for nothing. I should have found them first and then called you."

She lifted her noggin. "No, Neal. I'm not angry with you. I started counting my chicks before they hatched. I was so close. I have two witnesses seeing a carpet van. I have the tacks. It was all starting to fall into place!"

"I did talk to Detective Tanner and he's going to call back if he finds anyone else was a registered owner of the vans. If they can track them down, Tanner said they'll impound them and get the crime lab working."

Tracy sighed. "I guess that's something. I don't suppose you have an employee list for Waverly Carpet?"

"Well, that's the thing Tracy. They didn't really have employees. They contracted out their work, and I think they paid a lot of people under the table. I saw some of their financial records and the amount of money they were raking in didn't jibe with the contracted payroll or inventory numbers they were showing."

"Oh. Still though, had they been alive, we could have introduced them to some of the people involved in the case. Somebody may have recognized somebody."

"Possibly; unless your idea about the Pane murder being about *protecting* the original killer is right."

"This sucks!" Tracy blurted out. "This. Really. Sucks!"

Neal gulped. "I'm sorry Tracy."

Tracy shook her head. She looked at her watch. "It's past 5:00 Neal; you can go. If El calls you let me know and if he calls me I'll do the same for you."

"I don't mind staying."

"No Neal. You did really great work today. It's not any of our faults that it worked out like this. We seemed to be *this* close; *so* close! I'm ticked off sure, but not at anymore in particular; well, Pinkerton maybe. If he had made an effort to…Well, given what Alton told me, maybe Pinkerton wouldn't have ended up talking to him anyway. I don't know."

"Are you sticking around?"

"I think I'll call Brian; see what his plans for tonight are. He had some computer emergency last night and I don't know if it worked out for him."

Neal smiled. "I hope you get to see him. I'm sure he can make you feel a little better."

Now Tracy smiled. "Thanks again Neal. Go home to your family."

"Hey, I forgot to tell how much the kids loved the bunnies."

"Oh, sure; no problem."

"Well, again I'm sorry this didn't pan out like you hoped."

Tracy nodded. "Goodnight Neal. Say some prayers for us. Maybe we'll catch a break tomorrow."

"You bet. Try not to break something else in the meantime," Neal winked as he left her.

Tracy took a deep breath. "Crap," she thought. "Now it's too late to call the church office." She sat there feeling cynical and dark. Ugly thoughts and scenarios were forming. The Carruthers: nice people right? Except, at the time of the crimes past, Jon was slobbering over Brandy, and Janie was fooling around with Colin. If Jon was eyeing older women, could he have…? No, that's sick. He wouldn't get involved with Colin's mother, would he? Why *did* Janie end up in Colin's arms? The night of the killing though they both had alibis. Or were their alibis just each other? Jon was on a hospital board; did that mean he had connections? Married couples—should she be looking at married couples? He cheats on his wife with Amanda; the wife, the scorned woman, fights with Amanda and kills her; hubby covers up or at least helps. They alibi each other. This was getting *too* dark for her.

She switched back to Pinkerton; if it weren't for those damn carpet tacks. They had to be significant given what both Betsy Riggs and Jesse Alton had said; lone witnesses sure but…Wait a minute: Jesse Alton. He used to work for the post office. So what? They have access to some personal info…Oh come on Tracy, what'd he do: start ripping open mail that looked like birthday cards to find a Tim Pane? And who puts exact dates on cards anyway? Were Jesse and Amanda involved? Could he have lied about the van because he knew Betsy had told the police about what *she'd* seen, trying to lay some groundwork in case he needed an alibi? But he never told anybody about the van until he told Colin. But that's because the police never asked him; it might look suspicious if he *volunteered* the information. Tracy shook her head.

Now Tracy started wondering about Chrissy Jacks' husband, the late Mr. Wellman: could he and Amanda have had a thing before Chrissy married him? She said he had kids from a former marriage. If he fooled around on his wife with Chrissy, could he have first fooled around with Amanda?

And then what, Chrissy got jealous and killed her friend, and then killed Jackson because he found out something. And then Chrissy charmed Tim Pane somehow? She said she still liked to have a good time. Oh good grief, Tracy; that's crazy.

Bobby Sugarman: he knew the whole story from Pinkerton. His dad dies haunted by the case he never closed, or haunted by guilt that he helped squelch the tack evidence. Does Bobby blame Colin for something involving his father? Bobby's about Tim Pane's age; maybe Bobby met Pane at the bar Janice and Tim hung out at. Now we're getting into dark territory again. She liked Bobby; empathized with him. Even if she could believe Bobby wanted to punish Colin for something, it takes a certain kind of monster to bring in an outside party, a Tim Pane, and sacrifice him on some demonic altar of vengeance.

Bobby's father knew about Pinkerton's affair; cops do some rather dramatic things for their partners sometimes. Lord, what if it was Bobby senior that killed Amanda to protect his partner…And then Pinkerton found out and in turn covered for his partner. Is that what happened? Were Pinkerton and Bobby involved in this to protect Bobby's father? Did Bobby Sr. put the tacks in the box because he felt guilty about what he did to Amanda? Colin, an innocent man, tried to kill himself. Did Sugarman—possibly a guilty man—walk into that drug bust *wanting* to get killed? Did Sugarman tip off the druggies, effectively setting up his own suicide? Oh good Lord Tracy—Tanner was right: you are falling out of the tree.

Tracy sighed. Lots of people she had talked to recently knew about the past; lots of people were haunted by it. Somebody had been consumed with the past for 30 years when they launched the plot against Colin Richmond and involved Tim Pane. But is the original killer the one she's after or someone who's covering things up? Here she was once again: feeling completely stressed out and harried over a murder case. The last two cases had involved people she already knew and loved; she should have expected to feel this way in those cases. But she hadn't known Colin Richmond when she took *this* case, so she thought she'd be okay this time. Wrong again, Tracy. She needed cheering up; Tracy reached for her cell phone.

"This is Brian."

"I have an emergency."

"Oh really?"

"Yup. My hard drive's sagging."

"Your…Look I have people near me. I don't think it would be wise for me to try and match wits with the mistress of double entendres right now."

Tracy laughed. "Is that your nickname for me?"

"No comment. Where are you?"

"Still at the office. How has your day been?"

"Okay; we got our server issues worked out and things seem to be working alright."

     A Tracy Brubaker Mystery

"How late were you there last night?"

"About 2:00 a.m."

"Oh you poor thing."

"It was the getting back here by 9:00 that was the worst part. But I'm actually feeling okay."

"Still, you should get a good night's sleep tonight."

"I want to see you though. Maybe even go out to eat. I may find it easier to behave myself in a public setting."

Tracy laughed. "I see."

"How was your day today? Is everything okay?"

"Hard to say, Brian. But I think you'll be able to rest easier knowing that Pinkerton—the guy who was at my place last night—has had his dirty laundry exposed. El knows all about it. In fact El's actually working *with* me now."

The relief in Brian's voice was obvious. "Thank God. I'm really glad to hear that."

"So, when you coming over worry wart?"

"How about 7:00?"

"That sound you don't hear is me nodding."

Brian laughed. "Okay darling, I'll be there around 7:00 then. Love you."

"Love you too. Don't be late, or I might eat your bunny."

"No comment."

Tracy smiled as she returned her phone to its holder. Neal had been right; she was feeling better already.

"I got Chinese for us," Brian said shortly after greeting his beloved with a kiss. "That way you don't feel like you have to cook anything."

"Oh Brian I don't mind cooking for you. But this is awesome. Thank you."

"Well let's dig in then!" And Brian put the fragrant bags down, quickly hanged up his coat, and started removing plates, serving spoons, and utensils. Tracy tended to the water glasses.

"I guess I should fill a pitcher with water huh? I see lots of hot mustard baggies," Tracy grinned.

"I gotta have the hot mustard for my spring rolls."

"Chicken in garlic sauce is spicy too."

"Yup; hot and spicy just like you."

Tracy laughed heartily. "Oh you sweet talker. Or should I say sweet and sour talker? We *are* having Chinese."

"I don't like sweet and sour stuff, because I don't like sour stuff."

Tracy came up behind Brian as he was opening the containers. She put her arms around his waist and leaned the side of her head on his back. "I love you," she said starting to nuzzle.

He wanted to turn and face her, but he liked what she was doing. "I love you too." Then he felt her kiss his back. She released him and took her seat at the table. "Your plate, madam," he said placing a full dish in front of her: a heaping helping of the garlic chicken atop white rice. Brian sat across from her after making himself the same. The spring rolls sat on a small plate between them.

"I've been thinking Tracy," Brian said after taking his first bite. "What do you want to do about living arrangements; I mean, after we're married."

Tracy smiled. "Well, this summer, I'd like us to go house hunting."

"Oh? You don't want to keep your condo? I though you loved it here."

She nodded. "I do, but this place really isn't big enough for a family. Besides, I want where we end up living to be picked out by the both of us." She looked up and smiled at him.

"Ah. So, uh, how many bedrooms we talking about then? How big do you see this family you mentioned being?"

"Well, at least four: mommy, daddy, baby one, and baby two. I want at least two kids. I never had a sibling. I want our children to have at least one sibling."

"I see. You wanted one?"

"My parents wanted more kids. It just never happened. There were kids to play with on my block, at least when I was younger. But I always wished I had someone to talk to at nighttime, when I was supposed to be sleeping."

Brian chuckled. "Yeah, I hear you. I'm glad I have Crystal in my life; and not just because if it weren't for her I'd have never met you."

Tracy grinned. "I keep meaning to call her. We need to do lunch or something. But I guess that's hard for her given how busy she is."

"She'd make the time for you Tracy. She says the same thing every time your name comes up. Two busy ladies you guys are."

"Uh-huh."

"So do you want to live in the city or the suburbs?"

"The latter," she answered quickly.

"Any reason?"

"Schools. I think Howard County has one of the best school systems in the state. Of course, I guess we could send them to private school. But I like the idea of living in a place where DC and the city are just half an hour away."

Brian nodded. "Wow, you've really given this some thought."

Tracy looked up at Brian as she put her fork down. "I've been thinking about it for a long time. It's what I've always wanted; a nice house in a residential area; kids playing in the backyard; nice neighbors that you actually talk to and get to know. Sound corny?"

"It's not corny if that's what you want Tracy."

She smiled. "What about you Brian? What do you want our home life to be like?"

          A Tracy Brubaker Mystery

Brian sighed and put his fork down. He was looking at her. "You're going to think I'm nuts."

"I already think you're nuts, Brian. That's one of the things I love about you."

He cleared his throat. "Tracy, you have a very important job. I mean, you really help people. You saved me, you got Max out of his jam, and you're doing everything you can for this new client of yours. I mean, what you do really matters."

"I don't think I understand you."

"Well, I like my job and all that. Most of the people I work with are alright. But, Tracy, it's not that important, not like yours."

"Brian, you're not being fair to yourself comparing what we do. I'm sure what you do is important."

He shook his head. "No, that's not really my point. What I'm saying is I don't have the passion for my job that you have for yours. And like I said, you make a real difference in your clients' lives, and don't start any false modesty about it either. Don't forget: I'm not only your fiancé, I'm a former client too."

Tracy smiled. "So what *are* you saying Brian?"

"Tracy, I want to stay home with the kids."

Tracy's eyes widened. "You *do*?"

"Yes. I want to be a real father to them. I mean, kids are naturally tight with their moms, and that's how it should be. But there's no way I want you to stop doing what you're doing. And while I know daycare places are usually safe, I still feel a little uncomfortable sending the kids off to someone we barely know."

Tracy blinked. "Brian, I had no idea you felt this way."

"And think how cool it would be that I could bring the baby over to see you at lunchtime, or if you were working late. And I could go out to your mom's place anytime she was up for a visit. I mean, sadly, any kids of ours are only going to have one grandparent, Tracy. So it's important to me that they see their grandmother whenever they can, so she can spoil them whenever she can. Now, does *that* sound corny to *you*?"

Tracy gulped. "Brian, I just don't know what to say."

"Would you think me less of a man for doing this? It's not like I, I mean we, really need the money, unless of course the company suddenly went broke or something. I know my dad wouldn't have approved of such a thing if he were still alive."

Tracy got up from her place and went to Brian. "Stand up," she ordered; he obeyed. She put her hands around his neck and looked him in the eyes. "If you think I'm going to turn down the offer of my husband watching our children, then you *are* more nuts than I thought you were." And then she kissed him. And they kept on kissing. And soon they were on the sofa. "Brian," she finally said. "You know I want kids with you. But I want them *after* we're married."

Brian nodded. "Yeah," he said. "I guess we should stop huh?"

"I'm sorry. It's difficult for me, even if you don't think so."

"You've always been the practical one Tracy." Brian got up and offered his hand to Tracy so she could do the same. "I guess we both know what we're missing; it makes it hard. Oh, let me rephrase: it makes it difficult."

Tracy grinned. "Let's finish dinner. And then you can let me fall asleep on your lap."

"Ha. I guess I don't have many options here."

Tracy walked backed to the table and sat down. Brian soon joined her. "Brian, I know I've always said I wanted a May or spring wedding. But what if it were sooner?"

Brian gave her a curious look. "Uh, why do you ask? Didn't the church you want have anything available in May?"

"Well, to be honest, I still haven't called them. I keep meaning to but then things come up that I feel I have to deal with right away and the day gets away from me."

"Oh. Well, what are you thinking?"

"To be married in the church we have to wait at least six months. We could be married as early as October."

Brian straightened up; now it was his turn to be surprised. "Tracy, what's all this about? You've always wanted to married in the spring. At least, any time we talked about it you said that was, how did you put it again, *nonnegotiable*?"

Tracy laughed. "Did I really say that?"

"I'm pretty sure that's the word you used. Is something going on I should know about?"

Tracy took a deep breath. "I told you: not making love is hard for me too. And I'm having a real struggle here. Part of me wants to wait until we're married, like you're supposed to do. On the other hand, like you said, we know what we're missing. I know most people wouldn't even think of it as wrong, but I guess I'm not so sure. I try to do the right thing, but I'm not perfect. I'm just confused."

Brian nodded. "And I'm not helping matters by making it clear how much I want you."

"No. I guess I need you to be the practical one sometimes. I know that you love me and that it's not just about the sex. But I've read enough articles to know guys are wired differently."

Brian smiled. "You know it's dangerous to read all those articles, don't you?"

Tracy grinned. "I can't help it. I'm curious to know what guys really want. The funny thing is: most of those articles are written by women;

   A Tracy Brubaker Mystery

women who seem to have had a lot of boyfriends. I mean, if they know what guys want why haven't they found a guy they can hold onto yet?"

Now Brian laughed out loud. "Research, Tracy; research."

"Oh you're cute."

He smiled. "I'm sorry Tracy. I guess I really didn't fully appreciate what you were going through with this. I thought it was easy for you, and that I was just doing what I was expected to do: be the lustful male."

"It's a tough line to walk, isn't it?"

"Yes. And to be honest Tracy: you're putting me in a tight spot."

"What are you talking about?" she asked him skeptically.

"Well, on the one hand, you want honesty, don't you? To know what I'm thinking and feeling, right?"

"Yes, of course."

"On the other hand, if I'm honest that I want to be with you in the carnal way, then I'm not helping you deal with your own struggle, because I'm, in a way, putting pressure on you."

"Oh you poor man."

"Seriously Tracy: what do you want me to do? Pretend I don't want you? Should we just not talk about it? What should I do?"

Tracy managed a slight smile. "Can't you do both? By that I mean, go ahead and admit what you're feeling but also acknowledge that you're willing to deal with it because you know how I feel?"

"Oh. You make it sound so obvious when you put it like that."

"Brian, even if something's obvious that doesn't mean it's easy to do. I know there are times, like right now, that it's going to be a real challenge."

"You want me right now?"

"Yes," she answered quickly.

"Ouch. So this is where I say I want you too but I'm not going to do anything because I know how you feel about it."

"Yes."

Brian squeezed his eyes shut and then sighed. "Okay. Look Tracy, you need to finish your dinner so you grow big and strong and then you need to go to bed because the early bird catches the worm."

She started giggling. "Worm huh?"

Brian let out a cry of exasperation. "Oh, there you go! Mistress of the Double Entendres! You love doing this to me! Admit it!"

Now she was almost in tears. "I'm sorry Brian; I just can't help it."

"Oh you difficult fiancée!"

Tracy stopped laughing—well, almost. "Hey, don't you dare start with that."

"Eat your vegetables then; and then brush your teeth and go to bed. You're punished. No chocolate bunny for you tonight."

Tracy grinned. "I'd rather get a spanking."

"That does it!" He stood up, picked Tracy up and put her over his shoulder, and brought her to the couch. She started hitting his back playfully, squealing. He dropped her on the couch and started kissing her frantically. "You are the most desirable and challenging woman I have ever met," he said between his wet pecks.

"But you love me anyway," she said, still giggling.

"Yes, temptress. I can't help it."

"Then go clean up the dinner mess while I get my PJs on. Be practical!"

He pulled back from her, scowled, and then gave her another quick kiss. "Fine. The sooner I get out of this madhouse the safer you'll be. My practicality may not last too long." He stood up and went to do as instructed.

Brian left around 11:00. They had remained practical, but that didn't mean the playfulness stopped when the chores were done. She wasn't having any luck falling asleep though. So Brian had to go. She gave him an extra long goodbye kiss. Challenging though she may be, she knew how to reward good behavior.

Rebecca noted Tracy's high spirits the next morning. Tracy had not been a happy person when the secretary left the office yesterday. Something had seriously changed her mood.

"Did you have a good night last night, Tracy?" Rebecca grinned.

Tracy looked around her suite. They were both at the coffee pot near Tracy's personal office. "Hey Beck, come with me will you?"

"Uh, sure Tracy." She followed her boss as instructed, and then Tracy closed the door behind them.

"Beck, can I ask you something?"

"Sure Tracy. Why are you whispering?"

"Because it's personal."

"But we're all alone here. Neal won't be here for half an hour at least."

"Still…Look, I'm not sure why I'm asking you this, but you seem to have a real grip on things."

Rebecca grinned. "What is it Tracy?"

"Um, do you know if…well, do men really like lingerie?"

"What?!"

"Shhh…keep it down."

Rebecca started laughing. "Oh Tracy you're adorable."

"What? I don't want to be adorable. I'm serious here."

"You're thinking of getting some lingerie huh?"

"Well, I was just thinking in general." Tracy clasped her hands and started pacing. "You see, well you know I was brought up Catholic. And you don't fool around before you're married if you are. And I figured I'd be, well, untouched when I got married. I mean, that's part of the wedding night; the big reveal and all."

Rebecca was grinning. "Sure Tracy."

    A Tracy Brubaker Mystery

"Well, things didn't go as I thought they would on that score…I mean one moment I'm an ugly duckling and most guys don't want anything to do with me and the next moment…Well, then I met Brian and…I mean, the purity ship has sailed. In fact, it's sailed a few times. So, I guess I was trying to think of something special for the wedding night—you know: something that would be different."

"Brian's never seen you in lingerie before?" Rebecca asked surprised.

"Well, no. When we finally, well…it wasn't too long after that that things started turning bad. The first time he came home drunk, well he couldn't…what I mean is I just didn't want him when he was like that. And then we broke up. And now we're back. But I'm still not sure we should be resuming *all* of our old habits."

"Oh, is he in the doghouse or something?"

"No no. It's just that I'm trying to be good, you know what I'm saying?"

Rebecca sighed. "Tracy, not everyone believes that sex before marriage is bad."

"I don't want to get into the right or wrong of it Beck. Bottom line is that I was just trying to think of something special I could do. He's being, or he's trying to be, very understanding and patient. Now, I've read some articles that say men don't really care for lingerie. I mean, if I spend a lot of time and money on it, and it's uncomfortable to wear, and then it's on the floor in 10 seconds, I'm gonna be pissed. And then somebody's always *ripping* the damn thing off in the movies. That would seriously kill the mood if it got torn."

Rebecca started laughing. "Oh Tracy you are absolutely precious."

"I'm serious Beck."

"I know, and that's what's so endearing. Look Tracy: that kind of thing is very private. The only one who is going to be able to answer the question for you is Brian. And that really should be between just the two of you."

"I wasn't planning on modeling anything for you Beck."

"I realize that," Rebecca chuckled. "If you really want to do something special, find out if he has any fantasies."

"Excuse me?"

"You know, French maid and house boy."

"What?"

"Role playing, Tracy."

"Oh, of course. I knew that. I'm not *that* naïve."

"Talk to him; find out if he has things that he'd like to try with you."

"If I start asking questions like that now, when he's hanging by a thread, so to speak, as he is now…Besides if I do that it would spoil the surprise."

"Well, get several ideas then. He won't know which one you'll pick."

"I don't know Beck."

"Well, I did something along these lines with my husband as we were coming up on our first wedding anniversary."

"Really? Is it safe for me to hear?"

"Sure; the set up is anyway. I left a Victoria's Secret catalogue lying around where I knew he'd see it. And then I left the room and waited for him to give in to his curiosity. Well, I quietly reentered and looked over his shoulder and noted what things he seemed to like. Then, I picked one of them out and wore it the night of our first anniversary. Worked like a charm."

Tracy grinned. "I always knew you were devious. But, didn't you feel a little jealous? I mean the women in those mags are really, um, in good shape."

Rebecca chuckled. "Tracy, men look. You're going to have to face that fact. So why not use it to your advantage? Marriage is about commitment, but that doesn't mean he can shut off the natural male instinct to look. The thing is: he's choosing *you*. And even though he may look once in awhile that's *all* he's going to do. Otherwise, he's a bum."

"I hear you."

"Besides Tracy, you've got nothing to be embarrassed about when it comes to how you look. You gonna tell me you haven't noticed guys looking at you before?"

"Uh, well…"

"You see. Bottom line: everyone's sexual fantasies are silly and ridiculous to everyone else except to the couple enjoying them. So I can't answer you about the lingerie or anything else. Only Brian can do that. And frankly I think that's the way it should be."

Tracy nodded, suddenly turning red. "I shouldn't have even brought this up."

"Oh Tracy, don't worry. I won't tell anyone; promise. Job security is what I call it."

Tracy grinned. "Oh you're cute."

"No Tracy, you are. And sweet. And human; you shouldn't be embarrassed that you have a desire for physical contact with the man you love."

"I know that…But I never had someone I could talk to about that stuff. I wish I had had an older sister or something."

"Well, you have me. Any other questions: positions, fetishes—"

"Stop! I'm good."

"Okay; let me know." Rebecca grinned once again as she made her exit.

Tracy sat on her chair. "I have to stop reading all those articles," she thought. "They just confuse me." Then she grinned. She took out the piece of paper she had put in her drawer the other day, and then she left her office. "Let's see if this works."

Tanner gave her the bad news just after 9:00 a.m. "The vans ended up being traded in and junked," he told Tracy. "And there were no other names connected with the registration other than the Waverly brothers. I'll keep looking for other names of course. But that's where we are now."

Tracy sighed. "Thanks El. I was expecting the worst after Neal told me both brothers were no longer among the living."

"I'm not giving up quite yet, Tracy. I'm seeing if there are any cases that involved someone who worked for a carpet company, if that is this guy's MO. Truth is, Tracy: I had a pretty gruesome thought last night."

"What do you mean El?"

"Amanda Richmond's disappearance: if you wanted to take a body out of an apartment, how would you hide it?"

Tracy sighed. "You could roll it up in a carpet I suppose." Tracy had already had that thought of course, after speaking with Betsy Riggs.

"Bingo. I wished I had a way to access Waverly's appointment records from the days Colin Richmond's parents met with whatever it is they met with."

"No relatives to nag?"

"None local. I don't see their kids or widows lugging old business records with them when they moved out of state. I still made some calls though, reached out to some detectives who are going to see if there is anything to find. But I'm not hopeful."

"Okay El," she sighed. "Thanks for the update."

"Sure Tracy." Tanner hung up his phone. Tracy moped. She needed cheering up. She buzzed Neal.

"Neal, would you be a sweetie and get me one of those Danish thingies from down the hall? Come in here and I'll give you a couple bucks."

"Sure Tracy; I might get one for myself."

"Thanks Neal."

And it was around 11:00 in the morning, this Thursday, April 9, 2015, that a classic memory was born at the office of Tracy Brubaker: Attorney-At-Law.

"Alright which one of you two jokesters is responsible for this?!" Neal shouted. "I mean enough is enough!"

"What's wrong with you Neal?" Rebecca shouted back.

"Oh I think you know Beck! I think you know all too well. This sounds like something you'd write!"

Rebecca got up and went to Neal's office. "What are you going on about?"

"This," he said, waving a crumpled piece of paper in her face. "Oh, this was a nice touch: 'Don't you love me anymore?'. I mean, real cute." Rebecca took the paper and looked at it as Neal continued. "I've thrown this thing away three times already so you've had your fun." And then Rebecca started laughing.

"Neal, I swear this wasn't me. I'd like to take credit for it, but it wasn't me."

Neal's eyes narrowed as the mental light bulb turned on. "So that's why for the first time in five years she sent me for Danish." Neal left his desk and marched into Tracy's office with Rebecca right behind him. Tracy did not have Tim Pane's, the true author of this silly exercise, poker face. As soon as she saw the look on Neal's puss, she started laughing. And then Rebecca joined in. "Oh, I get it," Neal said angrily. "Pick on the male, huh?"

Tracy was red-faced but shaking her head. "No," she gasped. "I just knew it'd be funnier with you." She started coughing.

"Oh chill out Neal," Rebecca said. "You're a big boy. Take it like the boy you are."

"Oh sure — you wouldn't be saying that if I did that to you."

"Neal, I wouldn't get so upset about it like you are. I'd just get even."

Neal started nodding. "Oh, I'll get even alright. I'm going to give new meaning to the idea of getting even. I'll get so even that...well you'll... Hell I've got work to do." He turned quickly and moved toward his office, walking right into the visitor who had heard the noise in the back. "Excuse me," Neal said curtly. He then called out, "Hey Rebecca, get out here." And then Neal marched into his office.

Rebecca was looking at Tracy, shaking her head. "He must have gotten up on the wrong side of the couch this morning or something. Usually he's usually a pretty good sport." Rebecca left to attend to the visitor. "Hello, sorry about all of that. Can I help you?"

"Uh, sure; I'm here to see Tracy."

"And you are?"

"I'm Brian, her fiancé."

Rebecca widened her eyes. She hadn't recognized him from the pictures she'd seen of him in the news stories last year. "*You're* Brian. Well I'm Rebecca. We've spoken a few times on the phone. Let me introduce you to Neal." Rebecca popped her head into Neal's office. "Oh Neal, would you like to meet Tracy's fiancé?"

Neal gulped. "Terrific," he said. He got up, cleared his throat and moved toward the hall. "Hi; I'm Neal, office jester and resident buffoon." Rebecca started laughing, and so too then did Brian.

"Nice to meet you Neal," Brian said offering his hand, which Neal accepted. "We've talked on the phone too."

"Sure. Look, I'm sorry about all of that."

"Hey, don't worry about it. Uh, can I see Tracy?"

"She's back here," Rebecca grinned. "You can follow me, Brian."

"Thanks. Glad to meet you Neal."

"Likewise," Neal responded, slowly returning to his chair.

Rebecca entered the boss' office. "Uh, Tracy...Somebody here to *see* you."

"Who Beck?"

"Hi Tracy!"

"Brian!" Tracy practically shouted as she stood up like a rubber band that had just been shot.

"Well, I'll leave you two then," Rebecca said grinning. "Nice to meet you Brian." And then she closed the door.

"Tracy: why was Rebecca grinning at me like that?"

"Like what?"

"Like she *knows* something."

"Oh, she just looks like that naturally; probably because she knows a lot."

"Uh-huh."

"Well are you just going to stand there or are you going to come over and give me a safe-for-work kiss?"

Brian smiled. He trotted over and gave her a gentle hug and kiss. "Hey gorgeous: wondering why I'm here?"

She grinned. "Now that you mention it, why are you here?"

"I might have to work late again. So I'm here to take you to lunch."

"Oh; well, I *guess* I can break away."

"I think you should. Why was Neal yelling like that?"

"I'll tell you all about it at lunch."

"Is everything okay here?"

"Yes Brian. I guess Neal is having an off day and I picked the wrong time to…well, like I said, I'll tell you at lunch. Where are you taking me?"

"How about Pitt's Steak Pit? If we leave now we can beat the lunch rush."

Tracy smiled and then leaned in and kissed Brian. "Let's go then."

"Right." He took her hand and led her out of the office.

"I'll be at lunch Beck," Tracy said as she passed her secretary.

"You two have fun."

Brian looked at Tracy. "She's grinning at me again," he whispered.

Tracy chuckled. "I told you, she's like that with everybody."

"I don't think that's terribly funny," Brian said after Tracy recounted the practical joke.

"You don't? I thought it was cute."

"Irritating people is cute?"

"Oh Brian, stop being a stick-in-the-mud."

"Well, I just don't find that funny is all. Obviously I'm in the minority."

"My mother would agree with you."

"Oh, that's good to know," Brian said rolling his eyes.

"Hey, buddy; you've thrown the mother jabs at me too a couple of times."

"You're right; guilty as charged."

"Hi Mr. Shane. How are you today?" a friendly-faced man asked Brian.

"Oh hey Patrick: meet my fiancée: Tracy Brubaker. Tracy this is Pitt's owner, Patrick Shaker." Tracy lifted her hand and Shaker took it with both of his.

"Fiancée, huh? Congratulations! Both of you! Let me buy you a drink. What'll it be?"

"Oh a ginger ale for me Patrick, thanks," Tracy answered.

"Make that two," Brian chimed in.

"You bet. Hope you have a great meal."

"Thanks Patrick. I always do here," Brian said. Shaker left to get their drinks.

"I should have known you knew the owner," Tracy grinned. "You're just so *important*."

A server placed the ales on the table. "Oh, stop, Tracy. He's nice to all the people here, not just me."

"Uh-huh." Tracy leaned a little closer to her lover seated across the table. "Hey Brian," she said softly.

He leaned in likewise. "What is it Tracy?"

"I have a question for you."

"Okay."

"Do you have any, um, fantasies?"

"What: like world peace or a football league?"

"No, silly." She started rubbing his hand and tilted her head. "You know: fantasies."

Brian's eyes widened. "Tracy, if you're asking what I think you're asking this is no place to ask it, to talk about it."

"But if I ask it when we're alone, you're going to get all worked up about it and say I'm being mean."

"Tracy, I…"

"Well, do you?"

"You like this, don't you? We're in a public place and you're talking to me about private fantasies."

"If you have them I'd like to know about them."

"And then what, you shout nah-nah-nah-nah, stick your thumbs in your ears and give me a big raspberry?"

Tracy started chuckling. "No Brian."

"Look, Tracy. Right now I just want to be with you. I don't really have any fantasy besides that. Maybe after we've exhausted the usual, uh, avenues let's call them, then I can be creative."

Tracy smiled. "Oh you're so sweet."

"Well…"

"So no, like role playing ideas."

"Good Lord almighty…"

"Like nurse and doctor?"

 A Tracy Brubaker Mystery

"Stop it."

"Oh Brian, I'm serious. I can be adventurous."

"I don't want to talk about this here."

"Here you are folks," a pleasant young woman said while placing the couple's plates down. "Two lunch specials, medium well with fries and green beans."

"Thanks," they answered simultaneously.

"Let's eat," Brian said.

"How about lingerie?"

Brian rolled his eyes. "Tracy I...okay, yes to lingerie." He started cutting his steak.

Tracy grinned. "You answered that one easy enough."

"Well, an image of you in a teddy popped into my head. I couldn't help it."

"See Brian, isn't this fun?"

"Fun? You know, I think you're punishing me."

"Oh come on Brian."

"No, subconsciously you're still angry with me even though consciously you love me and say you've forgiven me. Subconsciously you've devised a way to drive me crazy, telling me how you want to be pure and then putting images of you in various states of undress in my head. You're punishing me I tell you."

Tracy started chuckling. "No Brian; that's not it. I will tell you all about my reasons eventually for the questions but I assure I'm not trying to drive you crazy." She grinned. "I wonder if you'll always feel this way about me, when things start sagging."

"I'll still want Saggy Tracy," he said. "You know they say couples always see the image they first saw; that couples retain a sort of eternal youth in the other's eyes."

Tracy smiled. "Well I guess we'll find that out won't we, Brian?"

He looked at her. "Yes, we will. Now eat and show mercy."

"Okay; but I may ask you again later. You really weren't very helpful."

"Eat, will you please?"

Brian and Tracy were putting their coats on preparing to leave. "I should thank Patrick again," Brian said looking around. "Hey Tracy, do you have a business card with you? You could win a free appetizer if they draw your card."

"Sure; why not?" she said searching her pockets and then handing him one. "I'm already in the running for some beer battered onion rings at Richie's Digs."

"Oh really? Is their food any good? I've never been there."

"Actually it *was* good. What appetizer do I win here?"

"Uh, I think you get to pick."

"Cool, I like that."

"Okay, let's go," Brian said putting his arm around her. They moved toward the parking lot. Tracy was keeping pace with Brian when she suddenly stopped, and then looked back at the restaurant. "Forget something?" he asked.

She looked at him. "No." Then she got a far off look in her eyes.

"Tracy what's wrong?"

"I…I just had a thought. I…" She looked at Brian and then smiled. "I just had the most interesting idea."

"Okay; what is it this time? You want me to put on clown makeup and stand in the middle of the street…wearing a diaper eating a Twinkie or something?"

Tracy didn't laugh; she didn't crack a smile. "Huh? No diaper clowns."

"Then what?"

"I think I know who killed Timothy Pane."

"You *what*?"

"We need to get back to my office, Brian. I have some research to do and possibly some people to find."

"Uh, sure; okay." And then Tracy moved zombie-like toward Brian's car. He almost had to push her into the passenger's seat. She uttered not a word, not a sound the entire trip back to her office. But Brian could hear the wheels spinning in her mind.

It was Friday afternoon and Tracy was back in Detective Tanner's office. He was looking at the list she had just handed him. "Can you arrange it El, my little dinner party?" she asked.

"Tracy, I thought you said you were thinking 10:00 in the morning."

"Okay, technically not dinner, but let's not argue semantics."

"And you want me to check Pane's credit card history for you."

"Yes. That's why we have to delay this thing until Tuesday. I want to have everything lined up, like a row of dominoes, so that once I get going everything's just going to fall into place. It's really just a bunch of little details that don't mean anything really in and of themselves. But if you put it all together El, then the picture is clear — very clear."

"And what are you planning on serving at this soiree, as if I couldn't guess?"

"I'll be serving up a murderer of course, El. And for some of the guests, they can also dine on some crow."

"Uh-huh. I guess I should bring a bib myself. And just what is it you're planning exactly?"

Tracy smirked. "Do you remember your Shakespeare, El?"

"My Shakespeare?"

"Allow me to quote the Bard for you.

"That's from *Hamlet*, El."

"*Hamlet*."

"Right."

Tanner looked again at Tracy's guest list. "You have everyone connected with Tim Pane and Jackson Richmond's murders listed."

"Yes. And Betsy Riggs too; she saw Amanda Richmond the day she vanished."

"Pinkerton's here I see."

"Yes, El. He has to be there."

"Who's Janice Grant?"

"A co-worker of Tim Pane's. Maybe someday, she would have been more than that. And there will also be surprise guests, El. Think of it as a *This is Your Life*, with the murderer not realizing he or she is the subject."

Tanner frowned. "I don't know if Shandi's going to like this."

"Well, technically you're in charge of the re-opened Jackson Richmond murder, so if she's going to play tough cop then we'll just pretend all of this has to do with the earlier murder. But at the end of the day both cases are related. In fact, Amanda Richmond's vanishing is tied to this too, so Pinkerton and Danbury *should* be there as a matter of courtesy."

"Uh-huh. And are you going to let me in on your suspicions?"

Tracy sighed. "Sorry El. It's my party and I'll play coy if I want to."

"You gotta give me something Tracy."

"Look, just have everyone at Denzinger's Steaks and Chops 10:00 a.m. on Tuesday. We'll wrap everything up before they open for lunch so we won't be interfering with business."

"And why there exactly?"

"Because that's where the alleged fight happened, setting the stage for murder. It's the key scene in the murderer's drama, El. Tim Pane played his part, and the diners and staff were his audience. But there was someone else directing all of this from behind the scenes."

"Oh right, the cunning of the scene."

"Exactly. And notice that I want Colin Richmond there too. I want him to be able to look the killer in the face, if that's what he wants to do when this is all over with."

"Now *that* will require Danbury's okay."

"Then you have to get it El. Look: you know me. And you know I was right about Brian being innocent and Max Paganini being innocent. And you *all* owe Colin something because of what Pinkerton pulled with the tacks. You *know* I'm right El. Just trust me this once more on this case."

Tanner nodded. "I know your résumé, Tracy."

"Then you'll get this done for me."

Tanner sighed again. "I may have to pull some favors but…Okay Tracy, consider it done."

Tracy beamed as she gave El a firm embrace. "You're the best El."

"Uh-huh; sure Tracy," he said smiling himself.

"Now I'm off. I have to start practicing my lines. 'The play's the thing' you know."

"*Hamlet* again?"

"A-plus – I'm gonna fly now, El." And she flew out the door humming the *Rocky* theme as she did so. Tanner had his hands on his hips chuckling. He realized though he couldn't wait until Tuesday's performance.

"Won't you tell *me*, Tracy?" Brian pleaded. "I *swear* I won't say a word to anybody."

Tracy smiled. "Sorry Brian."

"How about just a hint then?"

"Uh-uh."

"Not even a teensy weensy itty bitty something?"

"Nope; this is part of my work; I really need to keep this hush hush and on the QT for now. I will give you most, if not all, of the details tomorrow evening—like an exclusive one on one interview with Tracy."

Brian pursed his lips. "There you go with the double entendres again: one on one indeed."

Tracy laughed. "I didn't do that deliberately. *You're* the one with the double entendre *mind*."

"Look, why don't you rehearse your presentation with me as your audience? I can give you feedback; let you know if your speech needs some polishing."

"Give it up Brian; ain't happening."

"I guess I can't be there at the restaurant to watch."

"Sorry; special invitation-only event."

"Well, the next time you're in court I'm going to show up. That's open to the *public*, no invite needed; you can't stop me from coming—hah!"

Tracy kissed him. "Even if I say you might distract me?" They were seated on the condo sofa; Tracy was sitting on Brian's lap.

"I'll wear a disguise if that will help."

She kissed him again. "I'll know it's you, James Bond."

"Bond? He was a spy not a master of disguise."

"Exactly."

    A Tracy Brubaker Mystery

"Harrumph." He kissed her. "So are you ready for tomorrow, the big day?"

"Yes."

"Nervous?"

"A little; but I'll be fine once I get started."

"Sounds like when you were studying for an exam: once you started the test all the nervousness left you."

She kissed him again. "That's easy enough to explain: fear of the unknown. Once you know what you're facing, you can deal with it."

He kissed her again. "I bet someone else is nervous tonight."

Tracy grinned. "But they're not having as much fun as we are." She closed her eyes and kissed him passionately. Then she pulled back and stroked his cheek. "I'm afraid though our fun has to end now. It's nearly 10:00 and I need to get my zzz's."

Brian nodded. "I know. I won't give you grief since I know tomorrow is such a big day for you."

Tracy smiled at him. "Thanks Brian; I really appreciate your understanding that; and for everything else."

"Everything else?"

"Brian, I know I've been all over the map, so to speak, lately: the case, my personal feelings, us moving so quickly—it's been a whirlwind. And in spite of a few verbal tussles between us, you've been very patient and understanding. I love you and I want you to know that I appreciate you being with me, just like this. It means a lot to me; *you* mean a lot to me. I love you." And she kissed him again.

"I love you too Tracy. But you know that."

"I still love hearing you say it; that will never grow old."

"Now after all those lovely words you're going to tell me to shoo, aren't you?"

Tracy chuckled. "You know me so well." And she stood up, allowing her fiancé to do the same. They completed their departing ritual, and then Tracy was by herself.

Sleep wasn't coming as she lay on her back, staring at her ceiling. The butterflies were wide awake in her stomach. Everything was set for tomorrow; Tanner had helped see to that. Her exhibits were packed in a box at her office; Neal had helped see to *that*. Colin Richmond would be at Denzinger's too; Tanner had made sure Danbury saw to *that*. The rest would be on her. Tomorrow would see the closing of one missing person's case and two murders; Tracy herself would see to that. "All the world's a stage, And all the men and women merely players; They have their exits and their entrances" she thought. Yes, tomorrow Colin Richmond would be exiting his prison, and someone else would, soon thereafter, be making his entrance into same. Tracy smiled. "*As you like it*?" she asked herself. "Yes; yes I like that idea very much."

Chapter 13

Peggy Osher was escorting the people to the dining area as they arrived for Tracy's early morning dinner party at Denzinger's Steaks and Chops. Mike Denzinger himself was offering his sort-of patrons water as they were seated. He approached Tracy. "Look Tracy: you sure this thing will be done in time for lunch. I mean, I don't mind helping but..."

"Don't worry Mike. I'll make sure this goes by quickly. I don't want to interfere with your commerce."

He forced a smile. "Well, I gotta keep the customers happy I guess." But he was mumbling as he went back to get more water pitchers.

"Hi Jon; hi Janie," Tracy said as she passed by the seated Carruthers. "I'm glad you could be here."

"Sure," Jon said. "Anything we can do to help." Janie said nothing, choosing just to nod in agreement with her husband.

"Colin needs to have friends here; I think the three of us are it."

Janie gulped. "Tracy, what's going to happen today?"

"We're going to be looking into the past a bit; learning the truth behind what really happened to Colin's parents and Timothy Pane."

"I see," she said quietly.

"Don't worry Janie; the only people getting hurt today are the ones who deserve it."

Jon looked at Tracy quizzically. "I don't know what we can do to help."

"Just be here for Colin. Thanks for coming you guys."

"Can I get a beer or something?" Linda Schumacher called out. "I mean if I ain't at work I might as well enjoy myself."

"Yeah, that's a good idea," Jesse Alton loudly agreed. "And when are we going to get this thing going; Crenshaw doesn't like to be in his cage more than a couple hours at a time. He starts barking and then my damn neighbor will start complaining again."

"I promise to make this snappy, Mr. Alton," Tracy said. "But I'm afraid alcoholic beverages are out of the question. Technically the restaurant is closed."

"Hey, I won't tell if you won't," Alton said. And then he and Linda Schumacher shared a good laugh.

"Where should I sit?" Bobby Sugarman asked Tanner as he strolled through the entrance.

"Anywhere you want Bobby. Thanks for being here."

"I didn't think I had much of a choice," he said softly, moving quickly to an empty seat.

"Hi Bobby," Tracy said. "Any word on those onion rings yet?"

Bobby chuckled. "Not yet. But I don't handle the drawing myself."

"Rats," Tracy said while snapping her fingers. "I may just have to get me some and pay myself."

Tracy moved toward where Betsy Riggs was seated. "Good morning, Betsy; it's nice to see you here."

"Oh hi. What am I supposed to do?"

"Oh, I'll let you know when the time comes. You have a very important part to play."

"Really? This sounds exciting!"

"I have butterflies! I'll see you shortly."

Tanner moved quickly toward the mingling attorney. "Hey Tracy: who is Gail Riegert? She's here but she's not on the list."

"Oh, sorry El," she said whispering. "She's one of my surprise guests. Let's put her in the back for now. And there's another one, Christine Jacks Wellman, who'll be here too."

"Uh-huh."

"When will Detective Danbury arrive with Colin?"

"She's on her way. I just spoke with her." Tanner suddenly froze and stared in the direction of the entrance. Tracy followed his stare. "Hi Alex," Tanner greeted.

Pinkerton grunted. "What's this all about, Elias? You're really pushing it, you know?"

"Why don't you just sit down, Lieutenant Pinkerton?" Tracy asked sternly. "You'll know soon enough what this is all about; I promise you that. Have some water while you wait; my treat." Pinkerton curled his lip but said nothing. Peggy then led him to a seat. Tracy looked at her watch. Then she consulted her own list. "Damn butterflies," she thought. "They can't keep still so I can't keep still. Argh!" She resumed her pacing.

Janice Grant arrived at 9:50 a.m. "Hi Tracy," she said warmly. "I'm not late am I?"

Tracy smiled. "No Janice, not at all. How are you doing?"

"I'm alright, I guess. Is that Colin person here yet?"

"Not yet, Janice," Tracy answered sympathetically.

"Oh. So you think you know who killed Timmy; that's why we're here?" Janice asked, gulping.

Tracy didn't answer. "This woman—her name is Peggy—will take you to get you seated, Janice." Tracy then rubbed Janice's forearm.

"Is everybody here yet?" Neal asked having found his employer in the lobby.

"Almost everybody; are you ready?"

"Affirmative."

"Everything in the box?"

"All present and accounted for."

"Guard that box with your life Neal," she said smiling.

"You bet. Anything I can do while we wait around here?"

"Nope. Have some water or take a potty break."

"Okay; I'll just sit back down then." He turned and left her.

"Here Tracy," Raymond said handing her a glass of water. "I thought you could use this."

Tracy smiled. "Thank you Raymond. That was very thoughtful of you. Thanks."

"Sure, no prob," he said shyly, grinning as he headed back toward the kitchen.

Tracy was sipping her beverage when she heard the familiar giggles of Chrissy Jacks Wellman. She seemed to be flirting with Tanner, who was trying to find her name on the list. His obvious discomfort with the flirtatious Chrissy had apparently made him forget she was the other name *not* on his list.

"Hi Chrissy," Tracy greeted as she approached. "Thanks for coming."

"Oh sure. I've never been in one of these places before."

"I'm going to tuck you away for now, if you don't mind. Would you like some hot tea? I know we can have someone make it for you."

"Oh, you remembered! You're a dear but if I could just get some water I'll be fine."

"I'll do that. In the meantime you can go back to talking to Detective Tanner. He's a very nice man who will take care of you." Tracy grinned as she made sure Tanner overheard her.

"Oh that sounds fine."

"Here's Chrissy back, El."

"Oh thank *you*, Tracy," he said insincerely.

Tracy looked at her watch. It was after 10:00; where the hell were Danbury and Colin? And then seconds later the front door opened with the arrival of the last guests. Tracy immediately went to her client. "How are you, Colin?"

"I'm okay. I'm not sure what's going on though."

Tracy looked at him sympathetically. "Well, I think very shortly you're going to be a free man." Colin looked at his attorney curiously.

Detective Danbury scowled. "Let's not get the man's hopes up, okay? I'm still not happy about all of this."

"I know, Detective," Tracy said. "But I hope to make a believer out of you when all is said and done."

"A believer? Are you for real?"

Tracy just smiled. "Once you and Colin sit down we can begin."

"Fine," Danbury said.

"Oh Detective, could you do me one more small favor?"

"What's that?"

"Could you please take the cuffs off Colin? Please? For real..."

Danbury scowled a bit more, but she acquiesced to Tracy's request. Now cop and captive took their places in the dining area. Everyone turned to stare at Colin Richmond; some looked at him sympathetically, others with confusion, still others with anger. And some didn't know who in the hell he was. Colin just stared down, hands folded on his lap. Danbury sat next to him. She sipped from the water glass that was soon provided her. Colin didn't look up when Raymond placed a drink in front of him.

Tracy asked that the front door be locked; she had less than an hour now before the restaurant opened for business. The noise of the busy kitchen could be heard throughout the establishment as the cooks and servers were preparing for the day. She would have to try to shut these sounds out. Tracy took a last swig from her glass, draining all but the ice. She entered the dining room.

"Good morning everyone," she began, making her way through the crowd and ultimately standing beside Colin Richmond. "I think all of you know me." She put her hand on Colin's shoulder. "And most, if not all, of you know Colin Richmond. You know that in 1985 his mother vanished; that in 1987 his father was murdered and he was accused of the crime; and you know that he's been charged with the murder of Timothy Pane. Now what you may *not* realize is that all of these events are connected to each other. Today, I am going to show *how* they are connected. And I am also going to show you that Colin Richmond did not kill anybody. In fact, he is very much a fourth victim in all of this."

Tracy moved away from Colin and went to stand in front of Lt. Pinkerton. He looked up at her. "Almost 30 years ago you made an assumption that Colin was guilty of killing his father; you were so damn cocksure of yourself that you buried crucial evidence. Instead of doing your job and following up on a lead, you helped persecute an innocent man. Maybe if you had done what you were supposed to do, Timothy Pane would still be alive." Pinkerton and Tracy were glaring at each other. She wasn't going to be pulling any punches this morning; that quickly had been established. Gonna fly now. Tracy moved away from Pinkerton and back toward her client.

Then she looked at Bobby Sugarman. "Thank God for Detective Robert Sugarman, Sr., a man who must have realized that a mistake had been made; or at least he thought one had been. He made sure that the evidence that had been buried was not lost; made sure it was put away and stored. If he hadn't, another injustice may have been done."

Tracy looked around the room; then she again moved toward Pinkerton. "I thought it was you behind all of this at first," Tracy said, starting in on him again. "It all fit: you had Bobby working at the bar, listening in on Colin; you could have learned about the drunken reincarnation story; you could have found a list of names with birthdates that coincided with

Jackson Richmond's murder; you could have transferred fingerprints to the knife used to kill Tim Pane; you did in fact pay a visit to Colin trying to make him feel hopeless and desperate; you were in fact having an affair with Amanda Richmond, an affair that she ended; you contrived to get yourself assigned to the Jackson Richmond murder case all those years ago: a man investigating a crime *he* had committed, a plot right out of a 1940s film noir. You had motive and opportunity, the circumstances lined up against you. How does it feel lieutenant? How does it feel to hear all of this laid out in this way? I wonder if I presented this to a jury what their initial thoughts might be — their first impressions before any actual *evidence* was introduced. The way you *should* be feeling is the way Colin Richmond felt 27 years ago during his trial and the way he's feeling right now. That is, if you have any feelings; I'm not sure that you do." Pinkerton just continued staring at her, biting his tongue. He dare not confirm or deny anything she said or implied in front of potential witnesses. After all, he knew the drill very well. But he was usually doing the drilling. Now he felt like the screw going into the wall.

Tracy relaxed a bit. "I wanted it to be you. I wish you could be punished for what you did. I know you have an exemplary record, have closed many a case; I assume you did so honestly. But who knows really? I know you tampered with evidence in the Jackson Richmond murder. I wish it were you that killed Timothy Pane so you could spend time behind bars." Then Tracy sighed. "But I know it wasn't you that killed Tim Pane." Tracy moved back to Colin. Then she looked at Neal. She nodded and he brought over a Banker's Box that he then placed on the table in front of Tracy. She took the lid off. "I know it wasn't Lt. Pinkerton because of these." She pulled out a small bag of carpet tacks. She turned so that everyone could see her prop.

"These are carpet tacks. They were found at the scene of Jackson Richmond's murder. Now these aren't the *actual* tacks; they're locked away in evidence. But my point is that carpet tacks were found near Jackson Richmond's body." Tracy put the tacks back in the box and moved toward where Jesse Alton was sitting. She pointed at him. "This is Mr. Alton. He saw something the night Jackson Richmond was murdered. Can you tell everyone what I'm referring to, Mr. Alton?"

He looked up at her. "I guess you mean that van huh?"

"Yes."

"Well I was getting home about 7:30 when this van pulled out in front me and almost took my front end off; the bastard."

"What business name did you see on that van Mr. Alton?"

"Oh: Waverly Carpet Installers."

"Thank you Mr. Alton." She moved back to the box. "A van belonging to a carpet company is pulling out in a hurry soon after a man is murdered, carpet tacks found at the scene of the crime." Tracy turned to face Danbury. "What do you think Detective; would you consider that an intriguing co-

 A Tracy Brubaker Mystery

incidence, or would your first instinct be that the driver of the van had just killed someone?"

Danbury said nothing. Tracy shook her head.

"Now we have to ask ourselves: why would some carpet business owner or one of his contract employees want to kill Jackson Richmond?" She paused and looked around. "*I* think the answer is that Jackson Richmond suspected his wife had met with foul play." Tracy went toward Betsy Riggs. "This is Betsy Riggs, a neighbor of the Richmonds. Mrs. Riggs saw Amanda Richmond the morning she disappeared. She saw Amanda head to the Dumpster in the alley with her trash. Mrs. Riggs had just come from that alley way. Could you tell us, Mrs. Riggs, what happened to you in that alley?"

She looked at Tracy. "I almost got hit by a sports car."

"And why do you think the car almost hit you Betsy?"

"Oh, I think it swerved so it didn't hit the van that was parked there."

"What was in the back of the van?"

"I saw some rolled up carpets."

Tracy heard at least one gasp. "Thank you, Betsy."

Tracy looked toward Jesse Alton. "Mr. Alton, is it true that Jackson Richmond was asking his neighbors questions about his wife's disappearance well after the police assumed she just ran off with somebody?"

"Ah, well, he asked me questions and I know he was asking other neighbors 'cause they'd bring it up."

"Thank you again Mr. Alton. Mrs. Riggs, did you tell Jackson Richmond about the van you saw parked in the alley the day his wife vanished?"

"Yes, I believe I did."

"Thank you." Tracy sighed. "I think Amanda Richmond broke off, or was trying to break off, a relationship with one of her temporary companions; maybe a companion who didn't want their relationship to be temporary. Something happened, and Amanda was killed. I wouldn't be surprised if her killer really didn't mean to kill her; it may very well have been an accident. Regardless, he killed her. Now since her car was left at her home and a suitcase was packed and removed, the murder probably happened right there in the Richmond apartment, during a time Amanda's husband was at work and her son was at school. That fits with the last time she was seen alive by Mrs. Riggs: 11:00 a.m. The killer then could have rolled Amanda up in a carpet and dragged the body to the van outside. At least that's one possibility."

Tracy looked around again. She gave Colin a sympathetic rub of the shoulders; she knew hearing this couldn't be easy for him. But he was remaining quiet. Again, Tracy found herself looking at Pinkerton. "The Amanda Richmond disappearance was poorly handled, because a certain well-respected detective at the time was involved with her. It wouldn't look very good if he was being questioned about his relationship with a woman who had vanished. It was easy, given the missing suitcase and the knowledge that Amanda had lovers, to just assume she ran off with one of them; case closed." Tracy looked back to her audience. "But Jackson Richmond knew in his heart his wife didn't leave of her own accord." Tracy looked toward Tanner. "El, can you get Christine to come in?" Tanner nodded. Tracy continued. "Amanda Richmond would never have left."

"PINKY!" a voice cried out. "It's you isn't it!" Chrissy was smiling, looking at the dour-faced Pinkerton.

"Chrissy," Tracy interrupted, slightly grinning, "how did Mandy feel about her son?"

"Huh?"

"How did Mandy feel about Colin?"

"Oh, she loved him more than anything in the world."

"And do you, as perhaps her closest friend at the time she vanished, believe she would leave him without ever trying to contact him?"

Chrissy started shaking her head. "No, I don't believe she could ever do that. She wouldn't have left Colin."

"Not even if she fell in love with someone?"

"She wasn't looking for another permanent fella to run off with. It was just all supposed to be fun."

Tracy nodded. "Have a seat Chrissy; and thanks." Chrissy obliged. Tracy started again. "So: Jackson Richmond started talking to neighbors—doing his own investigation. He found out about the van from Mrs. Riggs. He may have talked to someone or someones who worked at the bar his wife patronized. Somehow, he got a line on one of Amanda's beaus who worked for or was associated with a carpet company. Or maybe he just started calling carpet companies to find out if anyone was scheduled to be at or near his building the day of Amanda's disappearance. But Richmond didn't go to the cops with what he found since they did such a piss-poor job the first time around. Now either the killer paid an unexpected visit to Richmond after learning he was asking questions, or Richmond asked this person over. We know what happened when the two met up. Unfortunately for the killer there was a librarian across the street who witnessed Richmond get hit and she screamed. It was August and it was hot, so her scream could be heard through the open windows all through the area. The killer panicked and fled, almost hitting Mr. Alton's car as he did so. And he must have spilled some carpet tacks while in the Richmond apartment, perhaps as he pulled gloves out of his pocket so as not to get prints on the trophy—the murder weapon." Tracy now, yet again, was eyeing Pinkerton. "And then the cops showed up; we know how that went. And the tacks never made it into evidence, because Detective Pinkerton was *so* sure he knew who the killer was and didn't want the jury *confused* by pesky tacks."

          A Tracy Brubaker Mystery

Tracy drank from Colin's untouched water glass that was in front of her. "But the jury hung anyway, not convinced that Colin was indeed guilty. And then he was free. And, like his father, wanted to know what really happened to his loved one. He talked to neighbors too, searched his own memory; he's put himself through an emotional roller coaster for the past 27 years that none of us, myself included, can fully appreciate or understand. Meanwhile he's being spied on; Lt. Pinkerton arranges for his late partner's son to get a job at the bar that Colin frequents; a bar frequented by officers—honest officers." Tracy turned to Bobby. "Tell us Bobby, what opinion have you formed of Colin in the years since you first met him?"

Sugarman looked at her curiously at first, then he answered, "I like Colin. I think he's a nice guy. I can't see him killing anybody."

"Thank you Bobby. I think your father agreed with you, or at least he had his doubts. Again, it's thanks to him that this puzzle will be ultimately solved." Tracy took a deep breath. "Now: Colin, a few years ago, perhaps drunk, perhaps feeling wistful, starts telling some of his friends at Richie's Digs that he thinks, or at least hopes, his dad will someday return; that since his murder was un-avenged that he might return to avenge it. Wishful thinking perhaps, but the murder is clearly still haunting him. And then, one day, Colin crosses paths with his former neighbor, Jesse Alton, when running a business errand. And Colin learns about Waverly Carpet Installers." Tracy took another drink.

"Now the killer, who's very unhappy that Colin didn't go away for his father's murder, has been keeping an eye on Colin. He knows about Richie's Digs. He learns about the reincarnation story and soon too hears Colin is asking people about Waverly Carpet Installers. The killer starts to panic. The killer has no idea what kind of records might exist for the defunct company. He—or she—has moved on. But our friend can't take any chances. His or her name could be on some kind of maintained record, buried in an old box somewhere. Killing Colin is risky though, because the killer doesn't know *what* exactly Colin actually knows, or has told people. Besides, this person has already killed two Richmonds; a third could get the other two deaths reopened. I think because of all the law shows on television *all* of us here know that there is no statute of limitations on murder. So what is the killer to do?"

Tracy looked around the room. "Well, just like the Grinch, he gets a 'wonderful, awful idea.' What if he were to set up Richmond for *another* murder? What if he takes advantage of the fact the police still think Colin killed his father? What if he could use the reincarnation angle to his advantage? What if he could find someone who was born on the day that Richmond was killed; advise him on some things he knew or later learned about Richmond, like the limp or a favorite tune, things he may have learned about Jackson while sleeping with his wife Amanda? Of course, this unwitting accomplice wouldn't know what the end game really was, wouldn't realize he was participating in his own murder plot." Tracy turned to Janice Grant. She moved toward her. "Janice here knew Timothy Pane very well, didn't you Janice?"

"Yes," she answered.

"Timmy loved a good practical joke, didn't he?"

"Yes. He…yes."

Tracy looked at Janice sympathetically. "Thanks Janice." Tracy straightened up; she took another sip of water. "So, a few months before the crime, probably last December—the time Janice noticed Tim practicing his limp while at work—the killer formally enlists Tim Pane; they arrange for Tim to meet Colin at Richie's Digs and other places too, supposedly by accident; Tim walks with a limp and hums a few familiar tunes that make Colin curious; Tim makes sure at one point to let Colin see his license, and more importantly the birth date listed thereon; and then ultimately there is the staged argument at a busy restaurant. The killer calls from a location he knows Colin is working and phones three places until he finds a spot available here at Denzinger's. Then, on that fateful Friday night, Tim Pane delivers the punch line. Out of the blue he stands up and starts yelling at Colin. Everyone assumes it's a lovers' spat." Tracy turned to Linda Schumacher. "Did Colin ever tell you he liked men as well as women, Linda? You were together for, what was it, six months?"

Linda furrowed her brow. "Colin's not like that. I don't where the hell you get that idea from."

"Thanks Linda. I mention it because it seems that almost everybody who was working at the restaurant that night assumed it was a lovers' tiff, which was probably part of the joke. Then, a couple nights later, when the killer knows Colin is alone at his place, he visits Tim Pane under the guise of sharing in the gloat and perhaps giving Tim the agreed-upon reward. He probably double-checks with Tim to make sure he hasn't said anything to anybody about all of this. And then Tim's visitor stabs him. And we all know what has happened since then."

Tracy blew out a breath and rubbed her eyes. "But there's a problem with this potential, creative approach to framing someone for murder that we haven't addressed yet: how on this earth did the killer find someone born on the day of the murder to make the reincarnation angle a convincer? Not only that, but how could he also find out that the person was born in the evening, close to the time of the murder. Now of course the killer certainly knew the actual time of death. He wouldn't need to read the papers or attend the trial to know that, would he?" Tracy sighed. "And, ladies and gentleman, that was my roadblock. It's why I thought a police officer might be involved, or someone who worked at a place where they could access such information—a hospital, the department of motor vehicles; something. I mean, the killer can't very well start walking up to total

                    A Tracy Brubaker Mystery

strangers asking when they were born; am I right?" No one answered her either way.

Tracy moved her head from side to side, stretching her neck. "And then last week, I suddenly had my own wonderful idea." Tracy looked at Detective Danbury. "I was at lunch with my *wonderful, kind-hearted* fiancé when something happened that sent my brain spinning. And then *everything* — and I mean everything — suddenly clicked. Little details started returning to my consciousness that made me realize that only one person could have done this. And then, when I followed up on my admittedly wild hunch, I had my hunch confirmed." Tracy smiled.

"You see, I formed a profile of my killer. I assumed he was in his early-to-mid-20s at the time Amanda Richmond disappeared. That would put him in his 50s now. He had to be in a position where he could arrange the argument and make sure things went as planned. He had to be able to secure a knife with Colin's fingerprints. He had to be a blue collar-type who had worked for Waverly Carpet and been strong enough to move a carpet with a body in it. Last, but not least, he had to have a way of learning about Tim Pane's birthday. I finally figured that part out last week." Tracy smiled.

"Amanda Richmond and Chrissy Jacks: two fun-loving ladies out for a few drinks and a good time; two women sure to capture the attention of a fun-loving guy looking for laughs and a little nookie too maybe; a real rugged-type guy, someone who was good at laying carpet as well as the ladies." Tracy paused. "How am doing with all this so far, Mr. Denzinger?" She turned to face him.

Denzinger blinked and then looked around. "What?"

"How do you like my history lesson so far — how close to the truth is it?"

"Now how would I know that?" he answered nervously.

"Well, given that *you're* the mystery man I've been speaking about you should know better than anyone."

"What? I didn't kill anybody."

"Oh yes you did." Tracy looked in the direction of Chrissy Jacks Wellman. "How about it Chrissy, do you recognize Mr. Denzinger here? Why not come over here and take a closer look?"

Chrissy rose and started to approach the seated owner. Then her eyes flew open. "My God, it's Mikey! *You* own this place?"

"You're crazy, lady!" Denzinger shouted.

"You were a lot skinnier back then, but I remember those lovely eyes of yours," Chrissy said.

"You've got me mixed up with somebody else!"

Tracy cut in. "You can go back to your seat now Chrissy. Thanks again."

"What she said doesn't mean anything," Denzinger grumbled. "It doesn't prove nuthin'."

"In and of itself, no it doesn't," Tracy agreed. "But I'm just getting started here Mikey." Tracy moved back toward her box. She pulled out what looked like a small magazine, because, in point of fact, that's exactly what it was. "Do you recognize this edition of *Excellent Eats Culinary Digest,* Mr. Denzinger?"

He squinted. "Uh, I'm not sure."

"It's the edition from about three years ago where they did a profile on your restaurants. My associate had told me his wife had told *him* about your steak houses based on this magazine write-up."

"Oh, yeah; sure. I remember that."

"They primarily profiled your Anne Arundel County location, the one that had recently opened."

"So what?"

Tracy opened to a yellow sticky-tagged page. "Here's a picture of you sitting down with some others enjoying your steaks." She held the magazine in front of him.

"Yeah, so?" he asked after quickly glancing at it.

"Well, let me have Detective Danbury take a quick look and see what she thinks." Tracy moved to Danbury and handed her the magazine. Danbury looked at the picture. And then her eyes widened.

"Oh my God," she whispered. "The knife…"

"Yes Detective: the knife." Tracy motioned for the detective to return the magazine. Danbury obliged. Tracy returned to Colin's side. "For those who are wondering what that was all about, I will tell you. Detective Danbury just recognized the knife in the picture as matching the knife that was used to stab Tim Pane. Denzinger discontinued that style of steak knife about a year after this magazine article appeared, about the time he learned what Colin had found out—about the time he started forming his plan." Tracy turned back to Denzinger. "But you made sure to hold on to one of the knives, didn't you Mike? You forgot about the article, or rather, its pictures, or did you just think that if you let enough time pass people would never look too far back?"

"No, you're wrong; you're wrong about everything," Denzinger said shaking his head.

"Shall I tell all these people how Colin's prints got on the murder weapon?" Tracy was glaring at Denzinger who was looking at the floor. "*You* told me the way you did it yourself; you told me how you served customers and removed their dishes sometimes to help out on busy evenings. So the night of the argument you made sure you served Colin and Tim their dinners. But you swapped out your store's standard steak knife with the D on it for the old one just before giving Colin his plate, figuring the substitute knife couldn't be traced back to you. And then you made sure to remove at least Colin's dishes so you could then put the knife away for safe

 A Tracy Brubaker Mystery

keeping, Colin's prints now secured. I mean the odds of him, or anyone for that matter, remembering the kind of steak knife they were served at a restaurant must be next to nothing. You just cleaned off the future murder weapon's blade later, taking precautions not to disturb the handle of course. And you took those precautions again when you stabbed Tim Pane with it a few nights later!"

"No no no no no no—"

"Yes, Mike; *yes*. It was very clever of you to call two other restaurants before your own, making it look like your place was chosen at random. It might look suspicious if Pane had so readily found a popular restaurant on such short notice with a reservation available on the first try. You probably made that initial phony reservation—the one that supposedly was cancelled—months earlier yourself. Then when things were all set up with Tim, you whited-out the phony reservation after the business had closed for the day. The very next morning you called early enough so that you could get Pane's name in the book. I wonder if we show your picture around the office building from where those calls were made if someone would recognize you."

"I…you can't…this is just wrong."

"Mike, I haven't even gotten to the best part! The part where I explain to everyone just *how* you found Tim Pane!"

"No—you're wrong! I never met the guy before that night!"

"Really? Well *he* liked *your* place." Tracy went back to the box and pulled out several pieces of paper. "Do you know what these are, Mike? Would you like me to tell you?"

"Please stop!"

"They're credit card statements; they're Tim Pane's credit card statements going back a few years, right around the time your Anne Arundel County store opened. And guess where he charged several meals to? Want to guess Mike?"

"I…"

"Denzinger's: your Anne Arundel County location! Pane's parents live in that county, in Pasadena; and until about two years ago, the time when Waverly Carpet came into play, he had visited your restaurant on several occasions. He took his parents there. But I didn't have the heart to bring them here today to tell us that. And then suddenly Tim Pane stopped coming to your place, or at least stop paying to come. Shall I tell everyone *why* Mike?" She paused briefly. "Because it had to appear like you didn't know Pane at all, that the two of you had no history, because if the police *did* know there was a history and looked into it, it might expose how you learned about Pane's birth date."

"I've had ENOUGH!" Denzinger shouted. He stood up and was now towering over her, red-faced.

Tracy glared at him. "Will Gail Riegert please make her presence known?!" Tracy shouted. And then Mike Denzinger's face went the shade of a white sheet, and he sat back down. "You remember Gail, don't you Mike?" Tracy turned and saw Gail standing next to Tanner. "Why don't you say hello, Mike?" He started shaking his head.

"Gail, you can sit down, thanks," Tracy said, her calm briefly returning. "Friends, this is Gail Riegert. She used to manage the Anne Arundel County Denzinger's. According to the article I mentioned earlier, Mr. Denzinger had nothing but praise for her; he credited her for the success of the store as a matter of fact." Tracy turned back to her target. "Why did you fire her, Mr. Denzinger, this excellent employee of yours? Could it be to cover your bases with respect to the knife and how you found Tim Pane?"

Detective Danbury stood up. "Ms. Brubaker: can you PLEASE let us all know what you're talking about? *How* did Denzinger find out about Pane's birthday?"

Tracy looked at Danbury. Tracy took another deep breath. "Ever go out to eat Detective?"

"What? I mean, of course."

"Ever put a business card of yours in a box or empty fish bowl, trying to win an appetizer or cocktail?"

"Uh, sure I...oh." And then the detective sat back down.

"So I was standing in the parking lot the other week with my fiancé, having just dropped yet another card in yet another box or whatever. And I started thinking about all the information I just handed over: my office phone line, my cell phone number, my email address, my name, my office address. And then I remembered that Mike Denzinger gave me a gift certificate when I interviewed him. And then I wondered if Mike ever ran contests at his restaurants; I mean people will sometimes do almost anything for a freebie." Tracy was now again in front of Denzinger. "So I thought what if about two years ago you ran a contest soliciting birth dates as part of the required information for entry. I figured I had a good time line to work backward from: Colin's Waverly Carpet discovery two years ago. And when I got a hold of Tim's credit card statements, the time that Pane stopped visiting your restaurant matched right up. I remembered my associate mentioning the article about you, and I had him find it for me, and there was Gail's name—along with a picture of the knife—right there for all to see. What luck! We tracked her down." Tracy moved back toward Colin.

"Gail remembered the contest; all one needed to do as an entrant was to fill out a little piece of paper with your name, contact phone number, and birthday. The winner would be chosen based on a randomly selected birthday. And she also remembered what information the winner would

     A Tracy Brubaker Mystery

have to provide in case there were several entrants with the winning birthday: the time of their birth. The prize was a full course meal including drinks. That's quite a good one, Mr. Denzinger."

Tracy rubbed Colin's shoulder; she then moved back to Denzinger. "But your true motive in hosting that promotion was to find a list of people who met your qualifications for the part you wanted to cast. It was probably a very short list. I wonder though if Tim Pane was your first choice or if there were others offered the part first, a part they turned down. I also wonder if the police were to start searching credit card records from around that time if they could come up with their own list of names of men born August 19, 1987, men who visited your restaurant. Would these men remember if you talked to them? Regardless you eventually found Tim — someone who we know was patronizing your restaurant and a guy who loved a good practical joke. So you see you *had* to fire Gail after you found what you were looking for; you couldn't have her around when your plan finally went into action. When you approached Tim with your idea of a great practical joke, he agreed to stop coming to your store, all part of the set up you must have told him. You waited two years hoping there would be no trail to lead back to you. I mean, it was two years after Amanda disappeared that you killed Jackson, and no one came looking for you then. Is that why you thought two years would be a good time frame for your plan? *Huh Mike*?! And then when you were ready you connected, or reconnected back with Tim Pane. I guess it didn't work out for you though this time, did it Mike?"

Now Denzinger was red faced, near tears, shaking his head. "No, no I didn't…"

"Yes Mike, you did. I just connected you to Amanda Richmond; I just connected you to Tim Pane; I just connected you to the murder weapon. Who else but someone in the restaurant business could surreptitiously find out about Colin's ramblings in the context of, say, sharing stories of drunks visiting their bars or pubs and the tales they told? Maybe someone from Richie's Digs will remember you asking questions. Even with the turnover, there are payroll records that can be traced. Maybe the cops can start talking to old buddies of yours; maybe one of them will remember you working for Waverly Carpet Installers. We have witnesses to a carpet van by the building on those two pivotal previous occasions. And don't forget about the carpet tacks. Maybe your DNA is on one or more of them. DNA testing has come a *long* way since 1987!"

"STOP!" Denzinger cried out. He had his fists pressed against their respective temples. He was rocking back and forth, tears pouring out.

Tracy wouldn't let up. "What happened with Mandy, Mike? Did she call you Mikey one too many times? I know you hate to be called Mikey. Or did she get tired of you bothering her after she broke it off? Did she threaten to tell her boyfriend Pinky the cop about you, to get him to pay you a visit? Did she *threaten* you with something, Mikey?!"

"STOP IT!" he cried out sobbing. "It was an accident! I didn't mean to hurt her. I loved her!"

"What about Jackson Richmond then? *That* was no accident. You wore a jacket and jeans like Colin when you visited, just in case someone caught a quick glance of you; you made sure to wear gloves or something like them to preserve the prints on the trophy. And let's not even mention poor Timmy Pane, a means to an end for you. Why don't you look at Janice Grant over there and tell her how *sorry* you are—she's yet another victim of your *love!*"

"I'm sorry...I'm so sorry...I never wanted this to happen...I'm not a bad person!" Denzinger was sobbing uncontrollably, still rocking back and forth in his seat.

Tracy looked at him; she felt no pity. She had a hard time thinking a person who killed three people, and was willing to let a fourth one rot for his crimes, was *not* a bad person. She took a deep breath. "Well, I guess Colin got lucky this time out Mike. I'm just like you in one respect: I want to keep my customers happy too."

Tracy turned away from him and saw everyone staring at her. She looked at the seated Danbury; the motionless Pinkerton; the standing-still Tanner. And her rage exploded. "WELL?" she seethed. "What the HELL are the three of you gawking at?! You couldn't *wait* to throw Colin in jail even though he said he was innocent! And now that a murderer has confessed, you just sit there, just stand there! Why doesn't one of you do SOMETHING?!" She looked at each of them, and felt contempt for each and every one of them, even, God help her, Tanner.

But it was Shandi Danbury who finally moved. She went over to Denzinger. "Alright Mr. Denzinger: why don't you come with me?"

"Yeah; good idea," Tracy hissed. "I know a lawyer who *loves* to make pleas if you want his name."

Danbury ignored her. "Elias, would you mind helping me out here? Maybe get some statements from Gail Riegert, Betsy Riggs, and Jesse Alton for starters."

"Sure," Tanner said softly. "What should we do about Richmond though?"

Danbury sighed. "Well, I'm afraid he has to go back to the detention center for now. But I'll talk to the State's Attorney; tell him we should drop all charges."

"You better do that right quick," Tracy said.

Danbury looked at Tracy. If the detective was thankful she showed no sign of it. All she managed was a brief nod before she led the now-quiet Denzinger away by the arm. Tracy watched them leave.

　　　　A Tracy Brubaker Mystery

"Are we opening today?" Peggy asked aloud, hoping someone would answer her. No one did. Tracy just rolled her eyes and shook her head.

Tracy went over to Colin and sat down next to him in Danbury's now-vacated seat. "I think you'll be going home tomorrow; maybe even later today if I can keep yelling at people. I didn't make any new friends with the police today probably. They're going to want me to shut up."

Colin Richmond looked at her. "They'll never admit they were wrong," he said sourly. "They'll find a way to keep me in there; you watch."

Tracy rubbed Colin's back. "Don't be so cynical Colin; Denzinger confessed. All of these people heard it. A trial would be an *impossible* win for them now, even if they did continue to refuse to admit their error. But like I told you earlier, I know Detective Tanner. He's a good man and a dear friend. He won't let you stay there any longer than he has to. Please believe me, Colin."

Colin smiled weakly. "Okay; how can I not trust you after today?"

"That's the spirit Colin. Not much longer, I promise. And I'll be there when they let you out to make sure everything goes smoothly."

Colin nodded. "Thanks Tracy."

Tracy got up and went over to Neal, who had finished repacking the box of evidence they had brought with them. He looked at her. "Are you okay Tracy? I don't think I've ever seen you so angry."

Tracy nodded. "I'm okay *now*. I guess I got carried away with my role. Part of it was for effect though; I saw Denzinger coming apart and so I thought if I kept after him that he'd break. And he did. I got lucky; again I got lucky. I guess I was born with a chocolate rabbit's foot or something."

Neal smiled. "There you go again, not giving yourself enough credit."

"I just can't help thinking that this shouldn't have happened. If certain people hadn't dusted off Betsy Riggs so quickly in order to protect Pinkerton, they may have looked into why that van was in the alley that morning. If Pinkerton had been an honorable man, and really did his job, he may have learned about the missing neighbor Jesse Alton and talked to him. And then maybe the carpet tacks would have meant something to him. A set of horrible circumstances—and now Tim Pane is dead. It never should have happened. I just got lucky that some people remembered things and were willing to talk to me; that the killer left a trail, if one was willing to look for it. Maybe it wasn't just luck; maybe it was my prayers. Maybe I was God's tool for justice. I…I just got lucky." Tracy gulped.

"I don't care what you say," Neal said softly, resting his hand on her shoulder. "You amaze me."

Tracy smiled. "So you're not mad at me anymore about the joke the other day?"

"Oh, that," Neal laughed. "No, I'm not mad. I had had a fight that morning with my wife and teenage daughter over something, they kind of ganged up on me about a dance curfew and I was really ticked off. I took it out on you and Rebecca. It was a pretty funny joke when I thought about it later."

"Oh Neal I'm sorry. I never would have done something like that if I had known about your fight."

"I know that Tracy. We're good, as always."

"Supreme. Another mystery solved! And now I don't have to keep looking over my shoulder wondering when you'll get even."

"Oh Tracy, I didn't say I wasn't going to get even; I never said *that*." Then Neal grinned and started making his way, box in tow, toward the front door. Tracy's mouth slightly opened.

"You're just kidding with me, right Neal?" she called out. There was no answer, only more laughter.

Janice Grant, who had been sitting silently waiting for a chance to speak to Tracy, approached after Neal had finished his cackling. "Tracy," she said quietly.

"Oh, hi Janice; how are you doing after all of this?"

"Um, okay I guess. I'm still kind of bewildered by it all though."

"I can understand *that*," Tracy said smiling.

"I feel really badly for Colin; I didn't know all of that about his parents. That's awful."

"Yes; it's a very sad thing."

"I hope he doesn't think badly of Timmy though. I mean, Timmy would never have wanted to hurt anybody."

"Oh I think Colin understands that, Janice. I think Colin feels bad for Tim like you do now that he knows everything."

"Uh, Tracy, do you think Colin would talk to me sometime? I feel like I should tell him about Timmy."

Tracy smiled. "I understand, Janice. I'll say something to him. I can tell him your name and where you work. Is that what you'd like me to do?"

Janice smiled back. "Sure." She turned and looked toward the door. "Well, I guess I should get back the office. I told my boss I'd be back right after lunch. Thanks Tracy. Thanks for bringing Timmy's killer to justice."

"You bet Janice. And I haven't forgotten that I owe you a visit to look at those wedding invitations."

"Okay; see you later then." And then Janice Grant gave Tracy another weak smile and headed for the exit.

"Say, your name is Linda right?" Tracy heard Jesse Alton ask Ms. Schumacher.

"Yeah."

"I'm Jesse. Want me to buy you a drink?"

Linda grinned. "Sure, but not here."

"No way," Alton chuckled. "I know a good place." And then Linda smiled and followed Alton out the door. Tracy grimaced and shook her head; then she started chuckling. "Did I just play matchmaker?"

"Bye, thanks for coming," Peggy said cheerfully as people started leaving. Soon it was just Tracy, Tanner, and Colin that remained from the party guest list.

"Alright Colin. I have to take you back now," Tanner said as he approached Richmond. "I'm sorry I have to, but it's procedure. But you should be going home no later than tomorrow. The SA is being apprised right now of the situation."

Colin nodded. Tanner then took Colin to his unmarked vehicle and placed him in the backseat. Tracy was watching from the sidewalk. After Tanner closed the door he approached the attorney.

"I don't know what to say to you Tracy.' I'm sorry' isn't good enough. 'Thank you' seems inadequate."

"Your guys' apologies are owed to Colin here. And you *did* help me out today, the credit card records and all. You got Danbury to show up."

"Well, I wish it hadn't turned out this way, a cop being mixed up in this and all—a heretofor good cop."

"What is going to be done about Pinkerton? Will he lose his pension? Or will he just be forced to retire?"

"He's already put in his papers. I'm not sure about the rest of it yet. When this gets out—and it will—any case he's been involved with is going to be subject to review. Convictions could get tossed."

"I'm sorry El; you know I mean that."

"Yes Tracy; I do. But it's his own fault and nobody else's. There are certain mistakes you cannot make on this job; mistakes you can't make even once. He committed the biggest one. He *will* pay for this Tracy."

"Unfortunately so will others, even if they don't owe anything. And what he did *wasn't* just a mistake; he did it deliberately. I can understand people making mistakes El. Not this."

"You gonna sue him Tracy—the department maybe?"

Tracy snuffed. "Since Colin didn't get convicted I'm not sure what would happen even if he did decide to sue. And Pinkerton really can't be blamed—in any court of law I mean—for what Denzinger did."

"All these years on the job, I hope nobody else is in jail only because *I* thought they should be," Tanner said.

Tracy shook her head. "Don't beat yourself up too much El. You weren't the one calling the shots on the Jackson Richmond case all those years ago. You'd never hide evidence. Besides, you had a super partner to keep an eye on you for a good many years."

Tanner gulped. "Not enough years."

Tracy cleared her throat. "No, not nearly enough." And then she hugged Tanner. "Get Colin out as soon as you can El."

"I will Tracy; I promise you that." And then Tanner left her and drove away with Colin Richmond quietly seated in the back.

Tracy watched them go. She turned and looked at the front door of the steak house. Someone had written in black marker on cardboard "Closed until further notice," and taped the sign to the window. "Huh," she thought. "I guess my gift certificate just expired."

At approximately 3:30 that same afternoon Colin Richmond was collecting his belongings at the discharge desk at the Baltimore City Detention Center. He signed for them, turned to leave, and saw his lawyer standing there smiling. "Hi Colin."

He managed to smile back. "Hi Tracy."

"Come on; there are some people anxious to see you."

He gave her a quizzical look but followed her as she turned and started their journey to the exit doors. Once outside Colin saw a familiar car and then saw its two familiar occupants emerge, smiles on their faces: Jon and Janie Carruthers. Colin froze. He swallowed. And then he started to weep. Tracy instinctively embraced him.

"Thank you," he said over and over again between deep breaths and snuffles. "How can I ever thank you?"

Tracy rubbed his back for a while, and then pulled away to look at him. "Well, there is something I'd like you to *try* to do."

"Anything Tracy."

"Try to move on with your life and put the past behind you. You have a great company with a great reputation, and you've got two people over there who love you and can't wait to spend time with you. Those are great things to have." He nodded. "As hard as it's going to be to do, you have to let go of the past; try to forgive and move forward. The past is hurtful, and you were treated unfairly. You have every right to be angry. But if you dwell in that place of hurt and anger, it will kill you a little more each time you think about it. It will kill you over and over again if you let it. Don't let that happen to you, Colin. As hard as I know — speaking from experience — it will be to do, do it anyway. Today and the future are where your life is, not the past. Am I making any sense?"

"Yes, I understand what you're telling me. I don't know if I'm going to be able to do that though."

"Don't misunderstand me Colin. It *will* be hard to do, especially in the coming months when it's still fresh in your memory. But at least now you should have no doubts anymore that your mother did love you, and that your father, in spite of everything, loved your mother, at least he did in his own way. I'm sorry this happened to you; so sorry. Maybe if I had been

     A Tracy Brubaker Mystery

practicing law when I was four years old it wouldn't have turned out like it did."

Colin started laughing, and wiping the tears from his eyes. "And I still have *you* right? I mean, we don't have a law firm we deal with so if something comes up…"

"You bet Colin. You give me a call if you need *anything*. In fact, if you think about it, give me a call in a few months to let me know how you're doing. I'd like to tell you I'll call you, but I've been telling my fiancé for the past week or so I'd be calling the church to set a wedding date and I still haven't done it."

Colin laughed again; he was all smiles now. "I think your fiancé is a very lucky guy." Tracy smiled and bowed her head. "Hey, if you ever need your office redone or anything you just call me. No charge."

"Thanks Colin; I may take you up on that someday. But you're a professional at what you do so you'd have to let me pay you. You could treat me to lunch while you're there though."

Colin cleared his throat. "Deal. Well, I better not keep Jon and Janie waiting any longer."

"One more thing Colin: there's a woman by the name of Janice Grant. You may remember her from this morning; she worked with Timothy Pane at Deggman's Printers and More."

Colin nodded. "Yeah; I think I remember her. She seemed nice."

"She is. She would like to talk to you. I think she feels bad about everything and she's afraid you might have a bad impression of Tim Pane."

"Oh; I don't have anything against him. I mean, the poor guy's dead because of me."

"No Colin, he's dead because Mike Denzinger killed him."

"Well, yeah. I just meant I feel bad for the guy."

Tracy smiled. "I figured that. But it might be nice to talk to Janice. You could make another new friend."

Colin smiled. "Well, I'll think about it. I guess she liked the guy huh?"

"Yes; there was no one there today to really speak for Tim. She wants to stand up for him in her own way."

"Sure; I'll talk to her."

"Supreme! Well, goodbye for now Colin. I hope your life is a happy one from here on out. You don't have to be a 'lost boy' anymore." Tracy winked.

Colin nodded and embraced Tracy again. Then he headed toward his friends. Tracy took a few steps forward so she could hear their exchange.

"Hey Colin," Jon Carruthers said. "I've missed you buddy."

And then Colin Richmond started weeping again, as Jon embraced him. Tears started falling from Janie Carruthers' eyes as she started rubbing Colin's back.

"Come on," Janie said, forcing a smile. "I know two boys who can't wait to see their Uncle Colin." Colin looked at her and nodded. Jon opened the front passenger door and motioned for Colin to get inside, while Janie seated herself in the back. Jon then took charge of the wheel and guided the Carruthers' vehicle out of the parking lot. Tracy watched as they all pulled into the street.

The noise of a car door slamming got Tracy's attention. She turned to see Brian Shane approaching her, a mixed look of sympathy and concern on his face. He had been there the whole time, having agreed to drive Tracy to meet Colin. Now that the coast was clear, he had emerged so he could put his arm around her.

"Are you okay Tracy? That looked pretty intense from where I was sitting."

Tracy gulped and looked at him. Then she twisted her face in an effort to avoid crying. "I just feel so bad for him," she said. "He was just a boy, and his mother disappears and then his father's killed, and because he didn't act like an adult, adults thought the worst of him, caused him more pain. One cop went so far as to taint his trial…And then as he struggles with this more than half his life, he finds himself accused again." Now the tears were flowing.

"I'm sorry Tracy," was all Brian could think to say.

"And do you know what the killer said, Brian, after he just basically confessed to killing three people? Do you know what he had the gall to say?"

"No Tracy."

"He said he wasn't a bad person. I know I'm not supposed to judge people but…He killed three people."

"You're right Tracy; he sounds like a less than good person."

"And he tries to frame someone else for it—another victim, who almost killed himself."

"Tracy—"

"And what about Janice Grant? Who knows what life she and Tim Pane may have had if one of them eventually made *the* move? I can't help but thinking of her too. Maybe Colin and she could become friends…Well, that's neither here nor there really."

"Tracy, do all of your cases get to you like this?"

"I'm sorry. I can't help it."

"I know you can't. How many times have I told you what a beautiful heart you have? How can such a person *not* feel for these people? But I don't like seeing you like this. I think I prefer Angry Tracy to Hurting Tracy."

     A Tracy Brubaker Mystery

She looked at him. "Sometimes I hate this world Brian; I know I shouldn't say that but I do. I've met some people over the last few weeks who thought the be all and end all of love was spending time with a beautiful prostitute, or people who gave up on love altogether because of prior bad relationships, or people whose egos where so big they let innocent people suffer, or people who get so sad they try to end their own life. I mean, this whole thing…I just…I just wonder about this world."

"You're forgetting about another kind of person, Tracy."

"Huh? What are you talking about?"

"I'm talking about the person who fights for those she believes in; a person who puts her own life on hold to help others; a person willing to actually *risk* their own life if necessary to see that justice is done; a person who won't give up, and will stand up to those who try and stop her. There are people like that in the world too. I *know* one. Her name is Tracy Elizabeth Brubaker. I kinda love her."

Tracy looked into Brian's eyes, and she smiled. But soon the smile cracked and the tears were falling again. She leaned her face into Brian's chest. "I love you Brian. I love you so much. Let's go home now."

Brian put his arm around his beloved and helped her into the car. Soon he was turning the key in the ignition switch. "Brian: that Janice Grant works at a print shop that does wedding invitations. I told her we'd stop by and look at her stuff sometime."

"Sure Tracy; whatever you want."

"Brian," Tracy said softly.

"Yes Tracy?"

"I want you to stay with me tonight. I want to be happy again."

He smiled. "Tracy, why don't we get you home and fed, and then we'll talk. And then we'll see how you feel. I don't want you thinking I'm taking advantage of the situation. I mean, tears are a not-so-secret weapon of both sexes."

She smiled at him. "Well, look at that: Brian's gone practical on me."

"I don't know about that," he said laughing gently.

"But you'll at least stay with me right? Even if it's just on the couch, holding each other like we used to, when we were…well, blissfully ignorant, let's say."

"Of course Tracy, you know I will."

"Then let's go so I can wash my face and rid the day's pains from it." Then she smiled at him again and said,

"Tears, idle tears, I know not what they mean,
Tears from the depth of some divine despair
Rise in the heart, and gather in the eyes,

In looking on the happy autumn-fields,
And thinking of the days that are no more."

"Who are you quoting now?" Brian asked her.

"The same person who said it was better to have loved and lost."

"Tennyson, right?"

"Right!"

"How can you remember all this stuff? I don't remember a thing I learned in any English class I ever took."

"Well, in this case it's because thinking of the past would always bring me to tears. That's what the poem's about and why it's so memorable to me. At least, life used to be like that."

"Oh; I see."

"But now I'm looking ahead, ahead to a future '…so bright, I gotta wear shades.'"

Brian laughed. "I sure hope I'm in it."

"Brian, my love, of course you are; you're its brightest star." And then they kissed again, not a tear in sight. And soon Brian was guiding their journey to a condo with a certain couch, a place where the couple could sit and hold and love, a place where all of life's pain — even that of others that one has allowed to become their own — could be set aside, blinded by the light of faith in a future filled with promise. Brian had returned to her to make good on his promises, and to make her new ones. But she was looking forward to the day when mere promises would be superseded by vows; when Brian would no longer be leaving her when night fell; when she no longer would have to struggle with the right or wrong of giving in to her desire. But tonight would bring what it would bring. Tracy found herself looking out the window as the car traveled its journey. She thought about wishing on a star, since it made no difference who she was. She thought about wishing for Colin Richmond's happiness; then she thought about world peace. Then she turned to Brian.

"Hey sweetheart, now that it's just the two of us, do you have any fantasies?"

Brian started laughing. "Oh no, not this again."

She grinned. "I'll tell you mine if you tell me yours."

He stole a quick look at her. "I think I'll have to ponder this a while," he said finally.

"Hey, what was that thing about clown makeup and diapers you were babbling about the other day? Oh, there was something about a Twinkie too."

"Tracy, stop."

"Twinkie, Twinkie, little star; I like it here in Brian's car…"

                    A Tracy Brubaker Mystery

"Tracy, stop that. You know how I have impure thoughts when you start getting playful like this. Besides, your poetry, in this case, is lacking. Stick with quoting the professionals, will ya?"

She grinned at him, as he shook his head. Then she ran her fingertips across his leg. "What color was the teddy that popped into your head at lunch the other day?"

Brian screamed in frustration, "Temptress!", and then he pulled the car over onto the shoulder. And then he kissed her while she giggled. And then she was kissing him in return. The couch would have to wait a while longer. Right now the car seats would do just fine, like they had in the past. There was still joy to be found in *some* parts of the past, and those are the parts to hold onto. The rest get tossed in the garbage, like used diapers and stale Twinkies. As for the clown makeup, that need not be applied, as tears send the makeup running—unless it's all part of the fantasy of course. But fantasies weren't on Tracy and Brian's minds right now. They would have time to indulge in them later. From where they were both sitting now, the present was a fine place to be.

***Tune in for the next exciting
chapter in the Tracy Brubaker
mystery series, Practice to Deceive.***

Visit www.midmar.com
for a complete list of titles!

www.ingramcontent.com/pod-product-compliance
Lightning Source LLC
Chambersburg PA
CBHW070950190726

48292CB00004B/1409